THE FEVER

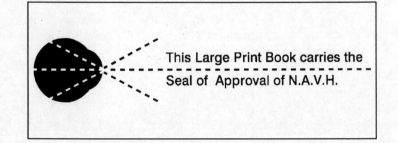

This Large Print Book carries the
Seal of Approval of N.A.V.H.

THE FEVER

MEGAN ABBOTT

THORNDIKE PRESS
A part of Gale, Cengage Learning

GALE
CENGAGE Learning·

Farmington Hills, Mich • San Francisco • New York • Waterville, Maine
Meriden, Conn • Mason, Ohio • Chicago

LIBRARY OF CONGRESS CATALOGING-IN-PUBLICATION DATA

Abbott, Megan E., 1971–
   The fever / Megan Abbott. — Large type books.
      pages cm. — (Thorndike Press large print peer picks)
   ISBN 978-1-4104-8347-8 (hardback) — ISBN 1-4104-8347-9 (hardcover)
    1. Epidemics—Fiction. 2. Family secrets—Fiction. 3. Large type books.
I. Title.
PS3601.B37F48 2015
 813'.6—dc23   2015024138

Published in 2015 by arrangement with Little, Brown and Company, a division of Hachette Book Group, Inc.

Printed in Mexico
1 2 3 4 5 6 7 19 18 17 16 15

For my brother, Josh Abbott

In all disorder [there is] a secret order.

— Carl Jung

BEFORE

"The first time, you can't believe how much it hurts."

Deenie's legs are shaking, but she tries to hide it, pushing her knees together, her hands hot on her thighs.

Six other girls are waiting. A few have done it before, but most are like Deenie.

"I heard you might want to throw up even," one says. "I knew a girl who passed out. They had to stop in the middle."

"It just kind of burns," says another. "You're sore for a few days. They say by the third time, you don't even feel it."

I'm next, Deenie thinks, *a few minutes and it'll be me.*

If only she'd gotten it over with a year ago. But she'd heard about how much it hurt and no one else had done it yet, at least not anyone she knew.

Now she's one of the last ones.

When Lise comes out, her face puckered,

holding on to her stomach, she won't say a word, just sits there with her hand over her mouth.

"It's nothing to be scared of," Gabby says, looking at Deenie. "I'm not afraid."

And she takes Deenie's hand and grips it, fingers digging into palm, their clasped hands pressing down so Deenie's legs stop shaking, so she feels okay.

"We're in it together," Gabby adds, making Deenie look in her eyes, black and unflinching.

"Right," Deenie says, nodding. "How bad can it be?"

The door opens.

"Deenie Nash," a voice calls out.

Four minutes later, her thigh stinging, she's done. It's over.

Walking back out, shoes catching on the carpet, legs heavy as iron, she feels light-headed, a little drunk.

All the girls look at her, Gabby's face grave and expectant.

"It's nothing," Deenie says, grinning. "It's just . . . nothing."

1

TUESDAY

At first, Lise's desk chair just seemed to be rocking. Deenie's eyes were on it, watching the motion. The rocking of it made her feel a little sick. It reminded her of something.

She wondered if Lise was nervous about the quiz.

The night before, Deenie had prepared a long time, bringing her laptop under her covers, lying there for hours, staring at equations.

She wasn't sure it was studying, exactly, but it made her feel better, her eyes dry from screen glare, fingers tapping her lower lip. There was an uncomfortable smell from somewhere in her clothes, musky and foreign. She wanted to shower, but her dad might hear and wonder.

Two hours before, she'd been at work, dropping dough balls in a machine and punching them out into square pans slick with oil. Lise and Gabby had come by and ordered the fat pizza sticks, even though Deenie warned them not to. Showed them the plastic tub of melted butter that sat all day by the hot ovens. Showed them how the oven workers stroked the sticks with the butter from that tub and how it looked like soap or old cheese.

As they left, oil-bottomed paper sacks in their hands, she wished she were going with them, wherever they were going. She was glad to see them together. Gabby and Lise were Deenie's best friends but never really seemed easy with just each other.

By the ovens, Sean Lurie clocked in late. Wielding his long iron grippers like swords, he started teasing her. About the fancy-girl arc of her hand when she'd grab a dough ball, like she was holding a kitten. The way, he said, her tongue stuck out slightly when she stretched the dough.

"Like my little sister," he teased, "with her Play-Doh."

He was a senior at Star-of-the-Sea, shaggy black hair, very tall. He never wore his hat, much less the hairnet, and he had a way of smiling lopsided that made her tie her apron strings tighter, made her adjust her cap.

The heat from the ovens made his skin glow.

She didn't even mind all the sweat. The sweat was part of it.

Like her brother after hockey, his dark hair wet and face sheened over — she'd tease him about it, but it was a look of aliveness you wanted to be around.

How it happened that two hours later she was in Sean Lurie's car, and a half hour after that they were parked on Montrose, deep in Binnorie Woods, she couldn't say for sure.

She always heard you looked different, after.

But only the first time, said Gabby, who'd done it just twice herself. *To make you remember it, I guess.* Deenie had wondered how you could ever forget.

You look in the mirror after, Gabby said, *and it's not even you.*

Except Deenie had never really believed it. It seemed like one of those things they told you to make you wait forever for something everyone else was doing anyway. They didn't want you to be part of the club.

And yet, looking in the bathroom mirror after she got home, she'd realized Gabby was right.

It was partly the eyes — something narrow there, something less bright — but mostly it was the mouth, which looked tender, bruised, and now forever open.

Her hands hooked on the sink ledge, her eyes resting on her dad's aftershave in the deep green bottle, the same kind he'd used all her life. He'd been on a date too, she realized.

Then, remembering: she hadn't really been on a date.

Now, in class, all these thoughts thudding around, it was hard to concentrate, and even harder given the rocking in Lise's chair, her whole desk vibrating.

"Lise," Mrs. Chalmers called out. "You're bothering everyone else."

"It's happening, it's happening" came a low snarl from Lise's delicate pink mouth. "Uh-uh-uh."

Her hands flying up, she grabbed her throat, her body jolting to one side.

Then, in one swoop — as if one of the football players had taken his meaty forearm and hurled it — her desk overturned, clattering to the floor.

And with it Lise. Her head twisting, slamming into the tiles, her bright red face turned up, mouth teeming with froth.

"Lise," sighed Mrs. Chalmers, too far in front to see. "What is your problem?"

Standing at his locker, late for class, Eli Nash looked at the text for a long time, and at the photo that had come with it. A girl's bare midriff.

Eli, for you xxxx!

He didn't recognize the number.

It wasn't the first time he'd gotten one of these, but they always surprised him. He tried to imagine what she was thinking, this faceless girl. Purple nails touching the tops of her panties, purple too, with large white polka dots.

He had no idea who it was.

Did she want him to text her back, invite her over? To sneak her into his bedroom and nudge her shaky, pliant legs apart until he was through?

A few times he'd done just that. Told them to come by, smuggled them to his room. The last one, a sophomore everyone called Shawty, cried after.

She admitted to drinking four beers before she came on account of nervousness, and even still, had she put her legs where she should? Should she have made more noise?

Secretly, he'd wished she'd made less noise.

Since then, he could only ever think about

his sister, one wall away. And how he hoped Deenie never did things like this. With guys like him.

So now, when he got these texts, he didn't reply.

Except sometimes he felt kind of lonely.

The night before, his friends at a party, he'd stayed home. He imagined maybe a family night of bad TV and board games moldy from the basement. But Deenie wasn't around, and his dad had his own plans.

"Who is she?" he'd asked, seeing his father wearing his date sweater, the charcoal V-neck of a serious man.

"A nice woman, very smart," he said. "I hope I can keep up."

"You will," Eli said. His dad was the smartest teacher in the school and the smartest guy Eli knew.

After one of those times sneaking a girl out of his room, Eli had gotten caught, sort of. In the upstairs hallway, his dad nearly bumped into her as she hitched her tank-top strap up her shoulder. He'd looked at Eli and then at the girl and she'd looked at him and smiled like the prom queen she was.

"Hey, Mr. Nash," she cheeped. "Guess

what? I got an eighty-five in Chem Two this year."

"Great, Britt," he said, his eyes not focusing on hers. "I always knew you could do better. Glad to hear you're doing me proud."

After, Eli shut his door and turned his music as loud as he could and hoped his dad wouldn't come talk to him.

He never did.

★　★　★

Dryden was the cloudiest city in the state, the sky white for much of the year and the rest of the time a kind of molten gray broken up by bright bolts of mysterious sun.

Tom Nash had lived here for twenty years, had moved with Georgia the summer after they'd finished their teaching certificates, and she'd gotten a job starting up the district's new special-education office.

Like many long-term transplants, he had the uncomplicated pride of a self-proclaimed native, but with the renewing wonder a native never has.

In the deep white empty of February when his students would get that morose look, their faces slightly green like the moss that lined all their basements, he'd tell them that Dryden was special. That he had grown up in Yuma, Arizona, the sunniest city in the United States, and that he'd never really looked up until he went away to summer camp and realized the sky was there after all and filled with mystery.

For Dryden kids, of course, there was no mystery to any of it. They didn't realize how much it had shaped them, how it had let them retain, long past childhood fairy tales, the opportunity to experience forces beyond their understanding. The way weather tumbled through the town, striking it with hail, lightning, sudden bursts of both clouds and sun, like no other place Tom had ever been. Some days, the winter wind moving fast across the lake's warm waters, the sun unaccountably piercing everything, students came to school, faces slicked in ice, looking stunned and radiant. As if saying: *I'm sixteen and bored and indifferent to life, but my eyes are suddenly open, for a second, to this.*

The first year he and Georgia lived here, Dryden had been this puzzle to them both. Coming home at night, the haze of the streetlamps, shaking off the damp, they would look around, their once-copper skin gleaming white, and marvel over it.

Pregnant with Eli and her body changing already, giving her this unearthly beauty,

Georgia decided Dryden wasn't a real place at all but some misty idea of a town. A suburban Brigadoon, she called it.

Eventually — though it felt like suddenly to him — something changed.

One afternoon two years ago, he came home and found her at the dining-room table drinking scotch from a jam jar.

Living here, she said, *is like living at the bottom of an old man's shoe.*

Then she looked at him as if hoping he could say something to make it not feel true.

But he couldn't think of a thing to say.

It wasn't long after that he found out about the affair, a year along by then, and that she was pregnant. She miscarried three days later and he took her to the hospital, the blood slipping down her leg, her hands tight on him.

Now he saw her maybe four times a year. She'd moved all the way to Merrivale, where Eli and Deenie spent one weekend a month and a full ten days each summer, after which they came back tan and blooming and consumed by guilt the moment they saw him.

In his middle-of-the-night bad thoughts, he now felt sure he'd never really understood his wife, or any woman maybe.

Whenever he thought he understood

Deenie, she seemed to change.

Dad, I don't listen to that kind of music.

Dad, I never go to the mall anymore.

Lately, even her face looked different, her baby-doll mouth gone. The daddy's girl who used to climb his leg, face turned up to his. Who sat in his leather reading chair for hours, head bent over his own childhood books on Greek mythology, then Tudor kings, anything.

"I'm taking the bus," she'd said that very morning, halfway out the door, those spindle legs of hers swiveling in her sneakers.

"I can drive you," he'd said. "You're so early."

Deenie hadn't beaten him to breakfast since she was ten, back when she was trying to be grown-up and would make him toaster waffles, with extra syrup he'd be tugging from the roof of his mouth all day.

Eli off to hockey practice at six a.m., Tom liked these drives alone with Deenie, the only time he could peek into the murky teen-girl-ness in her head. And get occasional smiles from her, make bad jokes about her music.

A few times, after dates like the one he'd had the night before — a substitute teacher divorced three months who'd spent most of dinner talking about her dying cat — driving to school with Deenie was the thing that roused him from bed in the morning.

But not this morning.

"I have a test to study for," she'd said, not even turning her head as she pushed through the door.

Sometimes, during those same bleak middle-of-the-nights, he held secret fears he never said aloud. Demons had come in the dark, come with the famous Dryden fog that rolled through the town, and taken possession of his lovely, smart, kindhearted wife. And next they'd come for his daughter too.

2

Deenie couldn't get the look on Lise's face out of her head.

Her eyes had shot open seconds after she fell.

"Why am I here?" she whispered, blinking ferociously, back arched on the floor, her legs turned in funny ways, her skirt flown up to her waist, and Mrs. Chalmers shouting in the hallway for help.

It had taken two boys and Mr. Banasiak from across the hall to get her to her feet.

Deenie watched them steer her down the hall, her head resting on Billy Gaughan's linebacker shoulder, her long hair thick with floor dust.

"Deenie, no," Mrs. Chalmers said, taking her firmly by the shoulders. "You stay here."

But Deenie didn't want to stay. Didn't want to join the thrusting clutches of girls whispering behind their lockers, the boys watching Lise turn the corner, her skirt hitched high in the back, her legs bare despite the cold weather, the neon flare of her underpants.

After, ducking into the girls' room, Deenie saw she was still bleeding a little from the night before. When she walked it felt weird, like parts of her insides had shifted. She could never have ridden to school with her dad. What if he saw? She felt like everyone could see. That they knew what she'd done.

As it was happening, it had hurt a lot, and then a sharp look of surprise on Sean Lurie's face when he realized. When she couldn't hide what she was, and wasn't, what she had clearly never done before — thinking of it made her cover her face now, her hand cold and one pinkie shaking.

You should have told me, he'd said.

Told you what.

Swinging open the lavatory door, she began walking quickly down the teeming hall.

"Deenie, I heard something." It was Gabby, sneaking up behind her in her sparkled low-riders. They never made any noise. "About you."

Gabby's face seemed filled with fresh knowledge, but there was no way she could know. Sean Lurie went to Star-of-the-Sea.

23

People couldn't know.

"Did you hear what just happened to Lise?" Deenie countered, pivoting to look at her. "I was there. I saw it."

Gabby's eyebrows lifted and she held her books to her chest.

"What do you mean? What do you mean?" she repeated. "Tell me everything."

At first they wouldn't let her into the nurse's office.

"Deenie, her mother isn't even here yet," snipped Mrs. Harris, the head of something called facilities operations.

"My dad asked me to check on her," Deenie lied, Gabby nodding next to her.

The ruse worked, though not for Gabby, who, lacking my-father-is-a-teacher privileges, was dispatched immediately to second period.

"Find out everything," Gabby whispered as Mrs. Harris waved her out.

The nurse's office door was ajar and Deenie could hear Lise calling her name. Everyone could hear, teachers stopping at their mailboxes.

"Deenie," Lise cried out. "What did I do? Did I do something? Who saw?"

Peering in the open door, Deenie saw Lise keeling over on the exam table, her lips ribboned with drying froth, one shoe hanging from her foot. She wasn't wearing any tights, her legs goose-quilled and whiter than the paper sheet.

"She . . . she bit me." Nurse Tammy was holding her own forearm, which looked wet. She hadn't been working there long, and rumor was, a senior athlete with a sore knee had scored two Tylenol with codeines from her on her very first day.

"Deenie!" Head whipping around, Lise gripped the table edge beneath her thighs, and Nurse Tammy rushed forward, trying to help her.

"Deenie," she repeated. "What happened to me? Is everyone talking about it? Did they see what I did?"

Outside the nurse's office, Mrs. Harris was arguing with someone about something, the assistant principal's stern jock voice joining in.

"No one saw," Deenie said. "No way. Are you okay?"

But Lise couldn't seem to focus, her hands doing some kind of strange wobbling thing in front of her, like she was conducting an invisible concert.

"I . . . I . . ." she stuttered, her eyes panicked. "Are they laughing at me?"

Deenie wanted to say something reassuring. Lise's mother, vaguely hysterical under the best of circumstances, would be here any second, and she wanted to help while she could.

"No one's laughing. Everyone saw your Hello Kitty undies, though," Deenie tried, smiling. "Watch the boys come now."

As Deenie walked out, a coolness began to sink into her. The feeling that something was wrong with Lise, but the wrongness was large and without reference. She'd seen Lise with a hangover, with mono. She'd seen girlfriends throw up behind the loading dock after football games and faint in gym class, their bodies loaded with diet pills and cigarettes. She'd seen Gabby black out in the girls' room after she gave blood. But those times never felt like this.

Lying on the floor, her mouth open, tongue lolling, Lise hadn't seemed like a girl at all.

It must have been a trick of the light, she told herself.

But looking down at Lise, lips stretched wide, Deenie thought, for one second, that she saw something hanging inside Lise's mouth, something black, like a bat flapping.

"Mr. Nash," piped Brooke Campos, "can I go to the nurse's office? I'm feeling upset."

"What are you upset about, Brooke," Tom replied. There was fidgeting in a dozen seats. Something had happened, and he could see everyone was looking for an advantage in it.

"It's about Lise. I saw it go down and it's a lot to take in."

Two jocks in the back stifled braying laughs. They seemed to go to class solely in the hopes of hearing accidental (or were they?) double entendres from girls like Brooke, girls eternally tanned and bursting from T-shirts so tight they inched up their stomachs all day.

"What about Lise?" Tom asked, setting his chalk down. He'd known Lise Daniels since she was ten years old and first started coming to the house, hovering around Deenie, following her from room to room. Sometimes he swore he could hear her panting like a puppy. That was back when she was a chubby little elfin girl, before that robin's-breast belly of hers disappeared, and, seemingly overnight, she became overwhelmingly pretty, with big fawn eyes, her mouth forever open.

He never really had a sense of her, knew only that she played the flute, had perpetually skinned knees from soccer, and appeared ever out of place alongside his own brilliant, complicated little girl and her even more complicated friend Gabby.

Four years ago, Gabby's father, blasted on cocaine, had taken a claw hammer to his wife's Acura. When Gabby's mother tried to stop him, his hammer caught her on the downswing, tearing a hole clean through her face and down her throat.

Gabby's mother recovered, though now all the kids at the community college where she taught called her Scarface behind her back.

Her father had served a seven-month sentence and was now selling real estate in the next county and making occasional, unwelcome reappearances.

In the school's hallways, Tom could see it: Gabby carried the glamour of experience, like a dark queen with a bloody train trailing behind her.

It was hard to fathom girls like that walking the same corridors as girls like Brooke Campos, thumbs callused from incessant texting, or even girls like downy-cheeked Lise.

"Mr. Nash," Brooke said, rolling the tip of

her pen around in her mouth like it hurt to think about, "it's so traumatic."

He tried again. "So what is it that happened to Lise?"

"She had a grand male in Algebra Two," Brooke announced, eyes popping.

The jocks broke into a fresh round of laughter.

"A grand mal?" he asked, squinting. "A seizure?"

Up front, antic grade-grubber Jaymie Hurwich squirmed painfully in her seat, hand raised.

"It's true, Mr. Nash," she told him. "I didn't see it, but I heard her mouth was frothing like a dog's. I had a dog that happened to once." She paused. "Mr. Nash, he died."

A hard knock in his chest in spite of himself, he looked at Brooke, at all of them.

He was trying to think of something to say.

"So . . ." Brooke said, rising tentatively in her seat, "can I see the nurse now?"

After second period, he found Deenie buried in her locker nearly to her waist, hunting for something.

"Honey, what happened with Lise?" he asked, hand on her back.

She turned slowly, one arm still rooted inside.

"I don't know, Dad."

For a second, she wouldn't look up at him, her eyes darting at the passing kids.

"But you saw it?"

"Dad," she said, giving him that look that had made his chest ache since she was four years old. "I don't want to talk now."

Now meaning here: *Not at school, Da-ad.*

Meaning he had to just let her go, watch her dark ponytail swinging down the hall, head dipped furtively, that red hoodie hunching up her neck, helping her hide.

3

Eli Nash was supposed to be in class. Practice had ended a long time ago, but he was still circling the rink behind the school. No sound except the faint hum of its refrigeration coils.

Looking up, he could see Gabby Bishop in the library. Back facing him, she was pressed against the windowpane like one of those butterflies under glass.

Deenie and Gabby and Lise. The Trio Grande. Always huddled together, whispering, a kind of closeness that interested him. He wondered what it might be like. He never wanted to huddle with his friends, though he guessed in a way he did it all the time, playing hockey.

Sometimes it was annoying. The way the three of them would be like this little knot in the house. He could hear them through the wall at night, laughing.

Lately, Lise and Gabby didn't seem to

come over as much, or maybe he'd just stopped noticing. But it always felt weird when girls were laughing together and you didn't know why. Sometimes it was like they knew all these things he didn't.

Other times he wondered if they knew anything at all.

They didn't know about guys, as far as he could tell. At least not the things he wished his sister knew. He would catch her looking at Ryan Denning or that guy who won Battle of the Bands. That dreamy expression she wore, her face showing everything she was feeling. Imagining big love and romance, he guessed. But she didn't realize what they saw, looking back at her: a girl, lips slightly parted, her head tilted hungrily. What they saw was *I'm ready. Let's go.*

"Nash," a voice rang out.

Eli looked up and saw A.J., the team captain, baseball cap low to cover his cigarette.

"Bro," he said, "you missed it. I got an eyeful of Lise Daniels's pretty white ass this morning." He tilted his head toward the school. "Come on. Who knows what's next?"

Eli felt the cold in his lungs, the ache of it. It felt good out here, and just looking at A.J. made him tired. All the effort, hat brim angled, jacket open. Smirk.

"Nah," he said. "Not yet."

A.J. grinned. "I feel you," he said.

Eli nodded, pushing off on his skates, gliding backward.

"Say hi to your sister for me," A.J. shouted.

Turning his head, Eli felt his skate catch a fallen branch.

★   ★   ★

The library was quiet, a glass-walled hothouse overlooking a narrow creek dense with mud.

Deenie found Gabby behind the gray bank of computers along the far wall. She was sitting on the floor, knees bent, her sneakers pressed against the tall reference volumes on the lowest shelf.

As always, she was bookended by two girls.

To her right crouched thick-braced Kim Court, in her usual pose, whispering in Gabby's ear.

And to her left sat Skye Osbourne, her blond hair spanning the musty world atlases behind her. Lately, Skye was always around, that web of hair, her long mantis sleeves.

All three looked up when they saw Deenie.

"What did you hear?" Gabby asked, fingers tapping on her lip.

33

"Nothing," Deenie said, sliding down to the floor next to Kim.

She wished it were just her and Gabby. No one else to hear them and they could talk about Lise alone.

This was their favorite place to meet. It always felt hidden, forgotten. The gold-lettered *World Book* encyclopedias from the 1980s. The smell of old glue and crumbling paper, the industrial carpet burning her palms.

It reminded her of what you did when you were a little girl, making little burrows and hideaways. Like boys did with forts. Eli and his friend, stacking sofa cushions, pretending to be sharpshooters. With girls, you didn't call them forts, though it was the same.

This was the place Deenie and Gabby first really spoke, freshman year, both of them hiding back here, heads ducked over identical books (something about angels, back when that was all they read). They'd snuck looks at each other, smiled.

"Did you see her before school?" Deenie asked Gabby.

"No, I was late," Gabby said. "Skye couldn't find her purse."

"Is she pregnant?" whispered Kim, her tongue thrust between her wired teeth.

"Lise?" Deenie said. "No. Of course not."

"Pregnant people faint all the time," Kim said, tugging her tights up her legs, inching as close to Gabby as she could without landing in her lap.

"She's not pregnant," Deenie said. Then, turning to Gabby: "Her mom came and took her home."

Gabby nodded, looking down at her hands, clasped over her notebook. Deenie knew she wished they were alone too. Ever since that first week of school freshman year, it had been hard to find Gabby alone — at least at school, where girls hung from her like tassels.

"How can we go to class when this is going on?" Kim said. "We should go to her house."

"Have you ever even been to Lise's house?" Deenie said. Kim and Lise occupied starkly opposite poles in a group of friends. A year younger, filled with hard sophomore ambition, Kim was eager to spread herself wide, offering car rides, expensive eye shadow swiped from her mother, free gift cards from her job at the mall. She was the kind of girl you end up being friends with just because. The opposite of Lise, whom Deenie had known since third grade, whom she traded clothes, even underwear, with. Three days ago even helping her unwedge a crooked tampon, Lise laughing the whole time, wiggling her pelvis to assist.

That was how she knew Lise wasn't pregnant. That, and other reasons, like that Lise was still a virgin, mostly.

"The point is," Deenie said, "they're not going to just let us leave school."

"Maybe it was an allergic reaction," Skye said, tufting her hair against her cheek thoughtfully. "Don't you get those?"

Everyone looked at Kim, who was in fact allergic to everything, a special page in the school safety manual devoted to her. Nuts, eggs, wheat, yeast, shellfish, even some kinds of paper.

"I don't think that was it," Kim said, unwilling to share her special status. Then, swiveling closer to Gabby, eyes widening, "Oh God, maybe it's something to do with that one guy."

Deenie paused. "What guy?"

"You know," Kim said, dropping her chin, lowering her voice. "Don't you know?" Her lips were shining, like when she had her sister's car, waving the keys at everyone like they changed everything. "Didn't she tell you?"

"There's no guy," Deenie said. "So stop

making stuff up."

Boy crazy, that's what Ms. Enright, the English teacher, called Lise. But who could blame her? No guy had ever looked at Lise until suddenly they all did. Last summer, she wore a white bathing suit hooked with bamboo rings to the big Fourth of July barbecue and someone's older brother, who was in college, started calling her La Lise and even e-mailed her a song he wrote about her and her Lise-a-licious bikini.

Lise's mother would never have let her go out with him, but it set something off among the other boys and a fever in Lise, who suddenly decided that all boys were a-mazing, every one.

After that, Lise had vowed she'd never get that baby fat back, and every morning she'd chew on parsley or drink swampy green shakes out of her Dryden Wind & Strings thermos. It was the only way, because her mom made her finish a full glass of buttermilk at night, which, no matter what her mom said, she was sure was full of fat. *Maybe she wants me to be fat,* Lise said, *because she always makes monkey bread too and she knows I can't stop eating it.*

"You must've heard," Kim said, looking to Gabby, then Skye, who didn't even seem to be listening, her fingers running along

37

the lacy hem of her many-tiered skirt, vintage and baroque.

Gabby shook her head. "Lise didn't have a boyfriend," she said, looking at Deenie.

"Okay," Kim said, smiling enigmatically. "But I didn't say he was her *boyfriend.*"

"What would a guy have to do with her fainting anyway?" Deenie asked. "She's not pregnant."

"It could be a lot of things that aren't pregnant," Skye said, gaze still resting on her hair, webbed between her ringed fingers.

"Like what?" Kim asked, squirming onto her knees with fresh vigor.

"I knew this girl who got this thing from this guy once, an older guy, a club promoter," Skye said. "He had a big house on the lake and he gave her all this great red-string Thai stick. He leaves for the Philippines, she wakes up with trich. That's a sexual parasite. It crawls inside you." She reached down for her bag, tangled with fringe. "So."

No one said anything for a moment. Skye was somehow to be trusted in these matters. It was part of her mystique. That white-blond hair and thrift-store peacoat, the slave bracelets and green vinyl cowboy boots. Sunny, the artist aunt she lived with but whom Deenie had never seen and who let

38

Skye's ex-boyfriend sleep over, even though he was supposedly twenty-six years old, though no one had ever actually seen him either. The rumor was he'd been one of her aunt's students, even her boyfriend. After they broke up, Skye wore his coat, a long leather *Shaft* duster, to school every day until a hard winter rain shredded it.

"Well, maybe it doesn't have anything to do with guys," Kim said, facing them again, twisting her lips. "Maybe she's just sick."

Deenie picked up her phone and began typing.

eye roll, she texted Gabby, whose phone burbled immediately.

Gabby looked at her phone, grinned. Kim looked at both of them questioningly.

Nobody said anything, Kim's eyes darting back and forth between them.

"Well," Kim said, rising, tugging again at her tights, the ones just like Gabby's favorite pair, silver striped, "I got stuff to do."

"See ya," Deenie said, and they all watched until she was gone.

Nestling next to Gabby, Deenie let her head knock against hers.

Skye stood up, grabbing her purse, and Deenie's chest lifted in anticipation. At last, she'd have Gabby alone.

But then Gabby rose too, looping her arm

in Skye's to gain footing.

"Bye, Deenie," Skye said, already turning away.

"See you, Deenie," Gabby said, smiling apologetically. "Next semester I hope we get the same lunch period."

"Yeah," said Deenie, watching them walk away, their hair — Gabby's dark to Skye's bone-white — swinging in sync, their matching metallic tights. Those two leaving together again. Which happened a lot lately, like last week at the lake, and other times. Leaving together and leaving Deenie alone.

★   ★   ★

"Nash, get your ass to class."

Coach Haller's face was always red, a tomato with a crew cut. Eli's dad said he looked like every coach he'd ever known.

"Yes, sir," Eli said, rising from the locker-room bench. He had that crazy cold-hot feeling from the practice drills in the makeshift rink outside, the hot shower after, the school always blasting with forced heat that groaned through the building.

He'd been staring a long time at the picture on his phone, the girl in the purple underwear. Something about it.

And then there was the other thing.

Something he'd overheard that morning, about his sister. Someone seeing her get into a car last night, with some guy. And then there was A.J., that smirk of his.

All of that and looking at the purple panties on his phone, the girl's skin shining like girls' skin always seemed to. He began to feel a little queasy.

Sometimes he wished he didn't have a sister, though he loved Deenie and still remembered the feeling he had when he caught that kid Ethan pushing her off the swing set in the school yard in fifth grade. And how time seemed to speed up until he was shoving the kid into the fence and tearing his jacket. The admiring look his sister gave him after, the way his parents pretended to be mad at him but he could tell they weren't.

These days, it was pretty different. There'd be those moments he was forced to think about her not just as Deenie but as the girl whose slender tank tops hung over the shower curtain. Like bright streamers, like the flair the cheerleaders threw at games.

Sometimes he wished he didn't have a sister.

"Tell me again what Lise said," Gabby said when they caught each other between classes. "When you saw her."

"She wanted to know what happened to her," Deenie said. "She was really scared."

She couldn't remember any more than that, it had happened so fast. And now Kim's grimy insinuations, and Skye and her deadpan cool, were laid over her own bad feelings. She couldn't think. She just kept picturing Lise's face, the way her bare legs jerked when she went down.

"We should go check on her," Gabby said, scratching her palm. "See how she's doing."

"Leave school?"

"Yes."

"We'll get busted," Deenie said. "You will." Gabby had earned two detentions in the last month, one for smoking clove cigarettes in the kiln room and one for wandering off school property, sneaking to Skye's house, just a few blocks away.

"You, then. You won't get in trouble," Gabby said. "Your dad would understand."

"I'm not sure," Deenie said, but she knew she would go. Gabby was right. Someone had to see.

The bus ride was quick, and no one saw her.

Lise lived with her mom in a duplex on Easter Way. Despite all these years of being friends with her, Deenie had spent little time there.

"My mom doesn't like me to make lots of noise," Lise always said. Though they had never been noisy girls. At her own house, they spent most of their time watching movies and lying on Deenie's bed, listening to music and talking about how someday they'd travel through Africa or hand-feed stingrays in Bora Bora or ride Arabian horses in some desert, somewhere.

But Lise's mom usually preferred Lise to be at home with her, especially lately, when her daughter seemed to look more and more like she herself looked in her old modeling scrapbooks, posing in the Spiegel catalog and at trade shows, gold-shellacked hair and breasts like globes.

"Yes, she's a lovely woman," Deenie's dad had said when Lise once suggested he date her mother. "Lovely."

He said it very politely, like the time Deenie showed him the two-piece bathing suit her mom had bought her last summer. After, Deenie hid it in the back of the drawer and never wore it.

"Mr. Nash, I think she'd be so happy if she found a boyfriend," Lise had added, watching Mr. Nash as he focused intently on their English muffins, the toaster buzzing red beneath him.

"Lise," Deenie said later, "you can barely stand her. Why should my dad have to?"

As soon as the words came out, she regretted them.

But Lise had just sighed, winsomely, her pretty face crumpling a little.

"I just wish she had something to do. Other than watch my Facebook page."

Walking the three blocks from the bus stop, Deenie knew this was the right thing to do.

By the time she reached the front door, though, it felt like a big mistake. Except she'd promised Gabby, and, anyway, it looked like no one was home.

A long minute passed after she'd rung the bell.

She felt a grim thickness in the front of her head, a feeling of knowing something very important without knowing what it really meant. It reminded her of the day her mom decided to move out. The stillness in the morning, the house keys sitting in the middle of the kitchen table.

Her dad had spent hours shoveling the driveway, the front walk. She hadn't thought he'd ever come back inside.

Suddenly, the front door swung open. It was an older woman, her short white hair closely cropped, coat half open, purse slipping from her arm.

Deenie was pretty sure it was Lise's grandmother, but friends' grandmothers all kind of looked alike.

"Oh!" the woman said, startled. "Honey, what are you doing here?"

"I came to see how Lise was," Deenie said. "I was there when she —"

"She's not here," the woman blurted, her hands shaking wildly, car keys tight in red fingers. "They took her to the hospital. I'm going there now."

Behind her, the coffee table was overturned and a rug askew. There was a sharp smell of vomit.

"What happened?" Deenie said, her voice high. "Where's Lise?"

The car keys seemed to spring from the woman's hands, clattering onto the cement porch. They both bent down to grab them. Deenie could hear the woman's hard, hurried breaths. She grabbed the keys from Deenie's hands and inhaled deeply.

"Sweetie," she said, hands on Deenie's shoulders like she was seven, "go back to school, okay?"

Before Deenie could say what she wanted

45

to — *Can I come too? I need to come too* — the woman was running down the steps and to her car, its door hanging open.

Deenie looked back into the living room. A slick of vomit, a torn latex glove. Imagined Lise lying there, head knocking against the floor.

Lise on the classroom floor, eyes black.

Deenie now feeling her own knees shaking, like she hadn't eaten anything. The sense, again, of a bigness to the day that was more than she could ever want.

Lise.

You spend a long time waiting for life to start — her past year or two filled with all these firsts, everything new and terrifying and significant — and then it does start and you realize it isn't what you'd expected, or asked for.

4

Standing in front of his students, his butane lighters on, Tom couldn't get anyone's attention, not even Nat Dubow's, who loved to demonstrate every day how much he knew, who shot videos of himself doing chemistry experiments in a laboratory in his parents' garage and then posted the videos on the web under the name Nat Du-Wow. Despite Nat's constant urging — he'd planted his open laptop on Tom's desk one day, tail wagging — Tom always claimed he was too busy at the moment to watch, sorry. One night at home, though, he looked up an episode and was surprised to see four hundred comments posted and more than twelve hundred thumbs-up. All of it made him feel unbearably old.

But even Nat was distracted today, talking about epilepsy and electrical currents and auras.

"Mr. Nash, what if it was a tonic-clonic?"

47

he burst out, voice breaking. "It can damage your brain forever."

"Nat," he said, "let's focus, okay?"

But Tom was having trouble focusing too. He'd even walked down the aisles summoning all his best jokes, teasing Bailey Lu about the doodles on her hand, which usually made her blush and giggle.

Nothing worked, and Bailey could only stare at her hands in distress, her inky palms sweat-smeared.

Clearly, and he felt it himself, it wasn't the kind of day one of Mr. Nash's awesome gummy-bear-and-potassium-chlorate or Mentos-and-Diet-Coke demonstrations would become the talk of the school.

So he surrendered, gave them a pop quiz, and gazed out the window while they moaned and protested, their hysteria giving way to cries of injustice and the cruelty of teachers.

Meanwhile, he thought about Lise, and what it must be like for her mother, worrying. Sheila Daniels worried constantly anyway: about school trips to the falls, vaccines, the sound of hydraulic drills by the water wells.

And he reminded himself it was likely nothing. Girls fainted, kids fainted, fevers could do things to them, stress too. Some of these girls never seemed to eat, floating through the hallways like wraiths, drooping under the bleachers during gym. There wasn't much he hadn't seen in twenty years of high-school teaching.

After fourth period, Tom walked outside to the wind-slapping corner by the practice rink.

The new French teacher with the tattoo on her nape was leaning against a heating duct, smoking.

The first time he'd met her, he tried to imagine how he would have felt as a high-school kid if he'd had a slinky thirty-year-old French teacher with leather boots and a tattoo of a peacock feather snaking around her neck.

He wondered why Eli didn't take French.

"Bad habits," she said, grinning, and he started a little.

She gestured to her cigarette. He smiled.

"There are worse ones," he said.

"Like what?" she said, still grinning.

"Crack?" he ventured. "High-fructose corn syrup?"

"Come on," she said, offering him the gold pack in her ringed hand. "Don't make me the provocateur."

Just then, his cell phone tingled to life.

Deenie, the screen flashed, the picture of her in the sock-monkey hat she used to wear.

"Hey, Deen," he answered.

"Dad," she said, her voice sounding very far away.

"What's wrong, honey? Where are you?"

"Dad, can you come get me? Can you take me to the hospital?"

He spotted her standing in front of the Danielses' duplex, headphones on, jumping a little in the cold.

Her parka, those skinny legs — she looked for all the world like she had at eleven years old.

Noticing her bluing ankles, he could imagine what Georgia would say. He only hoped she'd taken the bus to Lise's and not gotten a ride with an older student, some boy. Sometimes Tom found it hard to believe he was in charge.

He wanted to ask what made her think it was okay to leave school like that, but he didn't. The truth was, he was always glad when she asked for a favor because she almost never did.

"Hey," he said, "get in."

Just like her brother, she didn't seem to get in the car so much as tumble into it,

50

like it was a disappearing space she had to hurry in and out of.

Headphones on, not quite looking him in the eye.

"So," he said, turning the steering wheel as he backed up, "to St. Ann's?"

She nodded, leaning her head against the glass.

He was used to teen sullenness, even though Deenie's sullenness was only occasional and never sour. But this felt like something else.

He wondered how bad it had been for her, seeing Lise. What had she seen?

"Are you going to tell me what's going on?" he asked.

"Did they say anything at school?" she asked. Tom could hear a screeching from her headphones. "About Lise?"

"I didn't wait," he said. "I just left. Carl took my fifth period."

Pushing her headphones from her ears, she looked at him.

Her face seeming to wilt, flower-like, before his eyes.

"Dad," she said softly. "I think something really bad's happening."

He looked at her, nodded, pressed the gas harder.

"Okay," he said, hand on her forearm.

"One step at a time."

"My daughter is her best friend. She was there when Lise fainted. You can't tell me anything?"

The admitting nurse, glasses smeary, hair slipping from its clip, sighed and shook her head.

"You're not family, sir."

He looked at her, saw the weariness set on her, the feeling around her of fluorescence and confusion, a surly man with a mustache shouting at her from his chair about the president and single-payer health care.

"I know," he said. "I'm sorry." He gave the slightest of smiles, the one Georgia used to call the Charmer and eventually called the Croc, and set his palms lightly on the counter. "I'm being a pain in the ass. It's just, my little girl over there . . ."

He let the nurse's eyes wander over. He imagined how Deenie looked to her, her parka sleeves too long, her brother's old trapper hat slipping from her brown hair.

". . . she got spooked seeing her friend faint," he said. "Now she's just scared out of her mind. I promised I'd find out something."

The nurse wouldn't give him a smile in return, but she did let her gaze float down to the computer screen.

"What's the girl's last name again? Daniels?"

He nodded.

She typed a moment, then her face tightened.

★   ★   ★

Standing by the dusty halogen lamp in the corner of the waiting room, Deenie was watching her father talk to the nurse when the corridor doors swung open wildly.

A middle-aged woman bucked past them, a frizz of blond hair, her bright down coat flapping.

"Oh God," she said, spotting Deenie. "Oh, honey."

It was Lise's mom.

Rushing toward Deenie, she seemed to envelop her in the coat's puffy squares.

"My baby," she said, pushing herself against Deenie, a gust of perfume and sweat. "You should see what they've done to my baby."

At first, it was like on television.

On TV, this was when you find out your friend is dead. Her face punched through a windshield in a drunk-driving accident.

Strangled by her jealous boyfriend. Locked in a cage by a man she met on the Internet.

Even though it didn't seem real, Deenie found herself wanting to do what they did on TV, maybe sink to her knees, the camera overhead swirling away from her, the music cueing up.

But then a doctor arrived to talk to Mrs. Daniels.

And hearing him, it became real.

"Deenie," her dad was saying, "it's okay."

He was holding on to her shoulder, which was shaking. She felt her whole body shaking and wondered: *Is this how it felt for Lise?*

"We're very lucky she was here when it happened," the doctor was saying to Mrs. Daniels. "You did the right thing calling 911. Every second counted. A cardiac event of this kind at home . . ."

"Her heart stopped," Mrs. Daniels said, her face damp, mascara ashed across her left cheekbone. "I could feel it in my hands."

Seconds later, Mrs. Daniels and the doctor disappeared behind the swinging doors, and her dad kept trying to explain things to her.

"Lise had a seizure at home," he said, "a bad one. And her mom called an ambulance. When she got there, something happened to her heart, but they were able

54

to stabilize her. They're taking good care of her."

Deenie nodded and nodded, but all she could think was she wished he weren't there with her. All the smiling-at-nurses in the world wouldn't get her behind those doors to see Lise. If her dad were gone she could find a way to get back there. She and Gabby always found ways to get places: behind the tall fences at the shuttered train depot, into that room in the school's basement where they kept old VCRs so they could watch a mildewed cassette of *Romeo + Juliet* during Back to School Night.

"We can wait," he said, "if you want."

"Okay."

"Let me just drive over to the school and set it up with my classes. And tell Eli."

Deenie nodded.

"Are you going to be okay here, by yourself?"

"I am, Dad," she said, keeping her voice even, steady. "I have to stay."

Sitting in one of the metal chairs, as far from the angry man with the droopy mustache as possible, she tried to text Gabby but couldn't think what to say.

Then she saw a couple, the woman with a crying toddler in green overalls sobbing at her hip. They were talking to a doctor and nurse in front of the same double doors Lise's mom had exited.

Behind them, somewhere inside the belly of St. Ann's, was Lise.

She couldn't believe no one saw her walk in, but then many times she felt invisible. At school, the mall, she could feel people walk right through her. Sometimes, with boys, she realized they could see straight behind her head, to blond-lashed Lise, to long-legged Gabby, to anyone else but her.

★   ★   ★

His leg shook a little on the gas. He was thinking about Deenie in that waiting room with the growling man with the coffee-damp mustache and who knew what new arrivals. Downriver bikers with meth mouths, suburban predators prowling for teenage girls.

Lately, when he read the crime-beat section of the paper, he'd begun to feel his once-gentle town, their little Brigadoon, was teeming with endless threats imperiling his children.

He could hear Georgia's voice buzzing in his head.

So you left her there? You couldn't just call

the school? Call our son?

Sometimes it felt like parenting amounted to a series of questionable decisions, one after another.

At least his version of it.

It was just before lunch and the corridors were swollen with students, dozens of hunch-hooded sweatshirts, the boys shoving one another into lockers while the girls glided by in low-tops, skirts, and three layers of tights, their smiles nervous and intricate. Tom spent half his day feeling sorry for girls.

His phone vibrating, he thought it might be Deenie, but the minute he moved past the front entryway, the screen went black, his signal lost.

When he stepped out again, he couldn't get it back.

He waited at Eli's locker, and waited, and then the second bell rang, and everyone scattered, backpacks like cockroach shells.

There was a slight ripple in his chest. *Where is Eli, anyway?* As if Eli were as reliable as an elevator and not his shaggy, perennially late son.

He'll be here any second, he told himself, but a nagging fear came from nowhere: *What if, what if?*

Rounding the corner, he spotted his son's blaring-blue hockey jersey.

There he was, standing in front of his calculus class, shoving folded papers into a textbook.

Tall and carefree and more handsome than any son of his had a right to be. And late as ever, for everything. It was hard to explain the relief he felt.

"Dad?" Eli said, looking up, surprised. "Dad, why are you smiling?"

5

Walking through the cafeteria, Eli Nash was thinking about Lise, whom he'd known since she was bucktoothed and round as a tennis ball. She'd grown into the teeth, but not all the way, and the overbite made her look older, like her new body did, like everything did. She'd been one of those baby-fatted girls who laughed too loudly, covering their mouths, squealing. Then, at some point, overnight, she'd done something, or God had, because she was so pretty it sometimes hurt to look at her.

It felt like, whatever happened now, Lise was maybe gone. That maybe it'd be like his friend Rufus, who'd hit his head on the practice rink last year and who seemed okay but never laughed at anyone's jokes anymore and sometimes couldn't smell his food.

"Eli," his dad had said, finding him before calculus. Wearing a funny smile like the one he'd have after Eli had had a rough game, a cut over his eye, a stick across the face. "Can you do something for me?"

He said of course he would.

Right away, he spotted Gabby in the cafeteria's far corner, where she always sat, usually with his sister, their heads together as if planning a heist.

Gabby was the one all the girls puppy-dogged after at school, the kind other girls thought was "gorgeous" and guys didn't get at all. Or they got something, which made them nervous. Made him nervous.

All the stuff that had gone down with her family, it seemed to give Gabby this thick glaze, like the old tables in the library that shone golden-like, with dark whorls, but when you got close and touched them, they felt like plastic, like nothing. All they did was push splinters into your hand.

Eli didn't much like sitting in the library either.

She was spinning a can of soda between her palms, that girl Skye lurking behind her, the one with all the bracelets and heavy skirts, the one who got suspended once for coming to health class with a copy of the *Kama Sutra,* which she said was her aunt Sunny's, as if it were something everyone had at home, like the dictionary.

"Gabby," he said, tapping her shoulder.

Gabby's head whipped around and she looked at him, eyes wide.

"Oh!" she said. "Eli. You scared me."

Skye was looking at him, her eyes narrow, and Eli removed his fingers quickly from Gabby's shoulder.

"Sorry," he said. "Can I talk to you for a second?" He looked at Skye. "Alone?"

"Okay," Gabby said, slowly. "Sure."

They walked over to one of the far tables. Gabby was almost as tall as he was and had a big heap of hair on top of her head, like Skye and so many of the other girls seemed to be copying. Sometimes they'd put their hair in heavy braids they'd wrap across their heads and he didn't get it but figured it was a fashion thing beyond his grasp.

"Deenie's at the hospital," he said as they sat down, "with Lise. Something happened to Lise. I figured you might not know."

"I didn't," she said, shaking her head.

Three tables behind, Eli could see still Skye, her ringed fingers clawed around her phone, head bowed, typing something.

"I mean, I didn't know Deenie was at the hospital," Gabby said. "Or that Lise was."

He didn't think he'd ever sat so close to Gabby, her skin pale and that serious expression she always wore. He had the sense of so many things going on behind

61

that face.

"Yeah," Eli said. "They had to call an ambulance, I guess. She's there now."

Gabby's phone buzzed slightly on the table. They both looked at it.

"So, what happened? Is it . . ." Gabby started. "Is it mono again?"

Eli paused, licking his lips.

"I don't think so," he said.

★　★　★

Once she got behind the double doors, Deenie had no idea how to find Lise. There was a feeling to the place like in the basement at school, where they held classes for a while when enrollment ran too high. A furnacey smell and uncertain buzzing and whirring sounds. Turning the corners, the floor sloping, you felt like you were going down into something no one knew about, had forgotten about.

At the end of the first long hallway she could see an old man sitting in a wheelchair, his white hair tufted high like a cartoon bird. He was wearing a very nice robe, quilted, like in an old movie. She wondered who'd bought it for him and where that person was now.

The man's head kept drifting from side to

side, his mouth open in a kind of perpetual, silent panic. *How did this happen? Why am I here?*

"Hi," she said as she approached, surprising herself.

He looked up with a start, his swampy green eyes trying to focus on her.

"Not another one?" he said, his voice small and wavery. "Are you another one?"

One hand lifted forward from his silken lap.

She smiled uneasily, not knowing what else to do.

"Okay, well," she said, and kept walking.

Maybe that's what it's like when you're old, she thought. Always more young people, a parade of them going by. *Here's another one.*

"I hope it will be okay," he said, his voice rising as she passed. "I hope."

Far down the hall now, her head feeling hot, she turned to look back at him.

"I . . . I . . . ," he was saying, his voice like a creak.

She started to smile at him but saw his face — from this distance a white smudge — and stopped.

It took five minutes, and no one questioned her or even seemed to notice.

Rushing as if with purpose, she spotted Mrs. Daniels's turquoise coat in an open doorway, hovering just inside the threshold, Lise's grandmother beside her.

Walking in, she saw the hospital bed webbed with wires, a sickly sac hanging in one corner like a trapped mite. It reminded her of Skye once telling them that you should put cobwebs on wounds, that it stopped blood.

"Deenie," Mrs. Daniels cried out. "Look at our Lisey."

The puff of both women's winter coats, the sputtering monitor, a nurse suddenly coming behind her, and Mrs. Daniels sobbing to breathlessness — Deenie pushed past it all to try to get closer to Lise. Like people did in the movies, she would push past everything. She would not be stopped.

But when she got to the foot of Lise's bed, she halted.

All she could see was a violet blur and something that looked like a dent down the middle of Lise's delicate forehead.

"What happened," Deenie said, a statement more than a question. "What's wrong with her."

"She hit her head on the coffee table," the grandmother said. As if that were the problem. As if the purple gape on Lise's

64

brow were the problem here. Were why they were all here.

Though it kind of felt that way to Deenie too because there it was. A broken mirror where the pieces didn't line up. Splitting Lise's face in two. Changing it.

"That's not Lise," Deenie said, the words falling from her mouth.

Everyone looked at her, Mrs. Daniels's chin shaking.

But it felt true.

The nurse took Deenie's arm roughly.

"They always look different," the nurse said. "She's very weak. You need to leave."

Mrs. Daniels made a moaning sound, tugging on her mother's coat front.

"But are you sure it's her?" Deenie asked as the nurse walked her to the door. "Mrs. Daniels, are you sure that's Lise?"

6

Pulling into the hospital lot, Tom found his daughter standing out front, pogo-ing on the sidewalk to keep warm.

She climbed inside the car.

"Dad, I don't want to be there anymore, okay?"

"Sure," he said. "No one likes hospitals."

Her chin kept jogging up and down, but she wouldn't look at him.

"I don't like it there," she said. "I really don't."

"I know," he said, watching her scroll through text messages. One after another, they arrived, her phone sputtering in her hand.

She hadn't met his eyes once.

"Deenie," he said, "I think I should just take you home."

"I think . . ." she started, then set her phone on her lap. "I want to go back to school, Dad."

There was an energy on her that worried him, like right before she left for her mom's place each month. Sometimes it felt like she spent hours putting things in and taking things out of her backpack. Blue sweater in, blue sweater out, *Invisible Man* in, then out, biting her lip and staring upward. *What is it I need, what is missing.*

"A lot's happening," he tried again. "We can go home. Watch a movie. I'll heat up those frozen turnovers. Those fat apple ones you love. Your favorite Saturday-night special."

"When I was twelve," she said, like that was a million years ago. It had been their weekly ritual. She liked to watch teen movies from the '80s and make fun of their hair but by the end she would tear up when the tomboy with the wrong clothes danced with the prom king under pink balloons and scattered lights. It turned out he'd missed the perfect girl, right in front of him all along.

"I just want to be at school," she said, softly.

He guessed there might be something soothing about the noise and routine of school. Except she didn't know yet that the school didn't feel routine right now.

"Okay," he said, after a pause. "If you're sure."

His mind was full of ideas, ways to comfort her, all of them wrong.

"But Deenie," he said.

"Yeah, Dad."

"It's going to be okay," he said. The eternal parent lie, a hustle.

She seemed to hear him but not really hear him.

"I don't think it was even her," she said, a tremble to her voice.

"Was who? Did you *see* her, Deenie? At the hospital?"

She nodded, her fingerless gloves reaching up to her face.

"Just for a second. But I don't think that was Lise," she repeated, shaking her head.

"Baby," he said, slowing the car down. He wondered what she'd seen. How bad Lise looked. "It was her."

"I mean, none of it was Lise," she said, eyes on the traffic as they approached the school. "In class this morning too. Watching her. She looked so weird. So angry."

Her voice speeding up, like her mother's did when she got excited. Trying to help him see something.

"Like she was mad at me," she went on. "Even though I knew she wasn't. But it was like she was. She looked so mad."

"Why would she be mad at you, Deenie?"

he said, stopping the car too long at the blinking red, someone honking. "She wasn't. You had nothing to do with this."

She looked at him, her eyes dark and stricken, like she'd been hit.

★ ★ ★

It just wasn't a day for going to class.

It was nearly sixth period and, so far, Eli had made it only to French II — he never missed it, spent all forty-two minutes with his eyes anchored to the soft swell of Ms. Loll's chest. The way she pushed her hair up off her neck when she got frustrated, her dark nails on that swirling tattoo.

He never missed French.

But the idea of going to history, of sitting in class with everyone gripped in the talk of Lise Daniels and her rabid-dog routine and his sister seeing it — it all knotted inside him.

He didn't like to imagine what Deenie must have been feeling to ditch school, which wasn't something she ever did. She was the kind of girl who burst into tears when her fourth-grade teacher called her Life Sciences folder "unkempt."

So he found himself back behind the school, where the equipment manager kept the rusting bins of rubber balls, hockey pucks, and helmets.

The air heavy with Sani Sport and ammonia and old sweat, it reminded him of the smell when he'd put his skates on the radiator after a game, scorching them to dryness. As cold as it was, he could still smell it, and it soothed him.

He was sitting on the railing of the loading ramp when he heard a skitter, then the shush of a heavy skirt.

"You want some?" a crackly voice said.

He turned and saw that Skye girl again, leaning against the brick wall, a beret tugged over her masses of blond hair.

She was holding a brown cigarette in her hand, a sweet scent wafting from her, mixed with girl smells like hairspray and powder.

"What?" he said, stalling for time, watching her walk closer to him, her vinyl boots glossy and damp.

She waved the cigarette at him.

He wasn't sure what it was, but it didn't smell like pot. He wouldn't have wanted it if it was. It affected his play. A few times, though, he'd smoked at night, at a party, then picked up his skates, headed to the community rink. Coach had given him a key and he could go after closing, the ice strewn with shavings from the night's free-skate, the hard cuts from a pickup game. He could go as slow as he wanted.

He'd spin circuits, the gliding settling him, the feeling in his chest and the black sky through the tall windows.

Sometimes he felt like it was the only time he truly breathed. It reminded him of being six and his mom first taking him out on the ice, kneeling down to hold his quaking ankles with her purple mittens, stiff with snow.

"It's all-natural," Skye said, returning the cigarette to her mouth. Her lavender lips. "I don't believe in putting bad things inside me. It's musk root. It helps you achieve balance."

"My balance is good," he said, the smell of her cigarette drifting toward him again. Spicy, cloying. He kind of liked it but didn't want to. "But thanks."

"I heard Deenie went to the hospital," she said. "And that Lise's mom's freaking out and that Lise almost died."

Everyone knew things so fast, phones like constant pulses under the skin.

"I don't really know," he said. "You'd have to ask her."

She nodded, then seemed to shudder a little, her narrow shoulders bending in like a bird's.

71

"It's funny how you never think about your heart," she said.

"What?"

"About your real heart," she said. "Not when you're young like us. I heard her heart stopped for a minute. I never thought about my heart before. Have you?"

Eli didn't say anything but slid off the ramp. Looking at her hands, he saw they were shaking, and he wondered for a second if she was going to be sick.

"It's funny," she said, "because it's almost like I *felt it* before it happened. I've known Lise awhile. We used to share bunks at sleepaway camp. She has a very strong energy, don't you think?"

"I don't know," he said, heading toward the door, the blast of heat from inside.

"This morning I was waiting for Lise at her locker. I had my hand on the locker door and it was so freaky. I felt this energy shoot up my body."

She lifted her free hand and fluttered it from her waist to her neck.

He watched her.

"Like a little jolt. Right to the center of me."

She let her hand, blue from the cold, drift down to her stomach and rest, the dark-red tassels of her scarf hanging there.

"But that's how I am," she said. "My aunt says I was born with dark circles on my feet, like a tortoiseshell. Which means I feel things very deeply."

★　★　★

There was only one period left and suddenly Deenie couldn't remember where she was supposed to be.

She'd thought school would be easier, busier. She was trying to get the picture of Lise out of her head. The angry crack down her face. Lise was never angry at anyone. Even when she should be.

But now Deenie wished she were at home instead, sitting on the sunken L-shaped sofa watching movies with her dad, her fingers greased with puff pastry.

And so she walked aimlessly, the sound of her squeaking sneakers loud in her ears. A haunted feeling to go with the hauntedness of the day.

It wasn't until Mrs. Zwada, frosted hair like a corona, called out to her from the biology lab that she realized that was where she was supposed to be.

For a moment, Deenie just stood in the doorway, the room filled with gaping faces. The penetrating gaze of Brooke Campos, her useless lab partner who never did the write-ups and refused to touch the fetal pig.

"Honey, I think you should sit down," Mrs. Zwada said, her brightly lacquered face softer than Deenie had ever seen it. "You can just sit and listen."

"No," Deenie said, backing up a little.

Everyone in the class seemed to be looking at her, all their faces like one big face.

"I'm sorry," she said. "I have to find Gabby."

She began to edge into the hall, but Mrs. Zwada's expression swiftly hardened into its usual rictus.

"There's going to be some order to this day," she said, grabbing Deenie by the shoulder and ushering her inside.

So Deenie sat and listened to all the talk of mitosis, watched the squirming cells on the PowerPoint. The hard forks of splitting DNA, or something.

A few minutes before class ended, Brooke Campos poked her in the neck from behind.

Leaning forward, breath sugared with kettle corn, she whispered in Deenie's ear.

"I heard something about you. And a guy."

The bell rang, the class clattered to life, and Brooke rose to her feet.

Looking down at Deenie, she grinned. "But I don't believe it."

"What?" Deenie said, looking up at her, her face hot. "What?"

Her winter hat yanked over her long hair, hair nearly to her waist, Gabby was standing at her locker. Again, with Skye.

Until last fall, Deenie never really knew Skye, even though she'd been in classes with her since seventh grade. Skye was never in school choir, yearbook, French club, plays. She never helped decorate the homecoming float.

But she became Gabby's friend in that way that can happen, because the girl with the cool boots always finds the girl with the occasional slash of pink in her hair. The two of them like a pair of exotic birds dipping over the school's water fountains — you knew they would find each other. And, about a year ago, they had.

At first, Gabby told Deenie she liked to spend time at Skye's house because her aunt was never home and you could just hang out, listen to music, drink the fogged jugs of Chablis in the fridge or a stewed-fruit concoction her uncle used to make in the basement and called prison wine.

But Deenie knew it was more than that. Saw the way they'd exchange looks, how Gabby would come to school wearing Skye's catbird ring. She worried Gabby maybe shared things with Skye, personal things, like about her dad. Things she'd only ever shared with Deenie.

It's like you with Lise, Gabby once said. *You guys have this thing.* Which Deenie guessed was true because she'd known Lise forever and Gabby only since middle school, and Lise was part of her growing up and Gabby was part of everything newer, more exciting. And everything to come.

"Deenie," Gabby called out. "What happened?"

"It was bad," Deenie said. And then stopped. You couldn't talk about it the way you'd talk about a pop quiz or shin splints from gym. Your words had to show how big it was.

"What's wrong with her?" Gabby asked.

"Did you talk to her?" Skye asked.

"Talk to her? No. You don't get it. She's . . ."

Skye looked at her. They both were looking at her, both so tall and heavy-haired and clustered close. Waiting.

She didn't know how to talk about it, about what she'd seen. *Her face, it wasn't hers. It wasn't her. It was two pieces that didn't go together and neither of them was Lise.*

"Something happened," she finally said. "To her heart."

"Is she going to be okay?" Gabby asked, her chin shaking. "Is she, Deenie?"

Deenie didn't know what to say. Her mouth opened and nothing came out.

★　★　★

"We haven't been able to find out much," Principal Crowder said to Tom. "The hospital won't release information without her mother's permission, but Mrs. Daniels hasn't returned our calls. Understandable, of course."

"Right," Tom said, recalling the way Sheila Daniels had looked in the waiting room. He'd tried phoning her twice, thinking that's what one did. "If I can help . . ."

A teacher for nearly two decades, Tom still felt vaguely uncomfortable in the principal's office. Even though the principal — Ben Crowder, a shiny-faced former "curricular specialist" from the state education department — was only a few years older. Once, he'd flagged Tom down at a local gas station as he struggled to remove the frozen fuel cap from the tank of his Volkswagen.

Help a brother out? he'd asked, a desper-

77

ate gleam in his eye.

"I've talked to all Miss Daniels's teachers," Crowder said, tapping his fountain pen on the desk, "but I wanted to talk to you too. I heard you left campus to see her."

"Yes," he said, noticing his phone was flashing with that red zigzag of a missed call, something that always snagged at his nerves. "My daughter's best friends with her. But I guess I know about as much as you. It was a pretty chaotic scene."

"We followed all the procedures on our end," Crowder said. "But apparently things took a turn when she got home. Some kind of arrhythmia brought on by a seizure. Of course, there's already rumors."

"Rumors?"

"I wondered if you'd heard anything."

"No," Tom said. "Like what?"

But Crowder only leaned back in his chair and sighed.

"What a thing. I've only met the mother once, at a school-board meeting last fall. She seemed like a . . . cautious woman. The anxious type. So this has to be especially challenging."

"Well," Tom said, his fingers resting on his phone, "I guess all we can do is wait. I'm sure we'll know more soon."

"Right," Crowder said, tapping his pen on

the legal pad in front of him. "That's right."

From the entrance of the breezeway, Tom watched the throngs of woolly-hatted kids and pink-necked seniors pushing their way out of the school and over to the parking lot, the slightly rusting bus-stop sign quaking in the hard wind.

He sent Eli a quick text, hoped he'd get it.

Can you take D home and bring car back before yr practice?

He wanted to take her home himself, but he had detention duty.

And there was the missed call: Lara Bishop. Gabby's mom.

"Lara," he said, "how are you?"

It seemed like a silly question, but he didn't know what she'd heard about Lise. And he'd never felt particularly at ease with her. She had a look about her, a wariness, a watchfulness. He'd once heard the phrase *cop eyes,* and when he looked at Lara Bishop he thought maybe that's what cop eyes looked like. Or maybe it was just that he knew what she'd been through.

Maybe, really, it was the way he looked at her.

"Tom," she said, in that low voice of hers,

always barely above a whisper, "how scary. I got a message from Sheila. I don't even know her very well. I called back, but I just got voice mail."

"Maybe an allergic reaction?" Tom said. "Maybe epilepsy?" It was the first time all day he'd speculated out loud. It felt like a relief.

"She sounded kind of . . . off," she said. "But how else would she sound, right? She kept saying her daughter was the healthiest girl in the world and hadn't done anything to deserve this."

"People say all kinds of things," Tom said, but he felt a slight twinge behind his left eye. He was remembering Sheila from that school-board meeting now. Going on and on about vaccinations and autism. She had had some kind of petition.

"Is Deenie doing okay?" she said. "Did she talk to her mom?"

Tom paused for a second, realizing he had no idea.

"Everything's been happening so fast," he said, feeling a burr of irritation he couldn't identify.

"Of course," Lara replied quickly. "I haven't even had a chance to talk to Gabby. I'm heading over there now to get her."

"I'm sure everything's going to be fine,"

he found himself saying for what seemed to be the hundredth time that day. Each time, he felt like he made it worse.

"Well," she sighed, and Tom thought he could hear the click in her throat, a vestige from the tracheostomy after the accident. (The *accident* — is that what you called a claw hammer to the face?) She always wore a thin pearl choker to try to cover the scar, two curved lines, like an eye. Every time Tom had ever seen her, she'd put her fingertips to her throat at least once. Sometimes he saw Gabby do it too. That scar was so small compared to the one on her face, but she tried to cover that too, with a swoop of her dark red hair.

"Well," he said, offering a faint laugh — the nervous laughter worried parents share when they realize, jointly, there's nothing they can do. *You can't stop them, you can only try to keep the lines of communication open.* "I hear anything, I'll call you."

"Thanks, Tom," she said, the rasp there. "This stuff happens — you just want to *see* them, you know?"

★　★　★

Walking from the west faculty lot, hoping her brother's unprecedented offer would

81

wait, Deenie hunted for Gabby.

Amid the crush of pink-puffer freshmen, she found her by the front circle, talking on her phone, her eyes covered by large green sunglasses.

"Hey, girl," Deenie said. "Wanna ride?"

"Hey, girl," Gabby said, shoving her phone in her pocket. "My mom's on her way. She heard about everything."

"Too bad. Eli offered. He must've gotten hit in the head with a puck today."

"That is too bad," Gabby said, smiling a little. And they were both quiet for a second.

"I still can't believe it," Gabby said. "About Lise."

They spotted Mrs. Bishop's car, the only black one, like a carpenter ant.

"Yeah," Deenie said. "Maybe . . . maybe the two of us could go to the hospital later, if —"

"I can't go back there," Gabby said quickly.

At first, Deenie wasn't sure what she meant. But seeing Gabby's mother pull up, she realized what it was. It'd been four years since Gabby's dad did what he did, which wasn't a long time, really. Four years since she and her mother were rolled into the emergency room of St. Ann's. That was the last time anything big had happened in

Dryden. A thought fluttered through her head: *What are the odds that the two biggest things ever to happen here happen to my two best friends?*

"I'm sorry," Gabby said. "Am I a bad friend?"

"No," Deenie said, pushing a smile through her frozen face. "I get it."

Gabby tried for a smile too, but there was something under it, heavy and broody. You could feel it under your skin. In so many ways, knowing Gabby was like brushing up against something meaningful, pained, and grand. Before her, the only time Deenie had ever felt it was that time she was ten and the whole family went to the Cave of the Winds, which Deenie had read about in a book. Enfolded between a wall of rock and the falls, Deenie had held her mom's hand and felt the water and the winds and the cataracts mix. "A mysterious and indelible experience," the book had said, and that's how it felt. A thing that marked you. Like Gabby's history marked her, had marked her mother.

"Gabby, she's going to be okay," Deenie said. "Lise is."

Opening the car door to a blast of heat, Gabby turned and faced Deenie. "Definitely," she said. "She's our Lise."

Deenie watched as Gabby slid into the car, her sparkling low-tops, her knit ballet tights bright and jaunty, a day begun in a different place.

"Bye, Mrs. Bishop," Deenie said.

"Take care of yourself, Deenie," Gabby's mom said, waving a gloved hand, her sunglasses larger than Gabby's even, almost covering her whole face.

★ ★ ★

DETENTION CANCELED, Tom wrote on the sign, slapping it on the classroom door. It felt like a day for executive decisions.

He didn't know what he'd been thinking, leaving Deenie alone at the house after everything that had happened. And what if she decided to go to the hospital again?

Walking into the lot, he saw Eli had already returned his car, angled rather dramatically and nearly touching the French teacher's perky Vespa. Tomato red.

Seated behind the wheel, he made the call before he could stop and plan it out. Didn't want to always be readying himself to talk to her. Two years, it should be easier.

"Hey, Georgia."

He told her everything as quickly as he could, hearing her gasp, her voice rushing forward.

"Oh, Tom," she said, and it was like no time had passed. *Georgia, Eli fell off his bike, jammed his finger in gym, split his forehead on the ice.* Her hand on his. *Oh, Tom.*

"I thought you should know," he said.

There was a pause. He could hear her breathing. "I can't believe it. Little Lise."

And there it was: the immediate gloom in her voice, almost like resignation. *Life is so goddamned hard.* Near the end, she'd sounded like that a lot.

"I'm sure she's going to be okay," he said. "And Deenie's doing fine."

"Now all I can do is picture the girls in the backyard," she said. "Lise with her little potbelly, running through the sprinkler in her two-piece."

Tom felt his face warm. Last summer, Lise in a two-piece. From across the town pool, from behind, he'd mistaken her for one of Deenie's swim instructors. Carla, the graduate student in kinesiology who always teased him about needing a haircut.

"I thought probably you knew already," he said, his voice suddenly louder than he meant. "That Deenie'd called you."

"No." The drop in her voice gave him a second of shameful pleasure.

It had been a lousy thing for him to say.

85

Deenie almost never called her.

"Bad reception at the school," he said quickly. "You remember. The hospital too."

"Right. God, that town," she said, as if she had never lived here at all.

Turning the radio loud, listening to some frenzied music Eli had left for him, Tom drove home along Dryden Lake. There were other routes, faster ones, but he liked it.

He remembered swimming in it when they'd first moved here, before all the stories came out. He loved the way it shimmered darkly. It looked alien, an otherworldly lagoon.

Even then, there was talk of designating it a dead lake, the worst phrase he'd ever heard. At some point, people started calling it that, overrun by plants and no fish to be found, and the department of health coming all the time to take water samples.

It was almost ten years ago when the little boy died there, his body seizing up and his lungs filling with furred water. It was the asthma attack that killed him and the boy should never have been swimming alone, but it didn't matter. After, the city threw up high sheet fences and ominous skull-and-crossbones signs. Eli used to have nightmares about the boy. All the kids did. *It could happen to me, Dad. What if it's me?*

But for years, Georgia still liked to swim there at night when it was very warm. Sometimes, he would go too, if the kids were asleep. They felt like bad parents, sneaking out at night, driving the mile and a half, laughing guiltily in the car.

It was something.

The blue-green algal blooms effloresced at night. Georgia loved them, said they were like velvet pillows under her feet. He remembered grabbing her soft ankle in the water, radioactive white.

After a while, he stopped going. Or she stopped inviting him. He wasn't sure which came first.

One night, she came home, her face deathly pale and her mouth black inside. She told him the algae was like she'd never seen it, a lush green carpet, and she couldn't stop swimming, even when it started to hurt her eyes, thicken in her throat.

All night she threw up, her body icy and shaking, and by five a.m., he finally stopped listening to her refusals, gathered her in his arms, and drove her to the emergency room. They kept her for a few hours, fed her a charcoal slurry that made her mouth blacker still. She'd be fine in a day.

"I can't breathe," she kept saying. "I can't breathe."

★ ★ ★

Hey — U ok? Just saying . . .

That's what the text said, but Deenie didn't recognize the number.

She'd inherited Eli's old phone and often got texts meant for him. One night, that senior girl who always talked about ballet and wore leotards and jeans to school texted twenty-four times. One of the texts had said — Deenie never forgot it — my pussy aches for u. It had to have been the worst thing she'd ever read. She'd read it over and over before deleting it.

Except this didn't seem like one of those texts.

Who r u? Deenie typed back but stopped before she hit Send.

She leaned back on her bed. The house felt quiet, peaceful.

Downstairs, Dad and Eli were watching TV. Something loud and somehow soothing on ESPN Classic. The constant hum of the household for ten years.

It was nine thirty, and she wanted to stay off the computer. Red pop-ups in the bottom corner of her laptop.

The worst was the picture of Lise everyone was posting. Someone must have taken it with a phone right after it happened. A blurred shot of Lise's bare legs, a rake of hair across her face, that made Deenie almost cry.

There seemed no stopping all the texts jangling from her phone.

People she barely knew but who knew she was friends with Lise.

Kim C says she heard Lise was on Pill was she

Why did everything have to be about sex, she wondered. Didn't it make a lot more sense that it was something else? Like in sixth grade when Kim Court ate the frozen Drumstick and Mrs. Rosen had to inject her with the EpiPen in front of everyone. After, everyone called her EpiGirl or, worse, Nutz Girl, and since then no one could eat nuts anywhere at all.

Have u heard of toxik shok? tampax can kill u

Then came crazy thoughts, like what if, trying to help Lise dislodge that crooked tampon a few days before, she'd done something wrong? What if it was her fault?

She kept thinking about what Gabby had said: *Am I a bad friend?*

That morning, Deenie hadn't even met

Lise at her locker. She hadn't wanted to see her. Her head still muggy with thoughts of the night before, of Sean Lurie, she wasn't ready to tell. And Lise would see her, and would just *know*.

Tugging off her tights and jeans, she took a long bath, pushing her hand down on her pelvis until it burned.

She still felt funny down there, like things weren't right.

When you thought about your body, about how much of it you couldn't even see, it was no wonder it could all go wrong. All those tender nerves, sudden pulses. Who knew.

Right now, she couldn't even picture Sean Lurie's face.

She remembered, though, the oven grit under his fingernails, the grunt from his mouth, the rough shudder, jerking her back and forth beneath him so she thought something had gone wrong. And then the soft sigh, like everything was good at last.

It made her head hurt, and she put it all away in a high corner of her thoughts, where she wouldn't have to look at it for a while.

After the bath, she sprawled on her bed and opened her history book and read about ancient Egypt.

Mr. Mendel had told them that Cleopatra may have been a virgin when she smuggled herself in a hemp sack to meet Julius Caesar. Giving herself to him was pivotal to her rise to power.

The book explained how Cleopatra first enticed Mark Antony by dropping one of her pearl earrings into a wine goblet. As it dissolved, she swallowed while he watched.

Deenie read the passage three times, trying to imagine it. She wasn't sure why it was sexy, but it was. She could picture the pearly rind on the queen's lips.

In class, Skye said she'd read something online about how Cleopatra used diaphragms made of wool and honey, and a paste of salt, mouse droppings, honey, and resin for a morning-after pill, both of which seemed maybe worse than being pregnant.

Deenie wondered how it all came to pass, the virgin–turned–seductress–turned–sorceress of her own body.

She thought for a second about the snap of the condom Sean Lurie had used and she covered her face with her book, squeezing her eyes tight until she forced it out of her head.

By ten o'clock, she'd read all forty of the assigned pages, plus ten extra.

At some point, she could hear Eli in his room, his phone and computer making their noises, Eli clearing his throat.

Once, a few weeks ago, she'd heard a girl's voice in there and wondered if it was porn on the computer until she could tell it wasn't. She heard the voice say Eli's name. *E-liiii.*

She'd turned her music as loud as she could, held her hands to her ears, even sang to herself, eyes clamped shut. She hoped he heard her fling off her Ked so hard it hit the wall. She hoped he remembered she was here.

Tonight, though, the house was hushed. She was so glad for it she didn't even feel bad about not calling her mom back. And when her dad knocked good night and said he loved her, she made sure he heard her reply.

"Me too. Thanks, Dad."

At midnight, she felt her phone throb under her hand.

The picture of Gabby from when she had that magenta streak in her hair.

"Hey, girl."

"Hey, girl," Gabby said, a slur to her voice. "I just fell asleep. I dreamed it was tomorrow and she was back. Lise. She was laughing at us."

"Laughing at us?" Deenie said. She wondered if Gabby was still sleeping. She sounded funny, like her tongue was stuck to the roof of her mouth. "Why?"

"I don't know. It was a dream," Gabby said. "When I woke up, I thought maybe something happened. Maybe she called you."

Deenie paused, wondering how Gabby could ever think that. But Gabby hadn't been to the hospital. Hadn't seen Lise, seen her mom. Hadn't heard all that talk about the heart, Lise's heart. Deenie pictured it now, like a bruised plum in her mom's hand.

"No," Deenie said, carefully. "I don't think it's going to be that quick."

"I know," Gabby said, her voice sludgy and strange. "Listen, I'll see you tomorrow, Deenie."

"Okay," Deenie said. She wanted to say something more, but she couldn't guess what it would be. Then she remembered something. "Gabby, what was the rumor?"

There was a pause and for a second she thought Gabby had fallen asleep.

"What?" she finally said.

"This morning, before everything, you said you heard something about me."

"I did?" she said, voice faraway. "I don't remember that at all."

7

WEDNESDAY

When he woke up, Eli thought for a second that he was on the ice. Felt his feet in his skates, legs pushing down, grinding the blades hard. His chest cold and full. This happened sometimes.

It was still dark when he left the house for practice. It always was, and he never minded.

He rode his bike through the town, swooping under the traffic lights, counting the number of times the red signals would blink and no one would be there to stop.

It took him a long time to remember everything that happened the day before.

Morning practice felt like part of the dream and he woke up after, in the locker-room shower, his legs loosening and the heat gusting around him, his body finally stopping and his mind slowly rousing. Remembering all the things he'd forgotten.

"Principal Crowder's having a very bad time," Mrs. Harris whispered to Tom as he strolled through the administration office. "He can't get any information on Lise Daniels, and parents keep calling."

"Well," he said, reaching for his mail, "I'm sure Crowder's state of mind isn't a big concern for Lise's mom."

"Of course not," Mrs. Harris said. "But it would help us to know. To calm everyone down. When something happens in front of students . . ."

Tom nodded. He was looking at an interoffice memo: *Spring Will Spring (Soon!): A Morning Concert. All Faculty Expected to Attend.*

"So this is still happening today?" he asked. A picture came to him of Lise, rosebud lips perched on her silver flute, at the last recital, at every recital since fifth grade. She used to practice on a plastic water bottle. *You pretend like you're spitting a watermelon seed,* he once heard her tell Deenie, and they both giggled. All the talk of tonguing and fingering and the two girls laughing without even knowing why. These days, they didn't laugh about any of that —

a thought that made Tom nervous to ponder.

"Of course," Mrs. Harris said. Everything with her was *Of course* and *Of course not.* "They've been practicing for weeks."

Tom looked at the concert flyer, the graphic of the drunken music note swimming through flower petals.

Driving Deenie to school that morning, he'd felt the exhaustion on her, and a watchfulness. The waiting — which felt like it could end in a second or never, like waiting for all things out of your hands — seemed so weighty on her, her body so tiny next to him, her shoulders sunken.

Maybe a distraction was what she needed, what everyone needed.

★   ★   ★

"So you still have to play?" Deenie asked. "Without Lise?"

They were in the frigid girls' room, the high window always propped open. It was as if the school thought girls gave off so much heat and pungency that constant ventilation was required.

"I guess," Gabby said from behind a stall. She was changing from her jeans into her long performance skirt. "I think they want to do it."

"They should do it," Kim Court said, appearing from a corner stall. Kim again, like a bad penny. "For Lise. To send good thoughts to her."

Combing her fingers through her hair, Deenie didn't say anything.

"Deenie," Gabby said, her voice echoey from behind the door, "do you ever feel like something bad is about to happen, but you don't know what?"

"What do you mean?" Deenie said. Bad things, for her, were always a gruesome surprise.

"I bet Lise never guessed what would happen to her," Kim said, shaking her head. "Whatever happened to her."

"Maybe she did," Deenie said, always wanting to disagree with Kim. "Like when you're about to get your period, or when Lise got mono that time. The whole week before, she kept saying her neck felt thick."

"Yeah," Gabby said. Her voice sounded funny, like on the phone last night. Slow and soupy. "I felt a little like that this morning. Last night. My head felt so heavy."

Deenie turned and faced Gabby's stall, but she couldn't think of anything to say.

"I know just what you mean," Kim said, nodding fervently, as if Gabby could see her. "I feel funny too." She leaned toward the mirror, examining herself. "My teeth even hurt."

Deenie watched her. Kim's big tusks crowding her mouth. Guys called her the Horse, her braces elaborate, like the inside of your phone if you break it. Deenie wished she could feel sorry for her, but Kim made it impossible.

"We'll get good news today," Deenie said. "Our girl's strong."

"It's so messed up," Kim said, standing in front of Gabby's stall to make sure she could hear. "Lise should be on that stage with you today, Gabby."

Gabby opened the stall so quickly she almost hit Kim in the face.

Her performance shirt bright white, the hem of her dark skirt swirling at her feet, she was holding her vibrating phone open in her palm, staring at the flashing screen.

No one said anything for a second, Kim squirming a little.

Then Deenie's phone chirped, and less than a second later, Kim's squawked.

The texts seemed to come from three or four friends at the same time.

Lise's mom won't let any visitors & hospital called in s.o. from public health!!

nurse tammy reported something abt Lise

— what IS happening?!!

Health dept people here now — WTF?

"Health department?" Kim said. "Why . . ."

Gabby curled her fingers around her phone and looked at Deenie.

Kim was saying something else, but Deenie wasn't listening.

★ ★ ★

When Tom walked into first period that morning, the students were arrayed in little clumps of speculation. The back corner, the windowsill, the deep resin lab sinks. Bowed over their phones, a pinwheel of purple, pink, mesh, leopard, all their slick cases.

"Phones off and out of sight," he said. "Let's go."

Herding them through the hallways took a long time, all the last-minute stops at lockers, and a notebook slipped from sweaty hands, careering down the stairwell and making everyone jump.

But once they arrived, everything changed.

The solemnity of the auditorium always did something to students. Lights dimmed, you couldn't see the water-stained ceiling, didn't notice the squeaking risers. The darkened space, all the guffaws and giggles

99

brought low, to hushes and the odd screech. The stage lit a soft purple. The formal way student musicians always sat, their eyes locked on their easels or on Mr. Timmins, the sweaty, loose-shirttailed music teacher.

There was the feeling of something important about to occur, made all the more important by the circumstances of the day before. It all felt a little like church.

Instead of promoting a tentative freshman to Lise's second chair, Mr. Timmins had decided, in some gesture of something, to do without, leaving Lise's folding chair conspicuously empty. Its black metal base seemed to catch all the light on the stage. You couldn't take your eyes off it.

The music began, the dirge-y strain of "Scarborough Fair," which felt anything but springlike. Tom only hoped this number had been planned all along and wasn't a hasty replacement in honor of Lise. *She's in the hospital, for God's sake,* he thought, *she's not dead.*

Eyes wandering, he saw Eli standing in the back by himself, looking at his phone. A pair of long-necked freshman girls in front of him kept wiggling in their seats, trying to catch his attention. The kid could not manage it better if he was trying, Tom thought. The less interested he was, the harder they tried, their faces red and stimulated.

Up front, he spotted Deenie, her ponytail slipping loose, seated beside Skye Osbourne, with her great swoop of platinum hair. He'd never known Skye to show up for any school event, mandatory or otherwise. The drama of the day seemed to take all comers.

He imagined Deenie's eyes were mostly on the empty chair, but maybe also on Gabby, the cello between her legs, a dramatic skirt of violet lace, a floodlight at her feet.

Maybe it was the lights but her cheekbones looked touched with violet too. Her grave face and dark hair, the sound of the music, the captured angst of the students — so ready for angst anyway and now with the ripest of occasions — it made everything feel even more heightened.

He felt a stirring in his chest, and looking at Deenie, her slight neck arched up, he wanted to put his hands on her shoulders and promise her something.

★ ★ ★

Deenie liked being in the auditorium, like the bottom of a deep coat pocket, the warm hollow at the center of the quilt on the sofa in the den.

There had only been a few moments for her to think about the texts, the idea of the health department — what was a health department, anyway? What exactly did it do? — on the premises, investigating something. She wondered if they would want to talk to her. She'd been a witness, after all.

She pictured Nurse Tammy, her face struck with alarm, forearm wet with Lise's spit. Lise, face a vivid red, like she'd been painted. Deenie had been a witness, but she wasn't sure what she'd been a witness to.

"Can I sit here?"

Deenie looked up and, squinting, saw Skye through the spotlights, a blaze of white.

"Okay," Deenie said, pulling her bag from the cushion. "You never come to things."

Slinking into the seat, she shrugged. "Mr. Banasiak hooked me. And I was worried about Gabby. She's not feeling good."

Deenie looked at her, about to ask her what she meant, but then the lights dimmed again and the music rose up and she shook it loose from her head, turning to face the stage.

At first, she could only watch Lise's empty chair.

But then "The Sound of Silence" began

and she looked over at Gabby, who was staring off to one side of the stage, waiting to play.

When her cue came, Gabby lifted her white hand and it fluttered across the cello like a bird as her bow dipped and turned, the other hand bouncing and snapping against its neck.

Her eyes were focused straight ahead, into the back of the auditorium, into nothing.

★   ★   ★

Eli looked up suddenly from his phone, a shiver between his shoulder blades.

The music was so bleak and he'd been trying not to listen, but when he saw Gabby on the stage, she looked so focused, so intent.

Most times when he skated he felt like that, like there was no one else on the ice.

The only sound, the puck clinking on the post, thunking against the boards.

He would fix his eyes like hers were fixed. He would look toward the net with such intensity nothing could stop him from getting what he wanted.

★   ★   ★

Tom wasn't sure of the moment Gabby's

neck started to dip back because at first it felt like part of the performance, her knotted brow, her hand vibrating on the slender fingerboard, everything.

It started with her chin, then her whole jaw.

He watched as Gabby's face started to tremble, and then, the way the light hit, it was like her face itself was bending.

Her chair skidded loudly, her neck thrown back so far that, in the darkness, it looked like her head had disappeared.

For one terrifying instant, gone.

The cello still tight between her clenched legs, she lifted herself upright again, her face flushed.

Mr. Timmins had dropped his baton and was moving toward her, and Tom saw Deenie jump to her feet in the front row.

★　★　★

It's the same thing, Deenie thought, feeling herself rise, it's happening again. It's the same thing, the same time, the same everything.

She felt her legs hurtle up the steps, the stage lights hot on her.

Her dad seemed to be behind her in an instant, hands on her shoulders.

Mr. Timmins was leaning over Gabby, still in her chair, her legs twisted around its legs, its rubber feet clacking on the stage floor.

She was holding on to the cello and smiling oddly.

"I'm sorry," she said, her face like a flame. "I'm sorry."

★   ★   ★

Tom had one hand on his daughter as the other band members, instruments in hand, were closing in on Gabby.

Gasps, brass clattering on the floor, one girl tripping over herself, nearly teetering off the foot of the stage.

"Back everyone," Tom said, arms out. "Stand back."

Without thinking, he pushed Deenie back too.

Somewhere, a camera flashed, then another. Girls with their phones tucked in their long velvet skirts.

"Stop that!" shouted Mr. Timmins. "Phones away!"

"Gabby, honey," Tom said, leaning down in front of her. "Are you okay?"

There was a film over her eyes, like she might be about to cry.

Then her neck seemed to jolt back with

such force he expected to hear a pop, her body surrendering to thunderous motion, every limb shuddering and her torso slumping to the right.

He and Mr. Timmins gripped her, locking her between their arms, Mr. Timmins trying to take the cello from her.

"I'm okay," she said, dropping the cello at last, hand over her mouth.

"Dad," Tom heard a voice behind him say. "Dad."

8

Standing in the back, Eli had been the one who'd called 911.

Four minutes later, the back doors flew open and he showed the paramedics where to go.

"Oh, man," the taller one said, rubbing his winter-red face. "Another one?"

Onstage, Mr. Timmins was kneeling over Gabby, who was looking up at him, her hands around her own neck like she was trying to hold it straight.

All of them had their hands over their mouths, watching.

"Goddamn it, Jeremy."

Eli watched as his dad grabbed a phone from one of the boys' hands.

"I'm sorry," Gabby kept saying, her voice inexplicably loud, carrying through the space. "Did that happen? I just got confused. Are we in school?"

The cello kept getting knocked around,

wobbling and quaking like it was a live thing.

"Can you breathe, miss?" the paramedic asked.

"What," Gabby said, her voice high and puzzled. "Yes."

"Let's get everyone out of here," the tall one said, motioning to Mr. Timmins to help. "Clear this area. Give her some room."

They couldn't wrest the bow from Gabby's hand.

Tiptoeing, Deenie kept trying to see over the bear-shouldered paramedics, who were trying to snap an oxygen mask on Gabby's face.

"I don't need to go anywhere," she was saying, her fingers crooked over the mask, pushing it away. Her eyes landed on Deenie. "Deenie, I *don't*."

"I know," Deenie said, nodding, her neck thrusting almost as hard as Gabby's had. It hurt to look at.

"I just felt dizzy or something."

"But just to be safe," Deenie said. "Okay, G?"

★　★　★

Tom sat Deenie down in the car, windows shut tight. He asked her to breathe slowly.

He was trying to explain something he couldn't explain.

". . . and as soon as we can reach out to Gabby's mom, we will. They'll do some tests. It's just better if you stay here. With me."

"Why couldn't we go to the hospital?" Deenie said. "Gabby wanted me to."

Tom wasn't so sure about that. When Lara Bishop arrived, soon after the EMS, Gabby's embarrassment seemed heavy and tortured. She couldn't even look her mother in the eye.

"She didn't faint," Deenie said. "But her body. What was happening to her body?"

The pensive look on Deenie's face, like when she was small. Finding a cat drowned in the ditch by the mailbox. He didn't know how long she'd been staring at it, her brother next to her touching it gently with a stick, hoping to nudge it to life. That night she'd had nightmares, her mouth was filled with mud. He'd tried to explain it to her, how accidents happen but we really are safe. But there was, already, the sense that nothing he said touched what was really bothering her, which was the realization that you can't stop bad things from happening to other people, other things. And that would be hard forever. He'd never quite gotten used to it himself.

"And what does it all have to do with the health department?" she asked.

"They're just making sure everything's okay," he said.

Of course, he had no idea. When he'd learned about their visit, just before first period, he hadn't liked the sound of it.

"It was the nurse," Bill Banasiak told him. "She blew the whistle."

The new nurse, the peaked blond one whose name Tom could never remember, had called her supervisor at the hospital about a bite on her arm from Lise. Embarrassed, she hadn't told anyone at first. But now she was worried. What if there was some kind of virus at the school? One of those new kinds?

"Not the sort of talk you want to have at a school," Banasiak said, shaking his head.

Especially not coming from the nurse, Tom thought.

But he didn't tell Deenie any of this.

"I'm sure we'll know more soon," he told her now, realizing he'd said the same thing ten times about Lise. "Okay?"

"Dad," she said, looking down at his phone resting on the gear panel, "can we call Lise's mom again?"

"Sure," he said finally. "I'll call in a little bit."

"How about now?" she asked.

"Not right now, okay?"

Deenie nodded tiredly. For a second, she looked very old to him, the rhythmic chin wobble of his own grandmother.

But when she turned back to him, her chin had steadied. Tugging her jacket collar from her neck, she said, "But you will?"

"I will," he said. Then, "You feel up to class?"

Part of it seemed ridiculous to him, to have his daughter sit and listen to a lecture about the Panama Canal, but he couldn't think what else to do with her.

For a moment, only a moment, he wished Georgia were there. Georgia, at least the Georgia from before, would have canceled her own appointments, left work, and hijacked Deenie for a soothing schedule of girl time. Or their version of girl time: buying stacks of magazines and tall coffee drinks and curling on the den sofa together. Or something. She seemed to know how to do those things. Until she didn't.

"I can't get away," she had started saying the year before she left. "I'm sorry, Tom. I can't get away." That's how she would put it, as if home were "away." This was when

111

she was spending an hour a day at the Seven Swallows Inn on Beam Road with her coworker lover (What else could you call him? Married himself, with three kids, cat, dog, hamster). She confessed to this and everything, far more than he'd ever wanted to know, including how ashamed she was of keeping spare underwear in her desk drawer. And how she was "very — mostly — sure" that this coworker lover wasn't responsible for the pregnancy, and thus not for the ugly miscarriage, nine days of bleeding and sorrow. That was something else she had Tom to thank for, he guessed.

Later, after she was gone, he found himself driving to the Seven Swallows, sitting in the parking lot for hours, going through the bank statements, the separation agreement, divorce papers, filling in squares with a ballpoint pen, gaze returning again and again to the sign out front: CLEAN COMFORT HERE. He wanted to keep everything in his head all at once.

"I can go to class," Deenie was saying now, her hand on his arm. "Dad, I can."

Tom looked at her, saw her eyes fixed on him, searching. Like she had seen something on his face. Something that worried her.

"It's okay, Dad," she said, firmly. "I'll

be fine."

"Sheila," he said. "Tom Nash. Just leaving another message to see if there's anything I can do. Call me, okay? If I can be any help. Deenie sends her love to you and Lise both. We all do."

He thought of Deenie inside the school, wondering, worrying.

An uneasy thought came to him: If she doesn't find out something, what if she takes off for the hospital again?

So he had another idea.

"Billing, can I help you?"

"Hey, is this Diane? This is Tom. Tom Nash."

The harried voice on the other end eased into something soft, breathy.

"Tom. Well, well. I was hoping you'd call. I'd given up a little."

He cleared his throat. "I'd been meaning to. I had a great time. It's been a crazy couple weeks."

"Eight weeks." She laughed.

He'd met her at the post office, on the longest line either had ever seen. She'd told him her son was trying out for junior hockey and Eli was his idol. She didn't want her boy to play because she worked at the hospital and saw all the players come in with faces dented by flying pucks, teeth knocked out, cracked cheekbones, and, once, a blade to the neck. But what could you do, he loved it.

Tom said he understood.

She'd given him her number and they had dinner at someplace Tom couldn't quite remember. Maybe it was Italian. He'd meant to call again. A second date always felt like an announcement at his age. And he never felt ready for the announcement.

"Eight weeks, really? I'm sorry. But I've been meaning to and now I have a reason, a good excuse."

"You didn't need an excuse."

"Okay, but here it is."

It turned out all he had to do was say Lise's name.

"Oh, that girl."

There was a pause on Diane's end, and Tom wasn't sure what to make of it. It wasn't a large hospital, but still, he was surprised she knew who he meant.

"Yeah," Tom said. "We were over there yesterday, but they didn't know much then."

He heard a momentary clicking sound. "Let's see what I can find," she said.

Her lack of hesitation in breaking HIPAA regulations and various laws was a relief.

114

He felt a kick of revived interest in her, followed by wanting to kick himself.

"She's still not conscious," she said. "She's stabilized, though. And they're doing diagnostics. I can't tell you exactly."

"Oh," Tom said. It seemed like a long time to be unconscious. Unless *not conscious* was code for "coma."

"But the mother is a real problem," she said, her voice quickening a little. "Everyone's talking about it. First, she blamed the paramedics. Claimed they'd dropped her. They don't do that, Tom. Then she blamed the ER doctor. Now she seems to have darker theories."

"Darker theories?"

"I don't know. Crazy stuff she probably got off the Internet."

"Ah."

"We're hoping she doesn't find out about the other one."

"Gabby Bishop," Tom said quietly.

"You know her too?"

"I do." Part of him was expecting her to say Gabby was also unconscious. That maybe something had happened to her heart too.

"Jesus, sorry, Tom," she said. "But they're not the same. It's not the same thing. That's not a cardiac situation."

He could tell she was the kind of woman who told men what they wanted to hear. That didn't strike him as a bad thing, even though he knew it should.

"I saw it happen," he said. "It looked like a seizure."

"Well, they haven't even admitted her. They're doing tests."

"Diagnostics?"

"Yes," she said gently.

"Thanks a lot," he said, "for all this."

Then a lilt returned to her voice. "You know you left your doggie bag in my fridge. I gave you two days to call, then I ate all that peach cobbler myself."

★ ★ ★

Standing in the corner of one of the bathroom stalls, Deenie was trying to slow her breath.

Stop, she told herself. You're not one of those hysterical girls. You're not Jaymie Hurwich, who started sobbing in gym class and had to be walked to the nurse's office for hyperventilation. Jaymie, who went to the nurse's office for hyperventilation at least once a month, upset about a test grade, fighting with her boyfriend, grounded by her dad.

116

Kim Court said she'd seen Skye huddled by herself on the loading dock. "I didn't think Skye got upset," she'd said. "Did you?"

And Deenie's phone kept flashing with texts, one after another.

What is HAPPENING?

Gabby has it too!

Did u see her face??

And pictures of Gabby. Even videos someone took with the phone. A gruesome one of Gabby's head rearing back, her neck thick and purple under the lights.

And all Deenie could think of was Gabby and Lise in hospital beds, side by side, their arms connected to an elaborate blinking web of cords, tubes.

Both their heads somehow purple and split, their mouths open.

If it happens to both your best friends, the next one must be you. If it happens to both your best friends, it must be you.

But it wasn't the same. Gabby hadn't fainted, had never even fallen, exactly, never hit her head or bit anyone. Never had that look Lise had, like an animal trapped.

Gabby had only looked confused, lost, mortified. Which was how everyone looked some of the time, every day.

The door to the girls' room swung open.

"It was just like with my cat, I'm telling you," Brooke Campos was saying loudly. "Do they know if she was sleeping in a room with a bat? Or was around a sick bat? That's how it happens. We found one in our garage, hanging right over the cat bed. We had to have Mr. Mittens destroyed."

Deenie opened the stall door to see Brooke with a clump of senior girls, all waving their lip-gloss wands, passing them from one to another — watermelon crush, scarlet bloom.

"So you're saying they both just happened to get bit by bats?" one of the seniors said.

"It was probably the same bat," Brooke said, a little defensively.

The stall next to Deenie opened and Skye appeared. Deenie hadn't even known she was in there, those long crocheted skirts of hers, one layered over the other, muffling her movements.

"Hey," she said, nodding to Deenie.

And she started unhooking all her exotic bracelets to wash her hands, her fingers moving gracefully over the fasteners. It was strangely hypnotic.

"Hey," Deenie said, thinking about what Kim had said about seeing Skye curled up on the loading dock. She looked at Skye's face, hunting for a sign: red eyes, swollen face. But you could never see much through all the hair.

"I mean, think about it. What if they slept in the same place?" Brooke said, blotting her mouth with a paper towel. "Gabby and Lise."

"A place compromised by bats?" the same senior girl said, hand on hip.

"You can say what you want," Brooke said, digging her heels in. "I just know what it looked like. Her mouth was foaming and her tongue went like this."

Leaning into the mirror, she stuck her tongue violently to one corner of her mouth.

"That's not what happened," Deenie said, watching her. "You don't know what you're talking about."

"I heard Nurse Tammy got bit," Brooke added, ignoring Deenie. "Lise *bit* her. And she has big teeth."

"A vampire walks among us," whistled one of the girls, hooking her fingers under her mouth like fangs.

"So, Brooke, are you saying Lise bit Gabby too?" Deenie said, looking at Skye, trying to get some help. "Or that she just licked her?"

Brooke shook her head pityingly. "I know she's your friend. Both of them. But."

"There's bats down by the lake," Skye said

quietly, looking in the mirror, lifting her hair from her brow.

Deenie looked at Skye, shaking her hands dry.

"If it were rabies, they would have known right away," the most sensible senior girl asserted. "That's not hard to figure out."

Tugging loose three paper towels, Deenie rubbed her hands roughly, until they turned red.

"We'd be lucky if it was rabies," Skye said, twirling her bracelets back down her wet wrists. "They have a shot for that."

"So what are you saying it is?" the senior girl said, eyeing Skye, trying to up-and-down look at her, but Skye was not the type to be chastened by that.

Shrugging lightly, she shook a cigarette loose from somewhere in the folds of her skirt. "I don't know," she said. "I'm just thinking about the lake."

Deenie looked at her.

The senior shook her head dismissively. "No one goes in the lake anyway."

"No." Skye nodded, letting her eyes skate across Deenie's face, and keep going. "They never do."

★　★　★

120

Like after all school disruptions, there was a window during which you could do anything, and Eli took advantage, finding a corner in the back of the auditorium as teachers corralled the remaining students.

But soon enough, Assistant Principal Hawk — his real name, maybe — took Eli's shoulder in his talon grip and marched him to earth science.

No one was paying any attention to poor Mr. Yates talking about natural-gas extraction. Everyone in school had seen what happened to Gabby.

One girl, breathless, announced that Gabby's mother had arrived and that "her scar looked bigger than ever!"

"Let's try to keep our focus on the subject at hand," Mr. Yates said, straining.

"Mr. Yates, maybe it's the drilling!" Bailey Lu exclaimed, her palm slapping her desk. "My mom says it's poisoning us!"

Slipping in his earbuds, Eli stared out the window at the practice rink, bright with cut ice.

He wondered if it was one of those super-flus and was glad he and Deenie had had all those shots the month before, their arms thick and throbbing. Or maybe it was a girl thing, one of those mysteries, like the way the moon affected them, or like in some of the videos he'd seen online that, mostly, he wished he hadn't.

But it didn't matter what it was. It was going to be bad for his sister, who loved Gabby even more than she loved Lise. Who talked so much, always in a hushed voice, about the Thing That Happened to Gabby, about her cokehead father, who liked to show up at school every so often, begging to see his daughter. *Maybe you should have thought about that before you picked up the claw hammer,* Eli always thought.

The truth was, he didn't know Gabby very well, just as the tall, pale-faced girl all the other girls copied, her clothes, the streaks she'd put in her hair then dye away again, the way she spray-painted her cello case silver.

He did remember being surprised last fall when she started hanging out with Tyler Nagy, a hockey player from Star-of-the-Sea. Eli had never liked him, the way he was always talking about the screeching girls who came to all the games, the fourteen-year-old he said wanted him to do things to her with the taped end of his stick.

The only time Eli'd ever really spent with Gabby was when Deenie was a freshman and Gabby had stayed with them for a few weeks. Her mother was having a "hard time," which had something to do with all the empty wine bottles in her recycling bin and not being able to get out of bed, but no one ever told him the rest. It was soon after their own mom had moved out, and it seemed like having Gabby there was good for Deenie too, who'd spent hours reading by herself in her room back then.

As far as he could tell, Gabby never really slept. More than once, he'd spotted her hiding on the sofa in the den, watching TV in the middle of the night. Hour after hour of the same show where they dressed middle-aged women in new outfits, dyeing all their hair the same shiny red.

His dad told him he kept finding gum wrappers, dozens of them, trapped in the folds of the quilt.

One night, not long before she went home, he found her in the basement, lying on the Ping-Pong table, crying.

Girls — at least, the girls he knew, not his sister but other girls — always seemed to be crying.

But Gabby's crying was different, felt wild and broken and hurt his chest to hear.

Drumming his fingers on the Ping-Pong table until it vibrated, he tried to talk to her, to make her feel better, but the things that worked on Deenie — recounting graphic hockey injuries, popping his shoulder blade, trying to rap — didn't seem right.

Finally, he had an idea. Took a chance. Pulled one of the Ping-Pong rackets from under her left thigh, reached to the floor for the ball.

"Come on, little girl," he said, pointing to the other racket. "Show me what you got."

The grin that cracked — with tortured slowness — across her face stunned and rallied him.

They played for forty-five minutes, flicking and top-spinning and crushing that hollow ball, until they woke up everyone in the house.

★   ★   ★

I'm just thinking about the lake.

Deenie couldn't believe Skye had said it. In front of all those girls. In front of Brooke Campos, who stopped talking only while texting and usually not then.

At the final bell, Deenie found her at her locker.

"Skye, why did you mention the lake?"

"What do you mean?"

"It doesn't have anything to do with any

of this," Deenie whispered. "So why bring it up?"

Skye looked at her, shrugged. Skye was always shrugging.

"I don't think," she said, closing her locker door, "we really know what this has to do with."

They weren't supposed to go into the lake. No one was. School trips, Girl Scout outings, science class, you might go and look at it, stand behind the orange mesh fences.

Every spring and at the end of the summer, the lake would give over to acid green. It was called "the bloom" and Deenie's fifth-grade teacher warned them, pointing to the iridescent water, that it meant it was filled with bacteria and hidden species. With a stick, he would poke one of the large blades of algae that washed up on the shoreline. One year, during a conservation project for Girl Scouts, they found a dead dog on one of the banks, its fur neon, mouth hanging open, tongue bright like a highlighter pen.

When she was very young, she believed the slumber-party tales about it, that a teenage couple had gone skinny-dipping and drowned, their mouths clogged with loam, bodies seen glowing on the shoreline from miles away. Or that swimming in it gave you miscarriages or took away your ovaries and you'd be barren for life. Or the worst one, that a little boy had died in the lake and his cries could still be heard on summer nights.

A few years ago, long after it had been closed, Eli said he saw a girl swimming in it, coming out of the water in a bikini, laughing at her frightened boyfriend, seaweed snaking around her. He said she looked like a mermaid. Deenie always pictured it like in one of those books of mythology she used to love, a girl rising from the foam gritted with pearls, mussels, the glitter of the sea.

"It looks beautiful," her mom had said once when they were driving by at night, its waters opaline. "It *is* beautiful. But it makes people sick."

To Deenie, it was one of many interesting things that adults said would kill you: Easter lilies, jellyfish, copperhead snakes with their diamond heads, tails bright as sulfur. Don't touch, don't taste, don't get too close.

And then, last week.

It had been Lise's idea to go to the lake, to go in the water. She'd stood in it, waving at them, her tights stripped off, her legs white as the moon.

It was nine o'clock and Tom wasn't sure where the day had gone, other than to ragged places, again.

Deenie was hunched over the kitchen island, eating cereal for dinner.

Outside, Eli was slamming a tennis ball against the garage door with his practice stick. Sometimes it was hard to remember his son without that stick in his hand, cocked over his shoulder. Even watching TV, he'd have it propped on his knee. It seemed to have happened sometime during early high school, when the other parts of Eli, the boy who liked camping and books about shipwrecks and expeditions and looking for arrowheads in Binnorie Woods after a heavy rain, had drifted away, or been swallowed whole.

His phone rang: Lara Bishop.

"Tom, thanks for your message."

"Of course," he said. "How's Gabby?"

"We're home. They were going to keep her overnight, but she seemed to be doing okay. And she hates that place so much. So here we are."

"I'm glad to hear it," he said. "Really glad."

He could feel Deenie's stare, her hand

gripping her own phone.

"Well," she said, and there was a pause. "I guess I just wanted you to know. And, you know, to check in. See what you might have . . . I don't know."

"I understand," he said, but he wasn't sure what she was suggesting.

"I mean, we don't know what this *is,*" she said.

"No," he said, eyes on Deenie. "But I don't know anything. You mean about Lise?" He wasn't going to tell her what Medical Biller Diane had said.

"Or if maybe . . . Gabby's dad didn't call you, did he?"

"Charlie? No. No."

"I was worried he might have found out. From the school maybe. I don't want Gabby to have to deal with him right now."

"Of course not." But what he was thinking was, Weren't they obligated to notify him? He was still her dad.

"Thanks. It's just . . ." And her voice trailed away.

"And if he had called," he added, though he wasn't sure why, "I wouldn't have told him anything."

"Thank you, Tom." He could hear the relief in her voice. It all felt oddly intimate, in that parents-in-shared-crisis way.

Lightning hitting the Little League batting cage. Mall security agreeing not to call the police. Those "whew" moments fellow parents share.

After he hung up, he wondered how he would feel if he were Charlie Bishop. He would never, ever do what Charlie had done, even if it had been an accident. Once, before everything, they'd been teammates for a pickup baseball game, had cheered each other on, played darts after and drank shots of tequila with beer backs.

That was just a few weeks before the accident and it made Tom sick to think about now. How much he'd liked Charlie. How Charlie had slapped him on the back and said he knew just how hard marriage could be.

★　★　★

The minute her phone rang, Deenie began running upstairs to her room.

"Gabby —"

"Hey, girl," Gabby said.

"Are you okay, what —"

"Hey, girl," she repeated.

"Hey, girl," Deenie replied, slowing her words down, almost grinning. "What'd they say at the hospital?"

She leaned back on her bed, feeling the soft thunk of her pillow.

"They did all these tests," Gabby said. "They made me count and say who the last two presidents were. They gave me a tall drink of something that was like those candy orange peanuts that taste like banana. If you put a bag of those in a blender with gravel and old milk."

"Yum, girl."

Gabby snickered a little. "Then they strapped a mask on me and rolled me into this thing that was like the worst tanning bed ever. Everything smelled. Then they did this other thing where they put these little puckers all over my head and I had to lie there for twenty minutes while they shot electricity through my body." She laughed. "It was awesome."

"It sounds awesome," Deenie said, forcing a laugh. "So."

"So."

"What is it? What happened to you?"

"They don't know," she said. "They even made me talk to a headshrinker. She asked if I was under stress. She told my mom that sometimes this happens. Like maybe I was upset and my body just freaked out."

"Oh," Deenie said.

"I asked her if she meant 'stress' like hav-

130

ing your dad tear a hole through your mom's face."

Deenie felt her chest tighten, but Gabby was laughing, tiredly.

"So they don't think it's like with Lise?"

"I just need to relax," Gabby said, not really answering, a funny bump in her voice. "I guess maybe if I light some geranium candles and take a bath, like the doctors used to tell my mom when she couldn't breathe in the grocery store or the mall."

It was interesting to think about, the slender filaments between the worry in your head, or the squeeze in your chest, and the rest of your body, your whole body and everything in it.

Lise, the summer before, had lost thirteen pounds in less than two weeks after something had happened at the town pool with a boy she liked. She'd thought he liked her, and maybe he did, but then suddenly he didn't anymore.

She and Lise and Gabby had devoted endless hours to imagining him as Lise's boyfriend and then to hating him and the girl with the keyhole bikini they'd spotted walking with him by the snack bar. Deenie was sure he'd be at the center of their thoughts forever. But right now she couldn't summon his name.

Since then, there'd been so many boys they'd speculated about. Boys who liked them and then didn't. Or maybe a boy they didn't like until the boy liked someone else.

But Lise said the boy at the pool was worth it. Running her fingers over her stomach, she called it the Mike Meister diet.

Mike Meister, that was his name. Always a new boy, even last week, Lise at the lake, whispering about one in Deenie's ear. How could you believe any of it was real?

Lise, her head, her body, her flighty, fitful heart, were like one thing, and always changing.

But it was different with Gabby. Deenie knew all her beats and rhythms, had seen her through everything with her dad, her mom, her bad breakup. And this was not the way stresses played themselves out on her body. Everything stayed inside, her body folding in on itself.

"Well," Deenie said. "You're home now. That's good."

"I guess everyone was talking about it," Gabby said. "The whole school saw."

Deenie didn't say anything. She was thinking of Gabby on that stage, the way her body jerked like a pull-string toy. Like a body never moves, not a real body of someone you know.

"Deenie," she said. "Say something."

"What did it feel like?" Deenie blurted, her face feeling hotter on the pillow.

Gabby paused. Then her voice dropped low, like she was right there beside her. "There was this shadow," she said. "I could see it from the corner of my eye, but I wasn't supposed to look at it."

Deenie felt her hand go around her own neck.

"If I turned my head to look," Gabby continued, "something really scary would happen. So I couldn't look. I didn't dare look."

Deenie pictured it. That smile on Gabby's face after, when everyone surrounded her on the stage. Like something painted on her face. A red-moon curve.

"I didn't look, Deenie," Gabby whispered. "But it happened anyway."

I'm okay, she'd said. *I really am. I'm fine.*

That smile, not a real thing but something set there, to promise you something, to give you a white lie.

★ ★ ★

He waited until he couldn't hear the hum of her voice anymore through the floor. Then he knocked on Deenie's door.

133

"Hey, honey," he said, poking his head in.

"Hey," Deenie said, cross-legged on her bed.

As ever, her bed like a towering nest, always at least two or three books tufted in its folds. Deenie never fell asleep without a book or her phone in her hands. Probably both. When Georgia used to make her clean, Deenie would hoist the bedding over her head, shaking all the books, folders, handouts onto the carpet.

"They told her it might be stress," Deenie said. "Like you said."

Walking toward her, his foot caught on her white Pizza House shirt, ruched in the quilt where it hit the floor.

"Well," he said, picking up the shirt, sprayed with flour and forever damp, "when things like this happen, they can really knock around your body."

"I guess," she said, watching him closely. He wondered if he wasn't supposed to pick up her things. He tossed the shirt onto the bed lightly.

"What about you?" he asked. "What do you think?"

"I don't know," she said. "That doesn't seem like Gabby to me."

"I know, Deenie," he said. "We just gotta wait and see."

He sat down at the foot of the bed. She looked expectant, like she wanted something from him, but he had no idea what. He'd seen that look a hundred times before, from her and from her mother.

Then, nodding, she fumbled for her headphones, and he could feel her retreating, her face turning cloudy and inscrutable.

"Dad," she said, sliding the headphones on, "maybe I shouldn't go to work on Saturday. With everything that's going on."

He looked at her.

"I think maybe I just want to be home."

He didn't know what to say, her eyes big and baffling as ever, so he said yes.

★　★　★

The minute her dad left the room, Deenie wanted to jump up and throw the shirt in the laundry basket. She didn't know why she hadn't already.

But she didn't want to touch it or look at it.

It reminded her of the car, and Sean Lurie, the shirt wedged beneath her on the seat.

And then all the other things she didn't want to think about.

Lise's face. The lake. Everything.

There was too much already, without thinking about that.

9

THURSDAY

Just after six in the morning, Eli stepped into the dark garage, slung his gear bag over the front handlebars of his bike.

As the garage door shuddered open, he saw something move outside, in the driveway.

For a drowsy moment, he thought it might be a deer, like he sometimes saw on the road at night if he rode far out of town, into the thick of Binnorie Woods.

But then he heard a voice, high and quavery, and knew it was a girl.

He ducked under the half-raised garage door and peered out.

All he could see was a powder-blue coat with a furred hood, a frill of blond hair nearly white under the porch light.

"Who's there?" Eli asked, squinting into the misted driveway.

With a tug, she pulled the hood from her head.

Except it wasn't a girl. It was Lise Daniels's mom, the neighbors' floodlight hot across her.

"Eli?" she called out, hand visored over her eyes. "Is that Eli?"

"It's me," he said.

He'd seen her at the house dozens of times to pick up Lise, had seen her at school events, hands always tugging Lise's ponytail tighter, always calling after her, telling her to call, to hurry, to be on time, to watch out, to be careful. But Eli wasn't sure she'd ever said a word to him in his life. He knew he'd never said a word to her.

"Eli," she said, loudly now. "Tell your father I'm sorry I haven't called him back."

The halo of her hair, the pink crimp of her mouth. It was weird with moms, how you could see the faces of their daughters trapped in their own faces. Mrs. Daniels's body was larger, her shoulders round and her cheeks too, but somewhere in there, the neat prettiness of Lise lay half buried.

"Okay. Mrs. Daniels, are you okay?" he asked, and she moved closer to him, coming out from under the flat glare of the floodlight. "Did something happen at the hospital?"

For a moment, the vision of Lise fluttered before him, twirling in her turquoise tights, skirt billowing as she bounded up the school steps.

"I'm not supposed to talk about it," she said. "I've been advised not to speak to anyone associated with the school, and your father is a school employee."

He wondered how long she'd been standing out here. He thought of her looking up at the second-floor windows, waiting for a light to go on. Once, back when he played JV, he spotted a girl doing that after one of his games. A freshman on her bike, one sneaker flipping the pedal around, gazing up at his bedroom window. Until then, he hadn't thought girls did those things. When he'd waved, she jumped back on her seat and rode away.

"Oh, Eli," Mrs. Daniels said, shaking her head hard, her hood shaking too. "You're going to hear things. But I'm telling *you.*"

"Maybe you should come inside," Eli tried, the wheels of his bike retreating from her as if on their own. "I can wake Dad up. I bet he'd want to talk."

But she shook her head harder, shook that pale nimbus of hair. "There's no time for that. But I need you to pass along an important message. You know I've always

139

thought of Deenie as a daughter."

She was moving close to him, as if to ensure they were quiet, though her voice wasn't quiet but blaring.

"What does this have to do with Deenie?"

"Oh, Eli," she said, nearly gasping. "It has to do with all of them. All of them. Don't you see? It's just begun."

Before he could say anything, before she could get any closer to him, he heard the door into the garage pop open behind him.

"Eli, who are you —"

"Dad," Eli said, relieved, waving him over. "Lise's mom is here."

"My Lise," she said, not even acknowledging Eli's dad, her eyes, crepey and sweat-slicked, fixed on Eli. "It's already over for her. Now all we can do is hope. But it's not too late for the others."

Arm darting out, her red hand clasped him. "What if we can stop it?"

"Sheila," his dad said, walking toward her. "Did something happen?" He reached out to touch her shoulder gently, but the move startled her. She tripped, stumbling into Eli.

He tried to steady her, feeling her cold cheek pressed into his shoulder, a musky smell coming from her.

"Sheila," his dad was saying, more firmly now.

"Oh, Tom," she said, whirling around. "I need to tell you about Deenie."

"What about Deenie?" Eli thought he heard a hitch in his father's voice.

"They want us to believe they're helping our girls. They're killing our girls. It's a kind of murder. A careless murder."

"Sheila, why don't you come inside?" his dad said in that calm-down voice that used to drive his mom crazy. "Let's sit down and —"

"I can't do that, Tom," she said, her voice turning into a moan. "Our girls. I remember when I took Lise and Deenie shopping for their first bras. I remember showing them how to adjust the training straps. Those little pink ribbons."

"Sheila, I —"

"Who would ever have thought in a few years we'd be poisoning them?"

His dad was saying something, but Eli wasn't listening, couldn't stop looking at her, her mouth like a slash.

As if sensing his stare, she turned to Eli again.

"The things we do to our girls because of you."

Eli felt his hands wet on his bike handles.

"Me?"

Something was turning in her face, like a

141

Halloween mask from the inside.

"The dangers our girls suffer at your hands," she said. "We know and we'll do anything to protect them. To inoculate them. *Anything.*"

"Sheila, have you slept at all?" His dad put his arm on Eli's shoulder, gave him a look. "Let's get you some coffee and —"

She shook her head, eyes pink and large and trained on Eli.

"No one made *you* shoot yourself full of poison," she said, voice rising high.

She pointed her finger at Eli, below his waist.

"All of you," she said, eyes now on Eli's dad. "Spreading your semen anywhere you want. That's the poison. Your semen is poison."

"Sheila, Sheila . . ."

"Don't say I didn't do what I could." She turned and started walking away. "I hope it's not too late."

★   ★   ★

It had been a night of blurry, jumbled sleep. Deenie woke with a vague memory of dreaming she was at the Pizza House, standing in front of the creaking dough machine, Sean Lurie coming out slowly from behind

142

the ovens, looking at her, head cocked, grin crooked.

What? she'd said. *What is it?*

It's you, he said, standing in front of the blazing oven.

And she'd stepped back from the machine suddenly, the airy dough passing between her hands, soft like a bird breast.

It fell to the bleached floor, flour atomizing up.

Hands slick with oil, and Sean's eyes on them. On her hands.

And she looking down at them, seeing them glazed not with oil but with green sludge, the green glowing, the lights flickering off.

Deenie stood at the kitchen island, phone in hand.

Mom wont let me go to school tday, Gabby's text read. Sorry, DD.

After everything Gabby had been through, she was still worried about Deenie having to navigate the day without her. Because these were things they maneuvered together — school, divorces, faraway parents who wanted things. Boys.

The side door slammed and her dad came into the kitchen, shoving the morning paper into his book bag.

Something in the heave of morning air made her remember.

"Dad," she said, "did you hear something earlier? A noise."

Vaguely, she remembered looking out her window, expecting a barn owl screeching.

He turned toward the coffeepot.

"Mrs. Daniels came by this morning," he said. "She couldn't stay long, but Lise is doing okay. No change, but nothing's happened."

"Why didn't you wake me up?"

"There wasn't time," he said, lifting his cup to his face. "She couldn't stay. She had to go back."

"But can we go over there now?"

"No," he said, quickly.

Deenie looked at him, the way he held his coffee cup over his mouth when he spoke.

"I mean," he added, "we'll see."

Outside, it was bitter cold, the sky onion white.

Eli came with them on the drive to school, which never happened.

Riding together, it felt like long ago, fighting in the backseat until Dad would have to stop the car and make one of them sit up front.

She felt a wave of nostalgia, even for the

times he kicked her and tore holes in her tights with his skates.

"Eli Nash, skipping practice. I bet you broke Coach Haller's heart," Deenie said, looking at her brother in the backseat, legs astride, the taped knob white with baby powder, like Wayne Gretzky's. But he wouldn't look at her.

"I bet they didn't even have practice without you," she tried again. "I bet they all took their helmets off in your honor. I bet they hung black streamers over the rink and cried."

"I overslept," he said, facing the window. He didn't look annoyed. He didn't even seem to be listening to her.

She waited a moment, for something, then turned back around. The sky looked so lonely.

The car turned, and there was the lake.

"Deenie," her dad said, so suddenly his voice startled her, "Lise and Gabby haven't been in the lake lately, have they?"

★ ★ ★

He regretted it the moment he said it, and a hundred times more when he saw her body stiffen.

Wrung out from scant sleep, he wasn't

145

sure his mind was quite his own. All of Sheila's ravings, he hadn't quite pieced them together, but he could guess. It had something to do with vaccinations, a predatory attorney, the teeming Internet. She needed an explanation, badly, and he couldn't blame her.

Driving, though, he couldn't shake the feeling of something, some idea.

Then his eyes had landed on the lake, its impossible phosphorescence, even in the bitter cold, still half frozen over, the algae beneath like a sneaking promise. Remembering Georgia, her mouth ringed black that night years ago. She said she'd dreamed she put her own fingers down her throat, all the way down, and felt something like the soft lake floor there, mossy and wet and tainted.

She was never the same after that, he'd decided. Though he also knew that wasn't true. She hadn't been the same before that. No one was ever the same, except him.

So, his head still muddled, he'd found himself asking Deenie that ridiculous question about the lake, no better than Sheila's speculations.

He could see her whole body seize up.

"We're not allowed in the lake," she replied, which wasn't really an answer.

"Why are you asking me that?"

"No reason," he said. "I guess I'm just getting ready for today's rumors."

"Sometimes kids go in anyway," Eli said from the backseat. "I've seen it."

Deenie turned around to face him. "Like you, you mean. You and me."

"What?"

"We used to go in it, before. We used to swim in it, remember?"

"That's right," Tom said. "We used to take you."

When they were little, long before the boy drowned. Tom had a memory of pushing the corner of a towel in Eli's ear, hoping it wouldn't be another infection, that milky white drip down his neck. Why did he ever let them in that lake, even then?

He could hear Eli twisting his stick left and right. "But something happened to it. It doesn't even seem like the same lake. And it smells like the bottom of the funkiest pair of skates in the locker room."

"You mean yours?" Deenie said, like they were ten and twelve again, except there was a roughness in their voices Tom didn't like.

And Deenie's chin was shaking.

Tom could see it shaking.

He found himself watching it with exaggerated closeness, until she noticed him and stared back, her face locking into stillness.

"Dad!" she said. "You missed it. You missed the turn. It was back there."

You're a careless person, Georgia once said to him. He didn't even remember why. He didn't remember anything. She was always coming out of the water to say things, her mouth black.

★　★　★

@hospital did they ask u abt lake, Deenie texted Gabby. She was standing by the window in the second-floor girls' room, the best place in the school to get reception. But it still wouldn't go through.

It had been a week ago. Deenie and Gabby and Lise and Skye all in Lise's mother's Dodge with the screeching heater and the perennial smell of hand lotion. Lise said the steering wheel always felt damp with it.

As they drove along the lake, Skye told them she'd seen two guys in the water the week before, the first flicker of spring and their speakers blaring music from open car doors. One had a tattoo that began on his chest and disappeared beneath his jeans.

"Maybe they're there now," Lise had said, leaning forward eagerly, laughing. Boy crazy.

148

They all knew they wouldn't be, really, and they weren't. It was just the lake in front of them, its surface skimmed bright green.

And soon enough they were all in the water, just barely, ankle-deep, then a little more, all their tights squirreled away on the bank.

Wading deeper, Lise pulled her skirt high, and her legs were so long and skinny, with the keyhole between her thighs like a model.

You couldn't help but look.

She had a moon shape on her inner thigh that Deenie had never seen before. Later, Lise would say it happened when she lost weight, a stretch mark that wouldn't go away.

And then Gabby and Skye left, their calves slick with the water, thick as pea soup.

With Gabby gone, everything was less interesting, but it was easier. It was like before. Those days of just Deenie and Lise, and Deenie let herself settle into the sugar-soft of Lise's voice, and how easy she was and the water so delicious and Lise with stories to tell.

Now, remembering it, standing at the bathroom mirror, Deenie looked at herself.

Had the water done something? *Did it do something to me?* she wondered. *Do I look different?*

Then she remembered asking herself that question before, two days ago. How could you even tell, the way things kept happening to you, maybe leaving their marks in ways you couldn't even see.

She walked to her locker and opened it, stood there.

If she had to sit through first period, she thought she might explode.

"K.C.," she called out, spotting a familiar glint of braces in her locker-door mirror. "You have your car?"

Kim Court moved closer, smiling, nodding. Shaking her keys.

Gabby lived ten twisty miles from the school, an A-frame like an arrowhead snug in the Binnorie Woods. There was no regular bus route and the house was always hard to find. Deenie's dad had picked her up there countless times but sometimes he still got lost, calling Gabby's mom, who would laugh softly and give him the same directions again. *No, that's a right at the yellow mailbox.*

Gabby said living out here made her mom feel safer, tucked away like a nest at the top of a tree. But whenever Deenie was in the house, with its creaking wood and big windows, she couldn't imagine feeling more exposed.

"I always wanted to see it," Kim whispered, leaning over the steering wheel, gazing at the roof, its edges weeping with purple ivy. "It's like a gingerbread house."

They stood on the porch, hopping in their sneakers to keep warm. Kim in her rainbow-glittered ones, like the ones Gabby wore all last year.

It seemed to take a long time. Gabby's cat, Larue, watched them from the window with suspicious eyes.

Finally, Deenie saw a curtain twitch, and the door swung open.

"Hey." It was Skye, wrapped up in one of her fisherman's sweaters with the elbow torn through. "What's going on?"

"Hi," Deenie said, walking inside. She didn't want to show her disappointment that Skye was there again.

At some point, Deenie was going to have to get used to it. This new alliance.

After all, you could never be everything to one person.

Across the living room, Gabby was perched in the roll-arm chair. Larue hopped from the windowsill and stretched across her lap.

Kim's eyes were floating everywhere — at

151

the helix of books stacked in one corner, *Closing the Circle — NOW!* on top, and up into the wooden eaves, dark enough for bats.

Gabby and her mom had lived here for two years, but it still looked temporary, the furniture for a different kind of house, modern and sleek, beneath the heavy wooden ceiling fan, the faded stained glass.

"Where's your mom?" Deenie asked.

"Sleeping," Gabby said, her fingers picking at her scalp. "Look how gross this is. I can't get the glue out."

"Glue?" Kim asked, using it as an excuse to hover over Gabby.

"From the EEG," Gabby said as Kim leaned over Gabby, peeking through her long locks.

"It smells," Kim said.

"It's toxic," Skye noted, gazing out the window behind the sofa. "So it smells."

Kim shrank back from Gabby's head, her fingers wiggling like she'd nearly touched a spider.

"I've been texting you," Deenie said. "Gabby."

Gabby turned and looked at her.

"My mom made me turn off my phone," she said. "And computer. Because of the pictures and stuff."

"Right," Deenie said. She hoped Gabby

hadn't seen that video of her onstage. She'd heard it was on YouTube: "Cello Girl Possessed!"

"And Mrs. Daniels was calling me."

"Mrs. Daniels?" Deenie wondered if she'd showed up here too. "What for?"

"I don't know," Gabby said. "She wants us to come see her lawyer and some special doctor."

"So she thinks it's the same thing? What happened to Lise and what happened to you?"

"I guess." Gabby shrugged. "My mom says we shouldn't get involved."

"Sheila Daniels has a bad mojo happening," Skye said. "You can feel it coming off her. Maybe she doesn't want the truth. She just wants an answer."

"What do you know about it?" Deenie asked. "Do you even know Mrs. Daniels?"

"Not really," Skye said, walking to the sofa. "But maybe she's just not someone to be around right now. She's carrying a lot of pain."

"Tell them about the girl," Gabby said to Skye. "Skye was telling me this freaky story."

Deenie and Kim looked at Skye.

"Oh, just something I read online," she said. "This eleven-year-old girl a long time ago who got super, super sick. Her eyes sunk back in her head and she'd roll around on the floor. And her body started to do crazy things, like bending back on itself. So her parents called the doctor. And when he came, the girl opened her mouth and started pulling trash out of it."

"Trash, gross," Kim said.

"Not like our trash," Skye said. "Straw, gravel, chicken feathers, eggshells, pine needles, bones of little animals."

Kim's fingers touched her lips, eyes wide. "She was eating animals?"

"No," Skye said, shaking her head. "And she wasn't just throwing up things from her stomach. Because everything was always dry. The doctor could blow the feathers in his hand."

Kim gasped.

"Well, the Internet never lies," Deenie said, but then Skye loaded up the page on her phone. She showed them a picture, a girl with big haunted eyes, her mouth open. You couldn't really see anything, but her mouth looked gigantic, like a hole in the center of her face.

Gabby took the phone from Skye, stared at it, Larue spiraled on her lap, tail twirling.

"When the doctor put tongs down her throat," Skye added, "the girl spat out a cinder as big as a chestnut and so hot it burnt his hand."

Taking the phone back from Gabby, Skye showed them a picture of a stern-faced doctor, his hand out, a scythe-like scar in the center of his palm.

"What's a cinder?" Kim asked, teeth tugging at her lip. "Like a rock?"

"This is all very helpful," Deenie said. Gabby couldn't really want Skye here. She was only making it worse. Worse than even the pictures on the Internet. "Thanks, Skye."

"So then what happened?" Gabby asked, Larue's tail tickling her neck.

Skye shrugged. "I didn't read it all. Maybe they burned a bunch of people in the town square. That's what they usually do."

"No," Gabby said, "I mean to the girl. What happened to her?"

"Oh," Skye said. "I don't know. It doesn't say."

Deenie sat down on the roll-arm next to Gabby.

"Mrs. Daniels came to our house this morning," Deenie said.

Gabby looked up at her. "What for?"

"I don't know," Deenie said, realizing it herself.

Everyone was quiet for a moment.

Skye was kneeling on the sofa, looking out

the window. Larue leaped from Gabby's lap and winnowed between Skye's calves and scuffed boot heels.

"Gabby, are you going back to the doctor today?" Kim asked.

"We're waiting and seeing," Gabby said, her fingers flying back to her scalp. "For some results or something. I can't think of what more they could do. Or ask. 'Have you visited a foreign country recently? Have you been camping? Could you be pregnant?' "

There was a banging sound from somewhere in the house.

"That's Mom," Gabby said, jumping to her feet. "She's probably not going to like you guys cutting."

Skye didn't move, so Deenie didn't either. She hadn't had a chance to talk to Gabby and she needed to before it was too late.

"Gabby," she asked abruptly, "did they ask you anything about the lake?"

"The lake?" Kim looked at Deenie, her face animating. "What about it?"

Deenie watched the back of Skye's head, which didn't move.

"We were there last week," Skye said. "Isn't that what you mean, Deenie?"

And then something happened.

Gabby's jaw jolted to the left, then jolted again and again.

Grabbing the chair arm, she pressed her face hard against the back cushion to try to stop it.

Kim was watching, her fingers to her mouth as Gabby's jaw slammed into the cushion over and over.

They were all watching.

"Don't tell my mom," Gabby cried out, her jaw popping like a firecracker. "Deenie, don't."

★　★　★

Sitting in the parking lot, Tom spread the newspaper across the steering wheel and read the article. He hadn't wanted to read it in front of Deenie and he didn't want to be seen reading it in school.

Mystery Illness Strikes Best Friends at High School

There was a large photo of Lise and Gabby, cropped. In the original version — slapped, milk-spattered, to Tom's refrigerator door the previous fall — Deenie stood beside Gabby. In the newspaper, only Deenie's hand remained, resting on Gabby's shoulder like a ghost's. The girls, tanned and triumphant during a trip to WaterWonders last fall. Lise bursting from a star-spangled halter top that, no matter how she shifted or twisted, always seemed to land one of its biggest stars in the center of a breast, a bull's-eye.

He'd taken the girls himself, with Eli as company, both pretending not to hear the high frenzy of the backseat, the girls talking the whole eighty-minute drive in a language impenetrable and self-delighted. On the ride back, their bodies chlorine-streaked to numbness, a torpor set in and he and Eli could watch the twilit horizon stretched across the windshield, and not say a word.

. . . Lise Daniels, 16, remains unconscious at St. Ann's Hospital. Doctors would not confirm a connection between her condition and that of her best friend and fellow orchestra member Gabrielle Bishop, also 16. Bishop was given an EEG, among other tests. An unnamed source tells the *Beacon* that the results were "in the normal range," suggesting no seizure had occurred . . .

Midway down the page was another photo inset. A creamy lavender brochure he recognized:

Oh no, he thought. Here it is. What Sheila was raving about that morning. Alongside the photo came the subhead:

A Mother's Heartache Raises Serious Questions

. . . school and hospital officials have been tight-lipped. "It is not our role to speculate," Hospital Superintendent Bradford noted in an e-mail. "It's our job to get to the bottom of this and to see that these girls receive the best possible care."

This stance appears to carry little weight with Sheila Daniels, 43, mother of the first afflicted girl, who is still waiting for answers, especially about a controversial new vaccination that has had many parents nationwide crying foul . . .

There was a quote from Mindy Parker's father, Drew Parker, Esq., who was now speaking on Sheila Daniels's behalf.

"The situation has escalated beyond one mother's personal tragedy to a potential public health crisis," he said. "We can't rely on the public health department as our sole information source. After all, they were the ones who promoted this particular vaccination."

While officials at the health department had not returned calls at press time, one source there, speaking off the record, said the vaccine in question is "very safe. As safe as these things get."

Tom looked at the brochure inset again. *Protect her forever.* It had accompanied the letter all the parents in the school system had received the prior summer.

Parents of all rising sixth-grade girls are required to submit evidence of immunization or an opt-out notice, but all parents are strongly urged to vaccinate their daughters. The main cause of cervical cancer, HPV is easily transmitted via skin-to-skin contact during sexual activity. It is far more effective if girls get the vaccine before their first sexual contact. For your convenience, the department of health will conduct vaccinations on school grounds on the following dates . . .

So she'd done it, the whole series. Three boosters over six months. They sent text-message reminders. The final one had been just a few weeks ago.

He'd been glad for it, though he tried not

to think about it for long. He knew his daughter would eventually have sex. That any day now she might find a boyfriend and then it was inevitable. That wasn't the part that bothered him. It was the peril out there. Infections, cancer, a havoc upon his sweet daughter's small, graceful little body. One she held so closely, so tightly. Even hugging her, he felt her smallness and delicacy.

She liked the high dive and played soccer and, in gym class or touch football with Eli and himself, was always bold and fearless. Skinned knees, bruised elbow, *I can play too.* But sometimes he wondered if that was by necessity, a girl living with two males, a girl who might rather be up in her room with Gabby, with Lise, or with her books, that endless pile of novels with limp-bodied girls on the cover. Girls in bathtubs, in dark woods. Girls underwater.

And when he touched her, he couldn't help but think: What happens when someone touches her someday and doesn't understand these things about her? That she was both fearless and fragile and could be hurt badly in ways he could not fix.

And now, with Lise and Gabby, he was more glad than ever that he'd done what he could to take care of her. Whatever theories Sheila Daniels held in her fevered head, the shots were not to blame.

Vaccines, like all great scientific discoveries, are counterintuitive. You must take the very thing you are protecting yourself against. So your body remembers it, knows how to fight it.

You have to do whatever you can to shield their bodies. And sometimes that means you have to expose them to the very thing you want to protect them from. Which is the most unfair thing in the world.

★   ★   ★

"Oh my God, Deenie, did you *see* her?" Kim said, tearing open a bag of gummy worms from a warm spot under her car's heat vent. "Did you see what happened to her face? That sound?"

Nerves, Gabby had insisted, laughing lurchingly. *Stress.*

And now, heading back to school, Deenie wished she hadn't gone in the first place. She was going to make it just in time for third period and she hadn't even gotten to talk to Gabby alone. And she wished she hadn't brought up the lake.

"And why doesn't she want her mom to know?" Kim asked, teeth tearing noisily at the green worm dangling from her braces.

162

"I don't know," Deenie said. "Turn left."

"Here," Kim said, handing Deenie her phone. "Find some music. I can't think and drive."

Deenie scrolled down the playlist mindlessly with her thumb.

"You know," Kim said, mind-reading, "that lake water is in everything. It's not just in the lake. If you know what I mean."

"Is that some kind of riddle?"

"Do you ever drink from the water fountains in the school?" Kim said. "It's the same stuff. And remember that day in gym, when we played soccer in the field and we all got that orange stuff on our shoes?"

Deenie looked at her thumbprint seared onto Kim's phone, set it down on the gear panel.

"No," Deenie said, "I wasn't there."

Deenie's own phone began humming on her thighs. It was another text from the number she didn't recognize.

if I have the wrong # u can tell me

Who r u, she started to type. Then stopped. The thought came: *Could it be Sean Lurie?*

And then she pushed it away. Nearly shaking her head as if to shake the idea loose. She didn't have time to think about any of that.

"So," Kim said, looking at her from the

corner of her eye. "You guys went in the lake?"

"We were just there," Deenie said. "We weren't doing anything."

"But did you get near the water?"

"No," Deenie lied.

"Huh. Well, *you're* okay, right?" she said, looking at Deenie, maybe squinting a little.

"Don't I look okay?" Deenie replied.

Kim looked at her for a moment longer, then turned her eyes back to the road, tugging at a gummy worm, letting it snap against her lip.

Deenie's phone burred again, a text from Gabby, who must've gotten her phone back.

Don't worry. we didn't put our face under water. we were never all the way in.

But Deenie had. Though Gabby didn't know it.

It'd been after she and Skye left, disappearing up the bank.

Leaning back, Lise kicked her legs, her breasts bobbling from her cotton bra.

Swim with me, Deenie, she said. *Let's do it, huh?*

And she'd found she wanted to. Cool as Gabby and Skye were, with ex-boyfriends and birth control and complicated hair, maybe Lise and Deenie were cool too. Maybe they were lawbreakers. Rebels.

So they swam, even putting their heads under.

Afterward, lying on the bank, Lise had told her the story, whispering it in her ear. About the thing she had done with the boy, that he had done to her, in the bushes by the school. And she just had to tell Deenie about it. And how it had felt.

Deenie hadn't been able to put it out of her head for days after. She guessed she hadn't put it out of her head yet.

★ ★ ★

All during class, every time he walked by the window, Tom saw it, from the corner of his eye. Amid all the hay-brown thatch of late winter, a flash of neon pink, just outside, by the tall hedges.

Soon, he found himself teaching from that corner, trying to get a better look.

It looked familiar and he couldn't figure out why.

After the bell, in nothing but shirtsleeves, his face flushed from the cold, he crept along outside his own classroom windows like some kind of peeper.

Right by the dense, snow-furred hedges, there was a crumpled pile and first he thought it was a winter scarf swirling around itself, but when he reached out, he felt the thick knit of a pair of girl's tights, Fair Isles like Georgia used to wear on winter mornings, long ago. Vivid pink with fat white snowflakes.

He thought about tugging the wool loose from the brambles, taking the tights to Lost and Found, but he didn't.

Just looking at them, how small they were, he didn't know what to do.

★　★　★

Is everything ok? Your sister won't call/text me back. MOM.

it's ok, Eli typed, she will.

He hoped she would. He could still remember Deenie's tight, red-faced anger at their mom, all through the divorce. The way it sometimes seemed her forehead would split open. It had settled into something quieter, less vivid. Something worse, like grooves sunk deep, unfixable. It had been so much harder for Deenie. All because their mom couldn't control herself, she said. Which is disgusting.

Thrusting his phone to the bottom of his backpack, he opened the door to the loading dock.

And there, once again, was Skye Osbourne, prowling up the ramp from the parking lot.

He was beginning to wonder if she lived out here. But he guessed she could wonder the same thing about him.

She smiled through a crest of smoke. It smelled like honey.

"Sometimes a girl's gotta get some fresh air," she said. "Or she might go crazy."

He dropped his backpack to the ground, climbed up on the railing.

There was a heaviness to the sky, the whisper of something wet in the air.

"Hey," she said, tugging a fraying scarf from her neck. "Feel how warm it's getting."

She dropped her bag and climbed up beside him.

"I heard Lise's mom came to see you."

"Who told you that?"

"Deenie."

"Really?" he said. He had the impression Deenie wasn't really friends with Skye. Friends of friends. Sometimes Eli felt like that's all he had. Friends of friends.

"What did she want?"

"I don't know. She was acting pretty crazy."

"Huh," Skye said. "Did she say stuff?"

All those layers of sweater and scarf, and beneath those, her legs, boots climbing to

167

her midthigh. When she turned, her skirt whirled slowly, and, for a split second, he could see the inside of one of those thighs. Stark white through the skein of fishnets.

He watched her thigh. She watched him.

"Sort of," he said. All that came into his head was Mrs. Daniels saying *Spreading your semen anywhere you want.* "I don't remember."

She looked at him and he thought he saw a funny kind of smile there. He tried to imagine having sex with Skye, to picture her body underneath all those folds and seams. To picture her eyes rolling back, her skin flushed, her body giving way. He couldn't.

It made him feel relieved.

He didn't think he'd ever be interested in Skye, but he was glad girls like her existed. Ones who didn't need him to feel good, pretty, forgiven, safe.

★   ★   ★

There were marks on Lise's locker, like from a big claw.

"They didn't have her combination," Jaymie Hurwich told Deenie breathlessly. Class salutatorian and Most Self-Motivated Student, Jaymie said everything breathlessly.

168

"The janitor opened it with a bolt cutter."

Deenie put her finger on the metal-scrape scar.

"They looked, but then they didn't touch anything," Jaymie said, hand on the large padlock hanging from it now. "You missed geo, Deenie. How come?"

Deenie didn't say anything. She knew exactly what was inside Lise's locker: packs of highlighters, wild-berry hand sanitizer, the dented thermos containing sludgy remnants of yesterday morning's health smoothie. What could they learn from that?

Then Jaymie told her the other news: a silver-haired woman in a pantsuit had been spotted in the nurse's office. No one knew whether Nurse Tammy had quit or been suspended or fired, but she was gone. And the silver-haired woman was maybe not even a nurse at all but someone important. The lanyard on her neck read *Dryden County Health.*

"Do you think they'll cancel midterms?" Jaymie asked.

Deenie didn't answer. She was reading the newspaper article that had been making the rounds, the paper greased to near silk by now.

The picture of Gabby and Lise, best friends forever.

Which was all she could see at first until Jaymie spread her hand like a spider over the photo of the lavender brochure.

"It could happen to any of us," Jaymie said gravely. "We all have it in us."

The first shots were six months ago.

HPV vaccines are more effective if administered before sexual debut.

That's what the department of health poster in the nurse's office said. Gabby had read it aloud, making wide eyes at Deenie until she'd laughed.

Debut. Take a bow after. Hold your applause till the end, please.

Freshman girls were now required to have it before enrolling.

Brooke Campos said most of the fifth-grade girls had already had it. "Sluts," Brooke had said, annoyed at being beaten by her eleven-year-old sister. "The little sluts."

And here they were, high-school juniors with condoms hurled at their feet wherever they turned, it seemed. And they hadn't gotten the shots.

"The human papillomavirus can infect you anywhere," Ms. Dyer, the health teacher, announced before the first round of shots in September, "and can cause everything from benign warts on the hands and feet to cancer of the cervix, anus, mouth, and throat."

A papilloma, she explained, grows outward like a projecting finger and looks like cauliflower.

Deenie didn't see how a finger could look like a cauliflower but, watching Ms. Dyer holding up her pinkie, she knew she didn't want either of them inside her.

And then Ms. Dyer said that HPV had been around forever, even in those fairy tales you read as a kid, when the witches and trolls have bumps on their faces and hands.

"Can't warts just be warts?" Brooke Campos asked, grimacing. "Let's not get crazy." Brooke was always the person in English class who complained that Ms. Enright was "reading too much into things."

"This isn't a joke," Ms. Dyer said. No one would ever assume anything Ms. Dyer said was a joke. Twenty-eight years old with a master's in female adolescent something, she paused before she answered any question, pushing her oversize blue-framed glasses higher on her nose thoughtfully. Deenie's dad said, with women like her, a sense of humor comes a few years later.

"See how wide this area is?" she said,

171

holding a diagram of a cervix across her pelvis, making the girls in the front row flinch. "At your age, this is the area most vulnerable to invasion. It's utterly exposed. In a few years, it will retract. You'll be safer."

Lise whispered that it made her feel like her insides were on the outside and anyone could touch them.

"Until then," Ms. Dyer said, pointing to the sink handle on the lab unit, "you are as open as the mouth on that faucet."

Skye looked up for a moment from mild contemplation of her own fingers, bundled with rings — arrows, snakes, a silver seahorse.

"Ms. Dyer, I read something," she said. "Most people with HPV have issues with feeling grounded, with self-judgment, with their sexual energies."

"Where'd you read that, Skye?" Ms. Dyer asked, her fingers wrapped around the sink handle. Teachers never knew what to do with Skye, Ms. Dyer least of all. Whenever Skye spoke, Ms. Dyer tended to shift the weight on her feet back and forth until it made Deenie dizzy.

"Online," Skye replied. "It has to do with repression. Warts mean you're holding something back that needs to be released."

"Like what? Pus?" Deenie asked.

Everything was always so easy for Skye, with her older boyfriends, the way her aunt bought her cool old-time lingerie from vintage shops, the strip of birth control pills she once unfurled for them like candy.

"No," Skye said. "Sexual hang-ups. Hiding your erotic powers. Fear. Secrets. You have to release all that."

"But how?" Lise peeped from behind Skye. "What are you supposed to do?"

Everyone started giggling except Lise, her face puzzled and reddening.

"Don't worry, Lise," Skye said, not even turning around to look at her. "You'll know just what to do."

The first round of shots, Deenie was surprised how little it hurt, and disappointed.

All the rumors were that it hurt more than any other vaccine, ever.

She remembered Jaymie Hurwich. It had taken her ten minutes because the nurse couldn't calm her down.

Finally, she told me to watch the ladybug on the window, Jaymie said after. *And I said, What window? By then she'd stuck it in.*

Back then, the prospect of her or Gabby or Lise having sex seemed remote. None of them had boyfriends and there had been

173

the dramatic cautionary tale of a girl Deenie worked with at the Pizza House. The one who'd confided that she thought she was pregnant by the assistant manager at the ear-piercing booth at the mall. It turned out she wasn't pregnant but did have gonorrhea, which was disgusting to all of them in ten different ways, "starting with the name," Lise had said, shivering a little.

But the third booster round came after Gabby and Tyler Nagy. They'd had sex twice, but Gabby wasn't even sure it worked the first time, though she'd spent four summers at horse camp, so it was hard to know.

After the second time, Tyler broke up with her while she was still putting her jeans back on. "I should never have done it," Gabby said. "And now it's gone."

Around then, she'd started to spend lots of time with Skye, who sent Tyler a text message calling him an abuser of women. She told them there were secret codes embedded in the text and it was a hex. She shook the phone when she sent it, to increase the mayhem. And when Deenie thought about it now, it was then that Gabby and Skye's friendship was sealed.

Later, the brief reign of Gabby and Tyler — had it really only lasted a month? — became a sign to Deenie that there were entire dark corridors too awful to ponder. It wouldn't be that way for her, she decided. And she never would have dated anyone like Tyler, or any hockey player.

But it wasn't just Gabby. There was Lise, her body bursting with power and beauty, mere seconds away from a wealth of thrilling boyfriend possibilities, which would surely lead to romantic sex and never anything to feel bad about, ever.

Sexual debut. Sometimes it seemed to Deenie that high school was like a long game of And Then There Were None.

Every Monday, another girl's debut.

★　★　★

A sharp burst of screams erupted from inside the gym.

"Put your fingers in her mouth," someone was shouting, and A.J. and Scotty Tredwell were rushing down the hall, pulling Eli with them through the locker-room exit, following the noise.

The doors pitched wide, but all Eli could see was a band of girls' legs in all those colored tights like Gabby's, like the bright pegs in a game board, grouped so closely he couldn't see past them to whatever they were staring at on the floor.

175

Mrs. Darger, whistle jammed in her mouth, was shoving them aside like a pro lineman, and when the last clenched-face girl stumbled sideways, Eli spotted a pair of rainbow-colored sneakers twitching on the floor, heard the rapid sound of someone's head hitting hard wood, rat-a-tat-tat.

It was the red-haired girl, Kim someone, who used to trail after Gabby when she came to watch that jackass Nagy play. Laugh-filled braces, she'd flashed her shirt upward at him, but only as high as her white belly, freckle-sprayed. Once Gabby stopped coming to the games, Kim did too.

Suddenly there was a strong smell, a geyser of vomit from the girl's mouth, carrot-colored to match her hair.

"It's me," her voice came. "Oh no, it's me."

Eli had long gotten used to the screams of girls, their faces ruddy and ecstatic behind the throbbing Plexiglas.

You could never really distinguish them from the noise of everything else in the rink, the seashell roar under his helmet, the double-tap of a stick, the whistle shrieks, the sounds of his own breathing, ragged and focused.

But this wasn't the same anyway, the

sound that came from the girl's — Kim Court's — mouth as she saw the paramedics arrive.

It wasn't a scream, really.

More like a howl, a moaning howl that reminded him of something he couldn't name. An animal dying, something.

When they sat her up, there was a spray of blood down the back of her shirt from where her head had hit the floor.

"You're okay," Mrs. Darger had said, her face a funny shade of green. "You just spooked yourself."

Like you might say if she had gotten hit in the head with a volleyball.

"What happened," someone whispered, and Eli could smell the vomit on the floor. One of the paramedics stepped on it, smearing it as he wheeled Kim Court away.

"She was standing and then she wasn't."

"That is so gross."

"She was standing next to me," someone said, "and she was saying, 'Why are you so gray?'"

★ ★ ★

There was a long message from Gabby, broken across seven, eight texts.

Standing outside the east breezeway,

177

Deenie read them, one eye on her cell phone signal, her thumb pressing anxiously on the screen, *refresh-refresh-refresh,* for the next one.

I was scared he'd do this.

It was about Gabby's dad. Only he could make her like this.

She said he'd just showed up at the house, had learned what happened from Mrs. Daniels. Couldn't believe he had to hear it from a stranger on his voice mail. And wasn't that typical, Gabby said, because Mrs. Daniels was no stranger. Had in fact called the police on Mr. Bishop once, a year ago, when he'd come to pick up his daughter and driven right onto the front lawn, tearing out a porch light and insisting Gabby get in the car, now.

He went to hosp. looking for me, Gabby wrote. He just wants to show off. He doesn't care. He was yelling and mom wouldn't come from behind the dining rm table.

Then:

He started crying, big shock. Mom said what are you gonna do? Cry your whole life?

But Gabby's final text wasn't about her dad. It was short and the words seemed to flash at Deenie, her screen catching the sun's glare.

Also: I'm thinking about the lake. What if u r

right. What if it was in the lake. What if it is in us.

Deenie looked at the words, which seemed to float before her eyes.

But I'm okay, she wanted to say, to type. But she just looked at the screen instead.

That was when she heard the funny pant, someone rushing up to her, the hall echoing with new noise.

Keith Barbour was charging down the hall with another senior boy, both their necks ringed by monster headphones.

"Did you hear?" he barked, shoving Deenie in the arm. "Kim Court's getting wheeled out on a gurney."

"Kim?" Deenie asked, her phone smacking the floor. "What happened?"

"You're all going down." The other boy laughed, beats thrumming through the open mouths of his headphones. "One by one."

★　★　★

The whole school had a rabid energy, like nothing would settle again.

And then, a few minutes before sixth period began, Eli showed up at Tom's classroom door.

Tom hadn't even had a chance to talk to

him about what had happened that morning.

The dangers our girls suffer at your hands, Sheila Daniels had said to poor Eli. Eli, the sweetest boy in the world. *We know and we'll do anything to protect them. Anything.*

A woman who laid that charge at the feet of his son, a boy who couldn't even enjoy the girls, their avid eyes always on him, seemed outrageously cruel.

"Dad," Eli said, face pale, one hand tight on the door frame. "I need to talk to you."

Tom stepped outside the classroom and Eli told him what he'd just seen, the redheaded sophomore on the gym floor.

"The one with all the braces," Eli said.

"That must be Kim Court," Tom said. "It sounds like Kim Court."

Kim had been in his class last semester. She was one of the ones always trailing behind Gabby and who seemed years younger than her, mouth thick with orthodontia, skittering in her tennis shoes, spinning in the hallways like a red top.

"She didn't look good," Eli said. His eyes were glazed and wouldn't quite meet Tom's.

"This is just crazy," Tom said. "I'll see what I can find out."

Eli didn't say anything.

The bell rang.

"Okay," Eli said, swinging his backpack up behind him.

Something in his face when he turned away made Tom pause. An expression he'd almost forgotten. Back when Eli was ten or eleven, that time when he stopped sleeping. Georgia would hear him moaning, go to his room, and find Eli sitting in the dark, his arms wrapped around his shins. He'd say his bones felt like they were popping. The doctor said it was growing pains, which Tom hadn't realized was a literal thing.

"Kids can become very emotional when they don't sleep," the doctor had told them. "It's natural."

The only thing that seemed to help was when Georgia rubbed his legs, which she would do for a half hour or more, coming back to their bed her hands slippery with vitamin oil.

Driving him to school in the morning in those days, Tom would watch him in the rearview mirror, eyes ringed gray. It was hard to see. This, his easy child, none of the sweeping emotions of his daughter, her warmth and sorrow both heavy things. He wasn't used to it on Eli.

"Dad," Eli had asked one morning, "what if you woke up one day and you were gone?"

"If you woke up and I was gone? That

wouldn't ever happen, Eli."

"No, what if I woke up and I was gone."

Tom had looked at him in the backseat, his limbs growing so long, his face changing so fast you could almost watch it happen, and felt a fierce loss and didn't know why.

10

Eli sat, playing it and replaying it in his mind. The girl's head slapping the floor, the glare from all those braces, like a mouth full of tinfoil.

Horse. Now he remembered. That's what they called her.

Language lab should have started five minutes ago, but Ms. Chase, who gave out the peeling headphones, was nowhere to be found. Under the faded poster of the Eiffel Tower, A.J. and Stim, both in their jerseys, were sitting on top of their desks, speculating loudly that school would be canceled.

"They gotta do it now," A.J. said. "Quarantine. Lock your daughters up!"

"I'm telling you, it's some kind of mutant STD," Stim said, flapping the edge of the long gauze pad on his forearm, an acrid smell wafting from it. "I won't be hitting any of that. I'm sticking with Star-of-the-Sea girls."

"Oh, man, those girls *all* have STDs. They don't believe in condoms."

Eli looked longingly out the classroom door. Maybe he could just leave.

"Why don't you ask Nash?" Stim said, spinning the dials on the ancient analog tape deck. "He's the one who got a booty call from Mo McLoughlin after the Brother Rice game."

Maureen. The one who'd chugged hard cider on the way over and thrown up in his wastebasket after. So tiny, school gymnast, her fingernails looked like one of Deenie's old dolls', tiny as baby's teeth.

"I doubt Horse gets enough play to get a mutant STD," A.J. said, baring his teeth like a donkey, "or even a regular one."

"Speaking of, Nash," Stim said, still plucking at the gauze, "I saw your sister take off with her this morning."

"What do you mean?"

"Before everything. Your sister and K-Court were in a car, driving toward the woods."

A.J. smiled. "She's getting to be quite the little rebel, that sister of yours."

Eli placed his palm over his textbook, a different picture of the Eiffel Tower on it. *French in Action! L'Avenir Est à Vous,* it was called.

"It's evolution," Stim said. "With Lise Daniels and Gabby Bishop on the DL, somebody's gotta step up."

"Not even," A.J. said, shaking his head and laughing. "She's his sister, man."

Stim shoved a pencil under his gauze, scratching thoughtfully. "Did you see Lise in her bikini last summer? The top, it was just like triangles over her tits, and when she walked past . . . and sometimes the fabric, it'd kinda buckle. Man, I loved that suit."

"I think you should shut the fuck up," Eli said, throwing his bag down with a thud that made everyone in the lab look up. "I think it's time you do that."

Stim looked at him carefully.

Eyes darting between the two of them, A.J. seemed to be waiting for something, grinning a little.

Stim shrugged. "Lise isn't your sister, Nash," he said. "They're not all your sisters."

★　★　★

The teachers' lounge was the liveliest Tom had ever seen it, at least since Mr. Tomalla had been fired for taking photographs of female students' feet with his cell phone beneath his desk. He had posted them online and had twenty thousand hits, far more than Nat Dubow's YouTube science videos.

Everyone was waiting for Principal Crowder.

Laptops open, several teachers were hovering and gasping over photos of Lise and Gabby that had been posted online. A frightening snapshot of Lise's white thigh, her fingers locked around it. And one of Gabby, mid-seizure and curiously glamorous: jaw struck high, the auditorium's stage lights rendering her a pop singer, a movie star.

Tom didn't want to look, and didn't want to join in the tsk-tsking or the bemoaning of our social media–ridden culture.

Checking his e-mail at the communal workstation, he saw three messages from Georgia:

Why won't Deenie call me back? Is it true about Gabby?

What's happening?

Have D. call me ASAP, okay?

He told himself he would call her as soon as he could.

"A few other girls — I mean, has anyone else seen anything odd?" asked June Fisk, one of the scarved social-science teachers

— there were three of them, and they liked to sit in the lounge and drink from their glass water bottles and talk about the decline of grammar, the rise of bullying, the dangers of fracking.

"Jaymie Hurwich," said Brad Crews, rapping his fingers on his business-math textbook. "She kept blinking through all of sixth period."

"What, she shouldn't be blinking?" Tom asked.

"That's not what I mean," Brad said, looking slightly dazed — though he always did, the father of six-month-old twin girls who seemed to have ravaged him. "It was constant. And really hard. She's an intense girl to begin with."

Everyone knew vaguely about Jaymie's family situation, a long-estranged mother with emotional problems of some unspecified nature, which meant everyone was easy on her even when she was hard on them, crying over A minuses, over class critiques.

"They're scared," said Erika Dyer, the health teacher, snapping her laptop shut loudly. Tom couldn't look at her now without thinking of her presentation to parents last year: *HPV and Your Daughter.*

"Maybe because they feel like everyone's watching them," she added, poking her glasses farther up the bridge of her nose. "Their own teachers, maybe."

"I couldn't concentrate," Brad said, wiping his face, staring down at his shoes. "It was . . . unsettling."

"Of course it was," piped up Liz somebody, who wasn't even a teacher but an ed student from the community college. "You feel like any one of them might fly from their chairs at any moment." Tom couldn't help but notice how hard Liz was blinking.

"The sympathy in this room is affecting," Erika said. "Truly."

"I have nothing but sympathy for Lise Daniels," June Fisk insisted. "And as if Gabby Bishop didn't have enough trouble. But how are we supposed to teach like this? Pretend like nothing is going on?"

Carl Brophy groaned loudly. "Teenage girls fidgeting, high-school students trying to get out of class. Clearly, it's a supervirus. Call the CDC. Alert the World Health Organization."

At that moment, Ben Crowder swung open the door, which felt like a relief, though the look on his face, gray and tight, reminded Tom of the final years of Ben's predecessor, who'd retired at age seventy, skin like wet paper.

"First, an update on Kimberly Court," he said. "Her doctor said it looks to him like a panic attack. And the parents, in this case, seem to understand that. They had trouble at her old school with a few boys who teased her. Some bullying. They say she's always been a high-strung girl."

It seemed a funny thing for parents to say about their own child under these circumstances. Even if they might think it.

"So they released her?" Erika asked.

"She's probably heading home as we speak," he said, nodding firmly.

"But you don't know?" June Fisk said.

"I've been on the phone with the superintendent," Crowder continued, ignoring her, "and spent the past hour talking to the health department. What's important is this: Do not speculate, especially with students or parents. If parents come to you with questions, please direct them to me or the superintendent. And, in particular, if you have any contact with Sheila Daniels, please alert us immediately."

There was much exchanging of looks, but Tom kept his eyes on Crowder, trying to read him. He wondered if Sheila Daniels planned to sue the school district along with the health department.

Fleetingly, he wondered if it was possible

189

that she did know something none of the rest of them did. It wasn't a thought he wanted to hold on to.

"But this vaccine stuff she's talking about is everywhere now," Brad said. "I'm the parent coordinator and I have thirty-two e-mails about it in my inbox. What am I supposed to say to parents?"

Crowder took a deep breath, lifting his arms as if encouraging everyone to breathe with him.

"Our primary goal as educators," he said, his shirtsleeves furrowed with sweat, "needs to be containment of panic."

Erika Dyer, fingers still pushing those glasses up that dainty nose, hurried along next to him as they walked into the east corridor.

"Lise Daniels's mother called me," she whispered, not looking at him.

Tom felt like he had somehow been elected universal reassurer.

"Oh, don't worry," he said. "She's all over the place right now, and —"

"She told me I'd poisoned her daughter just as surely as the vaccine itself."

"She's just swinging wildly at anything. She came to my —"

"It's my job, you know?" she said, her

voice trembling slightly. "To protect those girls. Girls like Lise. She came to my office just last week. I was trying to help her understand her body. The feelings she had. Things happening to her. And now . . ."

"These girls trust you. Sheila should be thanking you. And when she settles down, she'll realize you don't have any say in public-health policy for the school system."

Erika looked at him, fingers cradled around her ear in a way that reminded him of Deenie.

"She said as sure as if I'd held the poison syringe in my fingers, I had harmed her daughter."

"She's hysterical," he began, then paused a moment. "Hold on. Lise came to see you last week?"

She looked at him. "Yes."

Tom waited a second.

"Of course, whatever she said, that's private," she added.

"Of course," Tom said, a little embarrassed. What did it matter now?

But it felt like it might.

Erika looked at him, her right eyelid trembling behind her clever glasses.

"You can't let it get to you," he said. "None of it's your fault."

★ ★ ★

Maybe it's from the funky ooze out by football field after it rains

Touretts like my uncle Steve no one likes him lost IT job after

Deenie wanted to turn her phone off, to stop the texts nearly rattling her phone off the kitchen island.

But it might be Gabby.

Let's meet up, she'd texted Gabby an hour ago, to talk abt Kim & lake.

So she was left with bad thoughts.

One, two, three girls. The way it was moving, like the way pink eye or strep would tear through the school, a blazing red mouth swallowing them one by one, it didn't feel like a vaccine. It felt like a virus, a plague.

She clicked to the latest news article and read it while she ate dinner, toaster waffles that were still cold inside.

Of the two hundred and seven girls in the school, the article pointed out, more than half had been vaccinated.

In her head, she kept running numbers. More than a hundred girls had had the vaccine. But what were the odds that she would be friends with all three of the Girls. *The Girls.* The *Afflicted* Girls.

"Police and public-health officials," the

article said, "are working together to determine commonalities among the girls: hobbies, medications, health histories, personal histories."

"Me," Deenie found herself saying out loud, washing her dinner plate, gluey with syrup, her fingers grating through it.

Lise to Gabby to Kim, and what did they all have in common?

They're friends with each other, sort of.

But how long before someone said, *All of them are friends with Deenie.*

Deenie is the thing they have in common.

It's Deenie.

"At that age, it's all about yourself," she'd overheard her mom say once. "You think the whole world spins around you."

Deenie had missed the context. All she knew was how it felt to hear that coming from her mom, the woman who'd overturned the family like a box of garage-sale toys to suit herself.

Maybe that's what this thinking was, her maternal inheritance. Something happened, anything, and it was all about *me, me, me.*

Her phone shot to life, buzzing across the counter.

The number flashing: Kim C.

Deenie grabbed for it.

"K.C., are you okay?"

"I can't talk long," came the choked whisper. "I'm not supposed to be on the phone."

"Why not? What happened?"

"I'm still at the hospital. They won't let me go."

"Why? They let Gabby go after. Are you . . ."

"I don't have time, Deenie. I just — look, I'm gonna have to tell them."

Deenie set down her fork, sticky in her hands. "Tell them what?"

"About the lake."

"Kim, you weren't at the lake. You don't know anything about it. You don't know what you're talking about."

"It might be why," she said. "It might be why it happened to me."

"Why *what* happened to you? Why you threw up in the gym? Someone throws up in gym every week."

Deenie knew it was mean to say. But what happened to Kim just didn't sound scary, like with Gabby or with Lise. At least not the way Keith Barbour had described it, twirling in a circle and gagging. And, privately, the thought had come to her: it's just Kim Court, anyway. Kim Court, who copied Gabby's tights, Gabby's shoes, lapped up everything Gabby ever said.

194

Kim didn't say anything, clearing her throat in a raw way that hurt Deenie to hear.

"You weren't even in the lake, Kim," Deenie added, dropping her plate in the sink, her right hand in the hot dishwater, swirling.

"But I was with Gabby. In her house. I touched her hair. You saw me."

"What?" Deenie asked, even as she remembered Kim's stubby fingers digging in Gabby's scalp, that dark swarm of Gabby hair threaded with glue from the plugs on her head. Frankenstein's creature.

"And —" She paused and Deenie could hear her breath coming faster. "And you."

"You didn't touch my hair," Deenie said, her hand stinging from the sink's hot water.

"We were together. You were in my car . . ."

Find some music. I can't think and drive.

". . . and then it happened to me."

Deenie pictured her fingers rubbing along the playlist on Kim's phone.

"It's not fair . . ." Kim gasped. "I didn't do anything wrong."

"No one did," Deenie said, coolly.

"And how come . . ." Kim let the question trail off for a second. "I mean, how come everyone but you, Deenie?"

Deenie looked down at her hands, red and

raw in the dishwater.

"What did the doctors say?" she asked.

"They don't know," Kim said, her voice dropping so low Deenie could barely hear it. "But I'm telling you: there was something inside me, and it was in my throat."

"Vomit, Kim," Deenie said roughly, her eyes stinging from the water.

"No, but that's why I threw up. Because I couldn't get it out. I couldn't stop it."

"Stop what?"

"The way it felt, the things I knew."

"Things you . . . What do you mean?"

"And it's *not* the vaccine, Deenie," she said, voice rising. "That's what I wanted to tell you. Don't listen to them about the vaccine!"

"Kim, what —"

Through the phone, Deenie could hear the crackling PA of the hospital, paging someone. She felt a click in her own throat but stopped herself from clearing it.

"I have to go," Kim said. "I can't explain it to you. It has to happen to you for you to understand."

★ ★ ★

Lying on his bed, three warm beers heavy inside him, Eli wished he'd just gone home

196

after practice.

Instead, he'd followed A.J. to Brooke Campos's house. They were all freaked out about Kim Court and everything, though no one would admit it.

Brooke took them to the basement, where there was a broken fridge. Laid flat like a glossy white coffin, it was packed with skunked Yuengling abandoned after her dad's poker game. They sat on it and drank and talked about everything.

Brooke said she used to go to camp with a girl who'd had the shots and her heart had expanded to the size of a grapefruit and she died. She said she always felt sorry for how she'd treated that girl and for pushing her off the diving board that time and now it was too late.

Then Brooke started crying, her head thrown back, just like Gabby in all those pictures. Leaning first against A.J., then Eli, with a kind of breathless warmth, she cried, her fingers clinging to their shirtfronts. Eli left before things got too crazy. Even A.J. seemed upset, talking about his brother, who died of septic shock when A.J. was five.

You never knew how things would make you feel. The kinds of people who might feel things.

That's what he was thinking, lying on his

bed, eyes on the spider cracks in the ceiling.

Reaching over, he grabbed his backpack, trying to shake his phone free. He hadn't looked at it in hours, afraid it'd be his mom again, texting about Deenie. He felt sorry for her, a little. And for himself.

Maybe he'd had four beers.

And the phone wouldn't shake loose.

Finally, lifting his torso woozily against his pillows, he turned the backpack inside out, scattering loose-leaf, handouts, practice schedules all over the bed and floor.

"Deenie," he said. "Can I come in?"

Through the door, he could hear her moving, thought he heard a sharp inhale, like she was deciding whether to answer.

"Okay," she said. "You can."

"You haven't seen my phone, have you?" he said, pushing the door open, surveying the room, the tangle of loose charger cords sprouting from the wall, jeans coiled at the foot of the bed, one long dust-streaked sock. And always the books, their covers creased, spines spread across the floor. He thought girls were supposed to be clean.

She was standing in the middle of the room, which surprised him. Her fingers were pinched red, latticed tight in the strings of her hoodie.

She stared at the knotted string ends in her hand for a second.

Then she looked up at him.

"Don't tell Dad," she said, voice so small.

"Tell Dad what?"

★　★　★

It was after seven o'clock, and Tom was sitting in the driveway looking at his house, holding his phone.

He'd just listened to another voice mail from Georgia: *Tom, maybe Deenie should stay with me. Maybe she'll be safer away from Dryden.*

And now, still not moving, not even taking the keys out of the ignition, he looked once more at the three texts from Deenie, asking if he'd heard anything about anything.

I'll tell you when I get home, he'd replied.

When r u coming home, she'd answered, more than two hours ago.

The meeting with Crowder had gone late, everyone with a great deal to say, and then talking to Erika and finally helping the French teacher — Kit was her name, he had to remember that — jump her scooter, stalled from the sudden damp in the air, the temperature rising twenty degrees or more since the day before in that weird way of Dryden.

"Isn't it something?" she'd said throatily, looking around, her cheekbones misted and her lipstick slightly smudged. "Like a fairy tale."

He'd said he knew just what she meant.

And she'd mentioned Eli's *magnifique* attendance, and Tom pretended he knew, even though he'd been sure Eli took Spanish.

Finally, they had talked about the image of Gabby posted everywhere, that curtain of hair, the theatrical arc of her neck, the inflamed cheeks.

"Like a ballerina," Kit said. "All the girls will want to steal that pose for their yearbook photos."

And now it was after seven, and he was still sitting in the car.

Did they tell u what is happening, Deenie's text read. Do they know yet.

Taking a breath, he picked up his phone one last time.

"Medical billing, Diane speaking."

"Diane," he said, "it's Tom. I wasn't sure you'd still be there."

"Tom," she said. "Well, I'm twelve-to-eight today."

"I'm sorry to keep calling," he said, sensing a tightness in her voice. "I was just wondering if you had any news."

There was a pause, then a sigh.

"Hey, I get it," she said. "If I had a daughter at that school, I'd want to know everything too. And a lot's been happening."

"A girl named Kim Court, she was there today, at the hospital, right?"

"Yes, she's here."

"Still? I thought they were sending her home. That it was just a panic attack."

"We have to keep her until she seems stable. After a seizure —"

"So it was a seizure?"

"No," she said, then lowered her voice. "I didn't mean that. But they have to rule out some things."

"Like what?"

"When teenagers come, and they're having hallucinations —"

"Hallucinations? I didn't know she was —"

"— we have to rule out drugs. Ecstasy, MDMA. There's a lot of ecstasy at that school."

"There is?"

"Or it could be the onset of schizophrenia."

"Jesus."

"Can I call you back?" she said suddenly.

"Sure."

A moment later, the phone rang.

"I'm calling from my cell," she whispered, a nervous titter in her voice, "from the ladies' room."

As if by magic, the smooth professional tone — professional biller, professional dater-slash-divorcée — was gone. She sounded suddenly younger, girlish.

"They wouldn't even let us leave for dinner because of the reporters out front," she was saying. "We're not supposed to be talking about any of this. They made us sign something."

"I'm putting you in a bad position," Tom said.

"I have a friend in ER," she said, words rushing, jumbling together. "She said the Court girl kept shoving her hand in her mouth. She got her whole fist in there. And when they put the restraints on, she started screaming that something was touching her from the inside."

"Touching her?"

"Well, people can say all kinds of things in that state. But they didn't find any drugs. I don't think."

Tom took a breath.

"How's Lise Daniels?"

A pause.

"I can't talk any more about her."

"What do you mean?"

"Listen, I just —" He heard the sound of another woman's voice, everything echoing, the rush of water. "I have to go."

"Right," he said. "I understand. It's just . . . when you have a daughter."

Her voice cracked a little. "Oh, Tom, I know. I wish . . ."

"No, I don't want to get you in any kind of trouble."

"It's just . . . Can I say something?" Whispering.

"Sure," he said, feeling a churning inside. There was a long pause, then the thud of a door.

"Tom. It feels crazy in here right now."

Tom could hear her breath catch.

"The mother, she walks the halls all night. That's what Patty, one of the nurses, told me. The mother walked by the nurses' station so many times last night, Patty thought she'd go crazy herself. She keeps telling them her daughter has been destroyed. That's the word she used. *Destroyed.* Like you do with an animal. After."

★   ★   ★

It didn't seem so bad to him. Nowhere near

as bad as Deenie seemed to think.

Sitting down on the edge of her bed, Eli watched his sister bobbing from foot to foot, just like she had during countless past confidences, shared reports of dirty deeds, stolen candy, a pilfered beer, running a bike over Mom's violets. Except that was a long time ago. It hadn't happened in a long time.

When she'd first started talking, he'd been afraid. He'd had this squinting sense, lately, of something. That she was different, changed.

A month or so ago, he and his friends had gone to Pizza House for slices after a game and he'd seen her in the kitchen. Her cap pushed back, she was carrying cold trays of glistening dough rounds, and her face had a kind of pink to it, her hips turning to knock the freezer door shut.

I didn't spit on it, Deenie had promised, winking at him from behind the scarlet heat lamps.

He'd stood there, arrested. The pizza box hot in his hands.

She looked different than at school and especially at home, and she was acting differently. Moving differently.

He couldn't stop watching her, his friends all around him, loud and triumphant, their faces swathed with sweat.

Next to her, by the ovens, was that guy Sean, the one who used to play forward for Star-of-the-Sea. Once, Sean had asked him about Lise, wondered if Eli knew her. *Her tits look like sno-cones,* he'd said. *Beautiful sno-cones.*

And now Deenie stood before him, her body tight, the zipper on her hoodie pinching that tiny bird neck of hers, saying, "Don't tell Dad. Okay?"

But what she told him had nothing to do with what he'd noticed at the Pizza House, whatever that was. Or the other thing — the thing he'd almost forgotten. Someone at school saying he saw his sister getting into a car with some guy.

Instead, it was just some crazy story about the lake.

"But Eli, we put our feet in. Last week. What if it did something?"

He shook his head. "If it did something, you'd be sick too. And Skye Osbourne, she was with you, right? She'd be sick too."

"Maybe it affected us in different ways."

She looked at him. The look he'd seen since they were small, like camping, her pale face in the tent flap when he'd spook her, telling her there were bears out there, hidden in the green daze of Binnorie Woods.

"Deenie," he said, "it's not the lake."

205

"How do you know?"

He looked at her. It was one of those tricks his dad always pulled off. He used to watch him do it with Mom over and over. *I promise you, I promise you,* a smile, a coaxing shoulder rub, spinning her around like dancing, *everything will be okay.* Mom used to call it the Croc dance, to go with the Croc smile.

"The doctors would know, Deenie," he said, the thought coming to him just as he needed it. "They've been doing tests, right? For toxins and stuff. They'd pick that up."

"Oh," Deenie said. "Right."

He could see her shoulders relax a little. He was surprised how easy it was. Just like when they were little. Taking her hand and dragging her out of the tent, promising her there were no bears out there after all. They were safe.

"So you feel better?"

She nodded.

"Okay, then," he said, leaning back, feeling his body loosen, the beer bloom returning.

Except there was something wedged under him, Deenie's Pizza House shirt, stiff with old flour or whatever it was they made pizzas with.

"Jesus, Deenie, don't you ever wash your

uniform?" he teased, fingering the shirt, feigning throwing it at her.

She didn't say anything, her hands once more gripping the ends of her drawstring. Tugging it back and forth. It was like it had lasted only a second, that brief spasm of relief.

Girls never stopped being mysterious, he thought, tossing the shirt to the floor.

Sinking back onto her pillow, he lay there for a moment, staring at her ceiling, wondering about his missing phone, or something.

11

Sitting at the kitchen table, Tom was trying hard to think of exactly nothing except the beer in front of him when he felt a hand on his shoulder.

His shoulder jerked, but it was just Deenie, her fingernails short and painted silver, like all the girls'.

"Dad," she said, "Gabby called. Can I borrow the car?"

She almost never asked. With only a learner's permit, she wasn't supposed to drive without an adult.

But it was the first thing she'd said to him since he came home and told her what Principal Crowder had said, or insisted. That everyone was working very hard to figure this thing out and that it was important not to get caught up in all the rumors. She'd given him a look that suggested what he knew to be true: he didn't really have any information at all.

So now, when she asked him for the car, something in him stirred, and, without even saying a word, he found himself sliding the keys across the table and dropping them into her palm, which closed over them instantly.

"Thanks, Dad," she said, grasping them so tight it hurt to look.

"But Deenie," he said, although she was already halfway to the door, "call your mom tonight, okay?"

She said she would.

★   ★   ★

It felt so warm outside, one of those weird nights when the temperature rises, making everything look strange and glowy.

Gabby's mom had taken pity on her and said she could go out for a while.

And, unaccountably, Deenie's dad had loaned her the car.

"The air," Gabby said, taking a few tight, sharp breaths. "Even the air hurts."

"It does?" To Deenie, it felt delicious. When she breathed, the warm seemed to swirl in her mouth. "At least your mom let you out."

Once they'd gotten a few miles from her house, Gabby, her face pale and puffy, said she didn't want to be in the car.

So they decided to walk through town, hands shoved in pockets and the sky a ghostly shade of violet.

For a few minutes, Deenie forgot everything.

No one was out, and there was a ghost-town feel, like no one knew winter was over, at least for the night, and the streets had a kind of fuzzy beauty, the air briny from four months of rock salt, the pavement spongy under Deenie's feet.

Across the street was the orange flare of the Pizza House. She wondered if Sean Lurie was at the ovens, grip in either hand, smiling.

"I can't believe Kim called you from the hospital," Gabby said. "I can't believe she's still there."

"Yeah," Deenie replied, shuttled out of her daydream. "They told my dad — they told all the teachers — that she's fine. It's stress."

"Do you believe it?" Gabby asked, leading them toward the misty blur of the elementary school, its bricks streaked with salt.

"I don't know," she said slowly. "I didn't see it. Eli said she just threw up."

"But, I mean, what Kim said to you.

About it being something in the lake. Do you think it's true?"

"Kim was never in the lake," Deenie said, her new refrain.

They arrived at the square across from the school, its olden-times town pump splintered and gray. Back in fourth grade, their teacher said it was the spot where they whipped people centuries ago. For months afterward, every time they stood there, waiting for the bus, Deenie and Lise talked about it, pretended.

Lise, color high, howling upward, chubby arms wrapped around that old pump, *Forty lashes, forty lashes, no, kind sir!*

"She wasn't in the lake," Gabby said, her face hidden behind her hair, her sunken hat. "But maybe that's why she's not as sick as Lise. Why it isn't as bad for her."

"But why would Kim be sick at all?"

"Because," Gabby said, and then she said the thing they hadn't said, not aloud to each other, "because maybe it's inside us now. And she got it. From us."

Deenie felt something twitch at her temple. For a moment, she felt like she had when she saw Skye at Gabby's house. Like everything was tilting and she'd only just realized it, but it had been tilting slowly for a while.

211

"But nothing happened to me," she said. "I'm fine."

"Well," Gabby said, looking down as their feet dusted along the glistening grass of the square, "some people are just carriers. Maybe that's what you are."

Deenie looked at her.

"Like those boys with HPV," she added, still not meeting Deenie's eyes. "They never get sick. They just make everyone else sick."

Deenie couldn't get anything to come out of her mouth, and they kept walking, and Gabby wouldn't turn her head, and then they were in the darkened center of the square, under the old elm.

It didn't even sound like Gabby and she wondered where it all came from. *Carriers.* In its own way, it didn't feel different from what Skye had said, all her talk about bad energy.

"So maybe that's what you are," Gabby added.

And they kept walking. And as they did, Deenie's lungs started tightening. Pressing her palm on the cold of the tree trunk, she had to stop.

It turned out the air did hurt, and Gabby was right.

"I'm sorry," Gabby said, stopping too, her eyes burning under the lamppost. Watching

Deenie. "I'm sorry."

★   ★   ★

When the phone rang, Tom was afraid it was Georgia again, asking why Deenie hadn't called. But it was Dave Hurwich, Jaymie's father, whose barking tone reminded Tom why he'd stopped coaching soccer.

"What kind of school endorses medical experimentation on its students?" Dave asked. "You're a man of science. I'm on the CDC website right now, Tom. I'm looking at the VAERS. Do you know what we're dealing with here with this vaccine?"

Tom sighed. There was no use talking epidemiology with Dave Hurwich, who always knew more about law than lawyers, more about cars than mechanics. And there was no use trying to explain the nuances of school-board recommendations versus forced government vaccinations of children.

A single dad, Dave prided himself on his parenting and on his daughter Jaymie's academic successes, which were due at least half the time to her ability to wear down all her teachers (*But I did the extra credit and I wrote twice as much and I never missed a class and I always contribute . . .*) as relentlessly as her dad. Whenever Tom began to lose his patience with either of them, he tried to remember the "family situation," Jaymie's out-of-the-picture mother — was it something to do with postpartum? The details were vague and it never felt appropriate to ask.

"It was a stressful day for all of us, Dave. How's Jaymie doing?"

"Let me tell you how she's doing," he said, a smacking sound like his tongue was dry from making phone calls all night. "She hasn't stopped blinking since she got home. It's like looking at a Christmas tree."

So why are you calling me? Tom wanted to ask. Except he got the feeling Mr. Hurwich was calling everyone, anyone.

"I've been reading all about that supposed vaccine. You're the chemistry teacher. You should know. It's loaded with aluminum and sodium borate. Do you know what that is? That's what they use to kill roaches. They treated my daughter like a roach. And yours."

"Dave, I'm sure your doctor —"

"That goddamned doctor doesn't know anything. He prescribed vitamins. None of them know anything."

There was a pause, a creaking sound.

"She says it's like a light flashing in the

214

corner of her eye all the time. She's my little girl," Mr. Hurwich said, and all the hardness broke apart in an instant. "She doesn't even look the same."

Tom swallowed. "What do you mean?"

"I don't know," he said, voice cracking. "The way she looks at me. Something. It doesn't look like my daughter."

★   ★   ★

"Let's just drive, okay?" Gabby said. "Can we drive?"

And they both knew where they were going.

Looping back and forth along the lake, three, four times.

At first, they kept the windows shut tight.

Finally, the fifth time, Gabby opened hers, her hair slapping across the pane.

The raw smell from the water, like a presence. Something furred resting in your throat.

It reminded Deenie of something, some school-retreat middle-of-the-night story Brooke Campos had told Deenie and Lise and Kim Court about how, when she was thirteen, her big sister's boyfriend had offered her ten dollars to "taste something she'd never tasted."

Clutching her throat as she told it, Brooke almost cried and couldn't finish the story. It was all anyone could talk about for weeks. Kim kept asking everyone, *But did she? Did she do it?* And nobody knew. They'd never gotten to hear the end.

"I should go home," Gabby said, looking down at her phone in her lap. "My mom's called twice."

"Does she know you're with me?" Deenie asked. *Carriers. Maybe that's what you are.* "She'd let you be with *me*?"

"Of course," Gabby said. "What —"

Before she could say more, Gabby's phone lit up: Skye.

But Gabby didn't answer, just stared at it. And then a text followed.

"What is it?" Deenie said, trying to sound even.

"She said there was a story on the news. About something happening at the hospital."

"With Lise? Is she okay?"

"I don't know," Gabby said, staring at her phone. "But I better go home."

"Gabby," Deenie said, turning the wheel hard, "we have to go there now."

"No, Deenie," Gabby said, her voice rushing up over the radio, the wind charging from the window.

But Deenie decided she didn't care and she was the one driving anyway and the hospital was only a few miles up the road, lit like a torch.

Lise. Lise.

"You don't have to go inside, Gabby," Deenie said, voice surprisingly hard. "But I am."

Deenie was driving very fast, the stoplights shuddering above them and her foot pumping the gas.

"She's all alone," Deenie said. "And we don't know what's happened."

Gabby looked at her, chin tight, like wires pulled taut and hooked behind her ears. Like the ventriloquist's dummy that used to perform at the mall, Deenie thought, then felt bad about it.

"Okay," Gabby said, as if she had a choice. "I'll go."

The white steeple of the hospital's clock tower gleaming, Deenie was walking Gabby, directing her in a way that felt unfamiliar and powerful.

But it wouldn't be like before, wouldn't be so easy.

As soon as they walked in, a lady in a gold-buttoned suit jacket at the welcome desk recognized Gabby.

"Oh no," she said, rising to her feet. "Not again. Let me page the ER."

The alarm on her face stopped both girls.

"We're okay," Gabby said. "We're here to see Lise."

"Oh no," she repeated, shaking her head, "that's not possible."

★   ★   ★

So they sat in the parking lot, three spots behind Mrs. Daniels's wind-battered Dodge.

They had the idea that if she came out, she might let them see Lise.

"Maybe she sleeps there," Gabby said. "Maybe she never comes out."

"She has to come out," Deenie said, flipping the radio dial, trying to find news. "Something's happening in there."

She wondered if Gabby was thinking about the night her mother was wheeled in on a gurney. The way Deenie heard it, the hammer prongs almost severed an artery and Gabby had had to hold the hammer in place until the paramedics came or her mom would have died.

Deenie didn't know if it was true, but she always remembered the one detail Gabby had told her, that the sound coming from

218

her mom reminded her of those slide whistles they'd give out at Fun Palace when they were kids.

Bad things happen and then they're over, but where do they go? Deenie wondered, watching Gabby. Are they ours forever, leeching under our skin?

She didn't even see the woman approach the car, and when the rapping on the window came, her body leaped to life.

★   ★   ★

Still thinking about Dave Hurwich's call, Tom was finishing his beer and considering a second, was half ready to ask his son to join him, when his phone rang again: Lara Bishop.

"Tom, sorry to call so late. Is Gabby there?" she said, voice raspy and anxious.

"Lara," Tom said, phone slipping slightly from his hand. "No. Deenie's not home either. Has it been that long?"

He looked at the clock over the stove and was surprised to see it was nearly eleven.

He didn't really know where the hours had gone, a stack of week-old tests on his lap, watching a documentary about people dying on Mount Everest along with Eli, whose eyes had a boozy luster, his long

219

limbs heavy. There was a feeling of warmth about Eli, his peculiar brand of gloomy nostalgia ("Hey, Dad, remember that time you took us to Indian Cave and we found those frozen bones with hair?").

"I keep calling Gabby," Lara said, "and she won't pick up. Can you call Deenie?"

"Of course." And he felt a surge of shame in his chest. The girls dropping like dainty flies at school, their limbs like bendy straws, their bodies collapsing, and he gives his daughter car keys and sends her out into the great dark nettles of Dryden with the girl who had violently collapsed in front of the whole school only the day before.

What made him think he could forget for an hour with his daughter out there, somewhere?

"Dad," Deenie answered, almost before Tom heard the call go through. "I'm coming home. I am."

"Are you okay? What happened?"

"We went to the hospital." Gulping, hectic. He thought he could hear someone in the background crying. "I think something happened."

★   ★   ★

At first Deenie thought she was hallucinat-

220

ing, that gigantic face at the car window, neck crooked down, hair like soft butter. A woman she recognized, something heavy in her hand like a metal flashlight, using it to tap on the glass.

"Deenie," Gabby was saying, next to her, "Deenie, don't."

There was an insignia on the flashlight, the numeral seven, with a lightning bolt like a superhero's, and she realized it wasn't a flashlight. It was a microphone.

"Don't open the window, Deenie!" Gabby said. "Don't talk to her!"

But Deenie had already pushed the window button, the woman's lips turning into a smile.

That's when she realized who the woman was. The lady from TV, the one who had emceed the big school fund-raiser to not quite pay for the new football field that never got built.

"Hey, I'm Katie," she said, her voice bell-clear. "Are you a friend of Lise Daniels?"

Deenie didn't say anything.

"Can you come out and talk for a second?" the woman said. Then, craning down, she peered at Gabby, who quickly turned away, her neck twisted.

"You're the second," the woman said, pointing with the microphone at Gabby.

"You're Girl Two."

A few minutes later, they were all standing by the car.

"Gabby," Deenie had whispered, "it's the only way we'll find out."

A man with a large camera hoisted over his shoulder appeared from nowhere, but the TV woman handed him the microphone and waved him away.

That was when Deenie noticed a truck and two vans with satellites like giant teacup saucers had pulled in behind them.

She looked at the TV woman, her hair crisp but eye makeup blurred in the mist.

"We got a tip from the Danielses' lawyer," she said, wiping her face with the back of her hand. "He's friendly that way. He's going to give us some camera time. He's got a statement to issue."

Deenie felt her chest pinch. "Something happened to Lise?"

"No. Not yet." She shook her head, her eyes as white as pearls under the parking-lot lights. "The mother is trying to move her to the medical center all the way down in Mercy-Starr Clark. Looks like she's going to be suing. Suing everybody."

"Suing for what?" Deenie said. "Over the vaccine?"

"You bet. We heard the state health department people were here today, someone from the DA's office, cops, who knows what's next."

There was a slamming of doors somewhere and the camera guy, his face concealed behind the great black box slung on his shoulder, was suddenly there again.

"Now?" the TV woman asked him.

He nodded.

"Wait," Deenie said. "But do you know about Lise, about how she is?"

The camera light went on and the woman's worn face sprang magically to life.

"Well, you two probably know more than anyone," she said, her voice newly smooth, buttery as her hair. "How about we just talk a few minutes. Have you ever been on TV?"

"No," Deenie said. "I —"

"Not you," the woman said. "Her."

Deenie turned to Gabby, who was facing the car.

"No," Deenie said, watching Gabby's body, wire-tight, her elbows clamped to her sides. It looked like she was trying to hold herself together, to keep herself from blowing apart.

The front doors of the hospital opened loudly and all the lights seemed to go on everywhere.

Listening to Rick Jeanneret's cracking voice on ESPN Classic, Eli was thinking again about what Deenie had said about going into the lake. In some ways, what she'd told him *was* like the thing he'd noticed about her at the Pizza House that night, or other nights, other things. Because the Deenie he knew wasn't the kind to break rules, take chances.

The lake was the last place he'd want to go. The smell, even from the car, felt wrong. It reminded him of the basement of their house.

Back when Deenie was in middle school, she was always having sleepovers. All that girly thumping and trills on the other side of his bedroom wall confused and annoyed and stirred him, so he'd sneak down to the basement and page through a mildewed 1985 *Playboy* he'd found under the laundry chute. The pictures were startling and beautiful, but he always felt ashamed after, standing at the laundry sink where his mom scrubbed his uniform.

And through the chute, he could still hear the girls, two floors above. The basement's drop ceiling porous and seeming to breathe. After a long rain, it smelled just like the lake.

Once, a senior girl from Star-of-the-Sea tried to get him to climb the safety fence, but he said no. Wiggling out of her halter dress, she said, her tongue between her teeth, *It's okay. We can always skinny-dip right in your car. Who needs water?*

"You're the luckiest mother I ever knew," A.J. said when Eli told him about it. "Screw that pretty face of yours."

Lying there, Eli fumbled for his phone before remembering it wasn't there.

★ ★ ★

"Dad," Deenie said, answering her phone. "I'm coming home. I am."

"You better be," her dad said in a tone he rarely used.

The car thudding along the road, the spatter of light rain, she and Gabby didn't say anything for a mile or two.

Finally, Gabby spoke. "They're going to want to bring me back in again, aren't they? They're going to want to talk to me again."

Deenie looked at her, passing headlights flashing across her face, and saw something pulsing there, from her temple to her jaw.

"I don't know."

It hurt to look at her, the way she was holding her body so tightly, her arms rigid

225

at her sides, a girl made of wood. "Maybe not."

When they entered Binnorie Woods, Deenie's heart started to slow down a little. No streetlights and the car dark, it was like being under your covers, your sleeping bag at camp. She'd always liked that feeling, and the smell of cedar coming through the vents.

"Maybe," Deenie said, "this means Lise is doing better. If they can move her she must be doing better."

Gabby nodded lightly, her head canting to one side.

"You know what I thought," she said quietly, "when the reporter came over, you know what I thought she was going to tell us?"

"What?"

"That Lise was dead."

★ ★ ★

"It's okay, Lara. She's driving Gabby home to you right now."

"Thank God. Tom, have you seen some of these pictures? And videos?"

"I saw a few," Tom said, thinking of that striking one of Gabby. "Wait, videos?"

"There's a video of Kim Court. Some kid must've taken it while it was happening. It's

226

all over. It's on the news now."

Tom grabbed the remote from Eli.

There, on Channel 7, was a grainy YouTube video of Kim Court, body twitching on the gym floor.

The screen crawl read: *Mysterious Outbreak: Parents' Rush to Vaccinate to Blame?*

And then, hands gripping her own neck, a blur of vomit, head thrown so far back you could only see the glint of her braces. The piano-tinkling score from *The Exorcist* played.

"Lara," he said. "Turn off the TV."

★ ★ ★

They were deep into the woods now and Deenie couldn't remember the way. Gabby had to keep saying, softly, *Right, right, left here. Left.*

"Deenie, remember what Kim told us in the library," Gabby said, resting her head on the window. "About Lise having a boyfriend?"

Deenie looked at her, not even remembering for a moment.

"In the library. Kim told us something about Lise and some guy."

"Why would Kim Court know anything

about Lise? Gabby, why are we talking about this now —"

"I think it might be true."

Gabby faced the window and Deenie could hear a faint rattling: Gabby's head against the glass.

"No," Deenie said. "It's not true."

Technically, it was not. There was the thing Lise had told her at the lake, the thing she'd done with the boy. But that boy was not Lise's boyfriend, not at all.

"Deenie, I've heard it from other people. I thought she might have told you. Sometimes she tells you things she doesn't tell me."

"No," Deenie said.

"Because lately, Skye and me, we've been noticing Lise has been kind of secretive. Like maybe she was hiding something. When I took her to the Pizza House the other night, I tried to talk to her, but —"

"Skye?" Deenie barked, so loud she surprised herself. "Skye doesn't know a goddamn thing about Lise. Why would you listen to her? Lise wasn't hiding anything." Taking a breath, she tried to calm herself. Then added, "No one's hiding anything, Gabby."

Gabby nodded, the worst, most thoughtless kind of nod Deenie could imagine.

Then she turned and faced Deenie. "I just

remembered what I heard about you," Gabby said. "The other day."

Deenie looked over at her, the car swerving slightly. "What?"

"That you were in a car with some guy. You never told me that."

Deenie faced the road again. "Because it's not true. It was probably Eli."

"Stop!" Gabby shouted, her voice suddenly loud, Deenie nearly jumping in her seat, words rushing to her head, flooding her mouth without emerging.

"My house," Gabby said, one hand dropping on Deenie's arm, the other pointing to the driveway.

Deenie turned the wheel.

The house blazing with lights, Mrs. Bishop was running out, her legs and feet bare, the headlights making her scar look red, alive.

Any anger on her face seemed to break to pieces the minute her daughter stepped from the car.

Backing out, Deenie watched as Gabby slumped into her mother's arms wearily, a veteran home from battle. Mrs. Bishop folding her in her arms in such a mom way. In a way that made Deenie blink.

★ ★ ★

Face drawn, hair half caught in her rubber band, his daughter looked half and twice her age at the same time.

Nearly midnight, on either side of the kitchen island, Deenie told him about the hospital.

"And so the reporter said Mrs. Daniels is trying to move Lise to the medical center."

"That probably means she's stable," he said. "So that's something."

Her mouth twisted, dubious, like Georgia somehow, that was the echo, and the way her shirt was riding up and her arm stretching tiredly and with dismissal.

"I'm going to bed," she said.

"Did you call your mom?" he said, holding out his hand for the car keys. A gesture stolen, he was sure, from his own father, a century ago.

"No," she said. "I didn't have time."

"Deenie," he said. "You were gone for hours."

"The reporter wanted us to talk on camera," she said. "She wouldn't leave us alone. But we wouldn't do it."

He sighed. "How did Gabby seem?"

He watched her try to pull the rubber band from her hair, her eyes down, and he wanted to reach over and help her untangle it, but her body looked so closed off, a tooth clamp.

"I don't know, Dad."

He found his hand reaching out to her anyway, and the flinch that came was sudden, terrible.

★ ★ ★

Trying to push herself, hard, into sleep, Deenie felt her toes cramp painfully, a pang in them she had to rub away, tangled under her own sheets, breathing hard until it stopped again.

Then her phone hissed: Skye.

She could have sworn she'd turned it off.

U still ok, right?

Yes, Deenie typed. She never got texts from Skye and she almost wondered if she had fallen asleep.

U saw Gabby tonite?

Yeah. Why?

We need to protect each other, came Skye's reply. We R surrounded by bad energy.

Staring at the words blinking hard at her, almost spasming, she had a sick feeling in her stomach and turned the phone off.

What made Skye think she could text her? Because they were the only ones left? Skye's words always felt cryptic. *Shake it off,* she told herself. *Don't let her get under your skin.*

And she grabbed for the bottle of antihistamine left over from the flu and drank three plastic cups.

Somewhere in the gluey Nyquil haze, the vision came of standing in the lake with Lise the week before, stomping their feet in the emerald thick of the water.

On the shoreline were Skye's hard-jeaned boys with the disappearing tattoos. They whistled at Lise, fingers hooked in their mouths.

Let's do it, Lise whispered in her ear, her tongue showing between her teeth. *Let's go in.*

When she woke up, in the purple of four a.m., she could still hear Lise's voice in her ear, high as a little girl's.

We went behind those tall bushes. He took my tights off first. It was so cold, but his hands . . .

Who was it? Deenie had asked, kept asking.

Then, finally, Lise whispered the boy's name, and Deenie was surprised.

Really? Him?

And Lise's smile filled with teeth, a giggle up her throat.

Like something inside opening, she said as

232

they sprawled on the shoreline, feet tangled in seaweed tickling up their legs, *and then opening something else.*

Don't tell anyone, she made Deenie promise. *They'll think I'm a slut.*

No, they won't, Deenie said. Though you could never be sure.

I told him not to do what he was doing. That it was disgusting. I don't know why I thought that, but I did. We put our mouths down there with boys, but . . . but he was down there and everything happened.

But she said his hands were cool, like a doctor's. And that made it seem okay. And soon enough she was so hot, a burning down there, and his mouth cool too, and the way, like — and she was so embarrassed to say it, to have even thought of it — like a flute, the flutter tongue. The move it takes so long to learn.

I don't know, she said, her fingers curled over her mouth like eating a candy. *I don't know.* And then she said the thing about how it was like an opening, an opening, and forever opening.

She never even knew before what it meant to see stars.

That was all she could say. Deenie wanted her to say more.

Since it was a boy she knew, she wanted

to picture it.

Is it disgusting? Lise asked, but she was smiling as she said it, face red. *Was it bad?*

Deenie didn't say anything. Their legs slimy from the water.

Deenie, she said, *am I bad?*

No, Deenie said. *Not you, Lise.*

Never you.

12

It was maybe five, the light looked like five, but without his phone, Eli had no idea.

There was a freedom in it.

It was warmer than in months, as if the temperature had risen during the night, and the bike ride through town felt delirious and wonderful.

His hand kept reaching for his pocket, the phantom buzz.

But nothing.

Maybe he'd never have a phone again.

He was nearly to school before he remembered everything from the night before, all the beer and ruminations and sinking to drunken sleep on the floor of the den, carpet burn on his face.

When he walked in the locker room, everything was unusually quiet. No clattering sticks or ripping tape or the low din of players rousing themselves to life.

But he could hear something, the tinny sound of someone's computer speakers, a soft voice and panting.

". . . my tongue is tingling, like, all the time. If you could see . . ."

He knew this was going to mean another speech from Coach about how important it was not to degrade women's bodies with pornography because what if they were your mothers, or your sisters.

". . . something in my throat. And it's getting bigger . . ."

When he reached the last bank of lockers, he saw seven, eight players huddled around Mark Pulaski's laptop, transfixed. A.J. was grinning and shaking his head. A.J. was always grinning and shaking his head.

"Get a load, Nash. Get a fucking load of this."

There was a stutter and hiss as the video began again.

It was the latest girl, that Kim girl, glowing from the light of her own phone screen.

Panting noisily, like her tongue was too big for her mouth, she couldn't seem to quite catch her breath. Her face looked wet, her eyes ringed vampire-brown and her mouth slickly red.

It was dark all around her, but you could

see the green fluorescence of some light somewhere, the hospital corridor.

And she was talking straight into the camera, her phone.

Her words slow and dreamlike.

"Hey, everybody, I know you're all probably worried about me and I wanted to let you know how I'm doing since it happened."

Breathing, breathing.

"I'm still at the hospital. They won't let me go."

Her fingers reached up to that glossy mouth.

"My tongue is tingling, like, all the time, and this side feels like it's got a lot of pressure and it's hard to keep my eye open on this side. It feels like this side of my face is slipping from me. Like it'll slip right off."

She started clearing her throat, and once she started it was like she couldn't stop.

"But most of all it's here," she said, clawing at her neck. "It feels like there's something in my throat. And it's getting bigger."

A scraping sound came from her mouth as she pushed her face closer to the camera, the lens distorting everything, fish-eyeing her.

When she opened her mouth, those teeth,

enormous and iron-girded, were blue.

"I'm sure you're hearing lots of things. About what's happening. Let me tell you: No one here wants to know the truth. That's why they won't let me go."

Suddenly, as if she'd heard something, a muffled sound too fast to recognize, Kim flinched, her eyes jumping to her left, pupils gleaming.

There was a long, long pause, her face palsied. Eli felt something even in his own chest: *What did she hear? See?*

Then her face turned slowly to the camera again, her throat a death rattle.

"But there's other girls out there. And they have it. Maybe ones you can't even tell. Who knows how many of us?"

"I know it by heart," A.J. said, leaping onto one of the benches. "Brooke and her sister were watching it all night."

" 'There's other girlth out there,' " he slurred, his tongue hanging from the corner of his mouth. " 'Who knowth how many of us?' "

Eli looked back at the screen, Kim's face caught. Beneath, there were 624 likes and dozens of comments: *oh, kim, be strong! kim, i've been feeling weird too, did u faint when you got the shot? Young lady: this is demonic*

238

possession. You can read about it in the New Testament. The solution is to find a True Man of God who can cast the demon out. Receiving Christ can cure you. Blessings to you and your family!

Eli fixed his eyes on the screen. It reminded him, in some obscure way, of those girls at the games, the younger ones who came in groups and banded behind the Plexiglas, bap-bap-bapping with open palms or the bottoms of their fists, their mouths sprung wide, their tongues between their teeth. *Me. Me. Me.*

"I don't . . ." Eli started. "Is she wearing makeup?" He was trying to figure something out.

"Maybe she'll get her own reality show," A.J. said. *"Kim's Wrecked World. My Toxic Sweet Sixteen."*

"And she didn't say anything about the shots," Eli said, just realizing it. "About the vaccine."

Mark Pulaski turned around to face Eli.

"You think she's faking it?" he said, his voice breaking. "Did you see her? My sister got her first shot last week. She woke up from a nap yesterday and couldn't turn her head. She's fucking eleven years old."

Eli looked at him, not knowing what to say.

"Just because your sister's bouncing around the school while all her friends are fucking dying, man. Your sister . . ." Mark's voice trailed off. "Jesus, man."

Eli watched Mark for a second, and everyone else watched Eli. He felt A.J.'s fist tap his shoulder.

"I'm sorry," Eli said. "Sorry, man."

He turned back to the computer screen, the big arrow over Kim's face, trembling.

★   ★   ★

Her backpack on her lap, Deenie talked to him the entire ride to school.

For the first miles, Tom let himself enjoy it. It felt almost like before, maybe a few years ago, when she always seemed to be bursting with giddy, nervous animation. *Dad, Dad, wait, listen, Dad, listen.* Telling him about a book, a science project.

But all the itchy squirming in her seat now, it was like she was trying to rally herself to get through the day to come. Or else she just needed to keep talking because she was afraid of not talking. He wondered if she felt guilty for the night before, for staying out late with the car.

"Dad," she said finally, after seven solid minutes about the algebra quiz, the rancid grilled cheese in the cafeteria, the stink of Eli's gym bag, "what do you think will happen today?"

He looked at the road, the steam from the streets, the crazy heat wave that had landed, the temperatures rising above sixty degrees, and tried to think of something to say.

The school felt anarchic inside, like the time Paul Lozelle let a pair of chickens loose in the cafeteria, a prank that had been musty when Tom was in high school.

Everywhere he looked, there were long bands of girls in their colored minis and tights, ropes of them, like the friendship bracelets that covered their arms, their faces tense and watchful. And the boys, in their own swells of confusion and bravado, stood apart, almost like in middle school, elementary school. Like they were suddenly afraid to get too close. Though maybe that was how they always were and he'd never noticed.

The teachers, in turn, were either spring-loaded, grasping their dry-erase markers like emergency flares, or slouched against doorways, filled with louche contempt.

Walking toward his classroom, its familiar formaldehyde smell, he tried to imagine how any of them were going to make it to three o'clock without spontaneously combusting.

A free first period, he spent a half hour in the dark auditorium, drinking coffee and watching one of the custodians trying to buff away the scratch marks the EMS gurney had left on the stage.

He couldn't stop himself from walking past Deenie's ancient civ class. She was in the back, so he had to move very close to the door to see her, but there she was, pen in mouth, brow tightly triangled.

It was when he finally stopped by the teachers' lounge to check his e-mail that he saw June Fisk and her chubby-cheeked teacher's aide gaping at the monitor, their mouths open.

On the screen, Kim Court's blue-lit face.

"It's not the only one," June said, rolling a chair toward him. "I've heard there's another one. Maybe more."

Tom watched it three times, silently.

He thought of Deenie sitting in that classroom and wondered if she'd watched it too, and what she'd thought.

★ ★ ★

Back to hospital today for more tests, Gabby's text read.

242

It felt a little like the days the orchestra went to regionals — no Lise, no Gabby at school. Except now there weren't even people like Kim, or Jaymie Hurwich, who would quiz Deenie before a test, her fingers always on her tablet, her flying-flash-cards app, her virtual periodic table.

And Skye was nowhere in sight.

Deenie wondered if she and Gabby were hidden away at Skye's parentless house, playing music or reading tarot or whatever they did together. All their private conversations.

Maybe it was for the best that Gabby wasn't there. It felt easier somehow.

★ ★ ★

Not having a phone at school didn't matter at all. You couldn't get reception most places, and you weren't supposed to use it anyway.

But what Eli liked about it was that when someone asked him, "Why didn't you text me back? Didn't you hear about the plan?" he could say, "Sorry, I lost my phone."

Except for the tickling sense in the back of his brain that there was something to it, that he might be missing something that mattered.

Like he'd felt after his mom left. All those days he'd walk past his parents' bedroom and still smell her smell, like those shiny orange soap bars she used.

Since then, his clothes had never felt the same, not soft like before, and no one ever slapped the kitchen table when they laughed hard, and all the blue flowers by the side door were gone. They smelled like grape candy.

He wondered if Deenie, who never seemed to miss anything about their mom, ever missed any of those things. After she moved out, two days after Christmas, Deenie piled her gifts into a trash bag and threw it down the basement stairs. For months, they were down there, the bag striped with mold.

The sound of the second bell jarred him and he was surprised to see the halls were empty, except for one freshman girl at the far end, leaning against the blasted brick.

One arm hanging to her side, she was breathing loudly, just like Kim Court in the video.

"Hey," he called out.

Her head flew up, scraping against the brick.

"Are you okay?" he asked.

She didn't move.

He started walking toward her, but before

he'd taken three steps, she scurried away, off into some freshman-girl hiding place.

Sliding on his headphones, he began walking to fourth period.

As he approached the classroom, he saw another girl lurking, but this one didn't seem sickly or afraid.

It was Skye Osbourne, wearing a long scarf the same color as her mouth, like those dark figs that hung from the tree by the practice rink every fall, the ones that split under your skates.

And this time it felt like she was looking for him.

"Ditch with me," she said, nodding her head toward the double doors.

He stopped, headphones still on.

"Why?"

"Because," she said, a slanting smile. "I'm pretty."

Funnily, Eli wasn't sure Skye was pretty.

If he saw her without all that hair, which looked like it'd been stripped from a corncob and massed thick, and without all the things she draped over and on top of herself, the scarves and snake rings and coiling bracelets, he wondered if he'd recognize her at all.

"What's the point of here," she added, waving something in her hand, a joint, a white Bic.

What's the point of here, he thought, looking at that fig mouth of hers.

Pushing through the doors swinging behind her, he stepped outside. The air felt hard, good.

★   ★   ★

There was a low rumble everywhere, even coming from his own classroom. The drum of confusion, skidding sneakers, a girl's lone yelp, a teacher trying to be heard.

He turned the corner and that's when he saw them.

A long line, like the one to get your school ID photo taken, your yearbook portrait. To get your shots.

Except they were all girls. Ten, twelve, he guessed, close to twenty wrapped around the hallway in groups and individually. Drooping against lockers, slumped on the floor, their legs flung out, doll-like, one in the middle of the corridor, spinning like a flower child.

Danielle Schultz, her right arm swinging like a baton every third second, synced to her own loud breaths.

Brandi Carruthers, junior-class treasurer and weekend pageant queen, her face streaked with a kind of gray sweat.

Two freshman girls who looked all of eleven grappling each other in that way very young girls do, as if the whole world were conspiring to ravage them.

"Pins and needles, pins and needles," stallion-legged track star Tricia Lawson was saying, over and over again, rubbing her long limbs.

Even strapping Brooke Campos was there, tan as ever in her buttercup-yellow tank top, but holding her pelvis in a way that made Tom look away.

The line hooked down one hall and then bottlenecked at the administration office.

Inside, Mrs. Harris, a swath of hair matted to her forehead, was hoarsely calling for quiet, the nurse's office door shut tight.

"He's not here," she whispered to Tom, nodding toward Crowder's office.

"Oh?"

Leaning closer, smelling of Pall Malls and desperation, she added, "He had a seven a.m. meeting at Gem Donuts with the superintendent. He must still be with him."

The door opened and Tom glimpsed two nurses and a badged woman from the health department, the back of her hand resting on her forehead and something unsettling in her eyes. Like a medic on his first day in-country.

Mrs. Harris tapped Tom's shoulder.

"They want to talk to you," she said.

"Who?"

"Are you Tom Nash?" the health department woman said, approaching him. "You were next on my list."

"Your list?"

"We'd like to speak to your daughter."

★   ★   ★

Standing in the breezeway, Deenie watched both the videos back to back on Julie Drew's smeary phone.

First there was Kim, her face sparkly with makeup.

Kim. Kim, a chilly voice inside her said, *this is the best thing that ever happened to you, isn't it?*

All your hard preening and social ambition has finally paid off. Forever craving attention, always the one dying to know the secret you don't, to have the gossip first, waving it like a peacock fan. And to use that gossip as her golden ticket to the inner circle, or its starry center: Gabby.

Except. Except the Kim on YouTube didn't quite seem like that Kim.

In spite of the makeup, the dramatic way

she'd tilted the camera to hide her braces, there was something that felt very, intensely real about the Kim on the screen.

The fear hovering in her eyes.

And that moment when she looked off camera, as if she'd heard something.

The way her body had been loose and liquid and then, in an instant, turned stiff.

She seemed to be looking intently at something for a moment. Whatever it was, it made her stop everything, her face frozen, her red mouth open, those glistening night eyes of hers.

The video had had 850 views since it had been posted, at two in the morning.

But then there was the second video, Jaymie Hurwich, who hadn't come to school that day.

Jaymie, Deenie's number-one study pal, who never, ever missed school, who once came even with strep because of a geometry test. Who came even the day after her sister overdosed on ecstasy at college.

Behind her the baby blue of her bedroom, the zebra lampshade by her bed, Jaymie was talking, and moving.

Blinking hard, so hard it hurt to look at it.

And incessantly stroking her hair. First with her left hand, then her right. Smoothing it over and over, her fingers moving as though playing a harp.

The video header read: *DON'T MAKE MY MISTAKE!*

"I'm Jaymie. I'm sixteen and I live with my dad and I go to Dryden High and I love school and my friends and playing softball. I pretty much have a great life."

Blinking rapidly, she let out a long sigh, tugging the fallen strap on her tank top.

"And I'm here to talk about the shots that changed my life forever."

Deenie took the phone from Julie's hand, pulling it closer.

"I've never done this before," Jaymie was saying. "But I don't know how else to deal with what's happening! Two weeks ago, I had my first HPV shot . . ."

Her fingers wiggled as if plucking her imaginary harp.

"I was okay for a few days. Then all this started happening," she said, her hand twitching, like she wanted to stop stroking her hair but her hand wouldn't let her.

"I kept quiet about it. But now I know I'm not the only one. You probably heard about Lise Daniels."

Blinking, blinking like an LED. Deenie felt her own eyes twitching.

"So my dad saw what was happening to me. He went and looked it all up and found out about the shots. About what they did to us. He got so scared. I've never seen him so scared."

She looked down, shaking her head, her fingers still wiggling in the air in front of her mouth, then grabbing at her hair, tearing at it.

"The doctor told us it was stress. There's no way that's true. There was nothing wrong in my life. I had the best grades in my class. I studied all the time. My dad treated me like a princess. My life was perfect. Until I got the shots."

Suddenly, her eyes snapped shut, then shuddered open, as if she'd startled herself. Her hand flew to her mouth, sparkle nail polish flashing, her head jerking hard three times, then her eyes rolled back in their sockets.

A beat, then Jamie's eyes landed on the camera again.

Her eyes wide with alarm.

"There was nothing wrong," she said, breathless now. "Everything was perfect. There was nothing wrong."

Shaking her head, looking down. Voice breaking.

"I don't feel like myself anymore."

When it was over, Julie Drew wanted to

251

watch both videos again. She said she'd heard there were more to watch, "*lots more.*" And she said this morning Jaymie's dad had parked himself in front of some congressman's district office and refused to leave until he got "some satisfaction."

But I have nothing to do with Jaymie Hurwich, Deenie thought, walking to next period, her head fogged. *All I ever did was study sometimes with her. We never shared anything. This one is nothing to me.*

For thirty seconds, she felt a swell of relief.

But then both videos began playing again in her head, those slumber-party voices.

My life was perfect, Jaymie had said. *Until I got the shots.*

Her head so filled with thoughts of the lake, Deenie had barely let her mind rest on the vaccine. Could that really be it?

It was the thing they'd shared, all of them.

The same lilac-walled clinic, side by side in the tandem seating, the laminated chair arms locked together.

One by one, going into the little room behind the lilac-painted door.

Slow deep breaths, and don't watch it go in. That was everyone's warning.

They'd all talked about it for days, the first time.

After that, no one talked about it much. But now Deenie could remember how it burned and that was all, and how part of her felt a little sad when the burning went away.

How could all this be about those little shots?

It had to be something else. A thing you didn't know you were waiting for.

Like something inside opening, and then opening something else.

The second bell rang, and she was going to be late.

Turning the corner fast, she nearly ran into the three of them, gloves on, clustered around Lise's locker, its door swung open.

There was a man holding Lise's gym uniform, wilted as a lily pad, and her thermos, its lip stained green from her morning health shakes.

The woman next to him, in a blue parka, was carrying a large bag with smaller bags inside.

The third person was Assistant Principal Hawk, his arms folded, missing the usual disdainful curl of the lip, the tan creases in his forehead thicker than Deenie had ever seen them.

"Is this yours?" the man said, pointing to Deenie's locker. She could see what looked like the hard corner of Lise's "purrfect cat" binder cutting into the bag's bottom.

"Hey, that's Lise's private stuff," she said, unsure where the defiance in her voice came from, the Hawk standing right there.

"That's her," Hawk told the others.

She drew her book bag close to her chest.

"She's the one," he added.

★ ★ ★

They were lying on the bed of Coach Haller's pickup truck, Skye on her stomach, legs waving in the air, the bottoms of her boot heels slicked with grass.

Eli took a long drag, his first since the summer before, that long family trip to WaterWonders. After the marathon car ride — Gabby and Lise and Deenie, high on sugar and new bathing suits, babbling in the backseat the whole time — his dad took pity on him, giving him thirty dollars and letting him wander alone. He met the guy operating the Tadpole Hole who shared his joint, teased him by saying some girl was watching him. "That one's in love with you, bro," he'd said, but the girl turned out just to be Gabby.

That joint had felt weak, easy, but this one was different. Skye said it wasn't pot but

254

the leaves from a plant used by Cherokees and other tribes. If you smoked it before bed, you would have lucid dreams.

"It clears away darkness," she said. "And banishes negative energy."

That sounded okay, and he took a long drag, closing his eyes.

Something passed suddenly, wind rustling above them, and Skye was showing him her bare back, her sweater pulled all the way up so he could see her twisting spine.

"When I was little," she said, "my uncle called me the Rattler. He said it looked like a rattlesnake."

Leaning down, Eli gave it a long look, the pale skin, bra Mountain Dew–green, that pearly white canal from her neck to the waist of her skirt. The swooping curve of the spine, an *S* for Skye.

All right there, for him.

What was he waiting for? Why didn't he set his hand there, flat on the center of that sloping spine?

Her skin would probably feel cool, like a smooth stone.

"When I was eleven they gave me the forward-bending test," she said, looking over her shoulder at him, sharp shoulder blade arching. "Did you never have one of those?"

"No."

"I guess it's only for girls."

Looking at her faint grin, he found himself speculating about figs. Sometimes he'd see one crushed open by the ice rink, its insides filled with dead wasps.

"He's an artist," she was saying. "My uncle. He took out his paints and painted up my spine. A diamondback coiling with my coil."

Coiling with my coil.

He was listening to her in a way, the joint working on him like warm hands. But he was wondering about something. Like what was stopping him from putting his hand on that skin of hers, displayed just for him.

"He told me to never be ashamed," she said. "That it was beautiful."

Looking at her, he could almost see the painted serpent squirming on her skin, ready to turn, mouth open.

He started thinking something about her uncle, but the thought drifted away before it could take hold.

"He kept rattlers in the old rabbit hutch. Did you know that baby rattlers have this tiny little button on the tip of their tail? It doesn't make any sound. It feels like velvet. I've touched it."

She turned on her side but kept the sweater hitched high. He could see the bottom edges of her green bra, half moons. But he didn't feel what he'd normally feel. It was like looking at a painting.

"They lose it when they shed their first skin," she said, her fingertips grazing her stomach. "After that, they grow the hard rattle. The one that makes all the noise. It doesn't sound so much like a rattle. It's softer than that. More like this."

She lifted her fingers over those dark lips of hers and made a sound.

To him it sounded like locusts deep in Binnorie Woods.

He didn't know how long they had been lying there, his head going to places, like that time he fell in practice and his cheek split open and his mom had to pick him up in the middle of the day.

Sitting in his mom's front seat, his skates on the floor in front of him, feeling the soft tickle of something, a pair of women's underpants, ice-blue, on the floor of the car.

He would never forget the look on her face. His mom's face.

Did that really happen? It did. Both of them sat there as if it hadn't, the entire drive home, the dull thud of the car over the wet streets.

He never told anyone, they never spoke about it, and six months later, two days after

Christmas, she'd moved out. Sometimes he could still feel it on his ankles, the sneaking sense that something had gone wrong and it was right there and it was touching you, rustling against you all the time even if you didn't look.

Then, through the fog of his head, Skye spoke.

"Have you gone to see her?"

"Who?"

"Lise."

"Lise," he said, her name sounding funny in his mouth. A picture of her coming to him, that pudgy Lise with her shirt always lifting above her belly.

"I heard she might be talking now. I wondered if she'd talked to you."

"Me?" he said. "Why would she talk to me?"

"Oh," she said, and he turned his head to her, her face suddenly so close, and the smell of something rotten from that dark berried mouth. It was like that fig, he thought. With something inside you didn't expect. "I heard some things. Maybe I was wrong."

"What did you hear?"

"I don't know. Something sexy. About you two."

"What?" He started to prop himself up on

his elbows, one of them tugging on her long hair.

She didn't move, her stomach still bare, her fingers dancing along it. "That you two were doing something. Before school."

"What do you mean, doing something?"

"By the practice rink, behind the bushes. You and Lise. You were both lying on the grass and you were taking off her tights. They said."

Those bushes, he knew them, their toothed leaves, thick-veined, and the seed pods laced with thorns. They grew wild and it was a place you could drink beer or do things.

"No way," he said, shaking his head, shaking the image of Lise, bare-legged, her skirt hitched high, from his thoughts. "Lise, she's a sister to me."

"Oh," she said, fingertips making circles just above the waist of her skirt. Wider and wider circles.

"A sister," he repeated.

He looked at her. There was something scratching again, in the corner above his eye, like those metal probes at the dentist clawing at your teeth.

"Who told you that?" he asked, his voice lifting to a new place. He didn't sound like himself. "Who's 'they'?"

259

Skye looked over at him, and in his head he could see the wasps.

"Listen," he said, grabbing for his bag. "I gotta get to class."

★ ★ ★

"Mr. Nash, we'd like to talk to your daughter."

She said she was Sue Brennan, deputy public-health commissioner.

"About what?"

They were sitting in Principal Crowder's vacant office.

Her bra strap was sliding down her shoulder and her hair looked dirty. She was wearing latex gloves. Her wrists were red.

"We're trying to trace as closely as possible Lise Daniels's movements prior to the attack."

"But why? You've got a public-health crisis here and —"

"We're looking into whether she may have come into contact with or been exposed to something."

"You think it might be something toxic?" Tom asked.

"Mr. Nash, we'd really just like to talk to your daughter." She folded her hands, then seemed to realize she still had the gloves on. Looked at them, not sure what to do.

"So you're talking to everybody?"

"We know Deenie was one of the last people with Lise before the event."

Tom looked at her, squinted. "So was a class full of other kids. A school full of people. Are you talking to everyone?"

"There's many parties involved, and we're pursuing all avenues."

"Who's the 'we' here?"

"You have nothing to be concerned about."

She was giving him a blank face. Like the woman at a car-rental desk, or an airline check-in. *Calm down, sir.*

"I have nothing to be concerned about?" Tom said. "Pardon me, but have you looked around you? Do you see what's happening here?"

"Mr. Nash," she said as she finally stripped the gloves from her hands, ashed with powder and trembling slightly. "We need to find out everything about Lise. About all these girls."

He leaned back in his chair.

"Why now, why three days later? Why weren't you talking to Deenie before? Do you have some new information?"

She crimped her file folders in her hand.

"Mr. Nash, I would think it would be

261

important to you. To try to help our investigation. Don't you want to understand what's happening to these girls? What if your daughter was next?"

"She won't be," he said, his voice suddenly hard.

She looked at him, paused. "No?"

"I know my daughter," he said, rising. He had no idea what he was talking about. What did it have to do with knowing his daughter? And was his answer, precisely, true?

"Of course you do," she said, glancing at her phone. "Anyway, it looks like they may have already gotten what they need from her."

★   ★   ★

They took her to the music room, empty except for a pair of orchestra stands on the floor. Deenie wondered which girl's raging spasm had knocked them down, emptying the room, which now smelled of fresh bleach.

"Did something happen to Lise?" she asked. "Something else?"

The woman in the parka shook her head. The man with Lise's uniform had left. So had Assistant Principal Hawk.

"We're trying to get some information about what Lise was doing before she got sick," the woman said. "Since you're pals, maybe you can help."

There were no chairs, so they sat on either end of Mr. Timmins's coffee-ringed desk.

"I don't know anything about that," Deenie said. "She was in class, and she jumped up and then she fell down."

"Did you see her before class?"

"No."

"Did you usually see her before class?"

"Not really," Deenie lied. She didn't want to explain that she hadn't gone to Lise's locker like she usually did. That she hadn't wanted to talk about what had happened with Sean Lurie. And she'd been worried Lise might see her and just know.

"And did Lise use any drugs that you know about?"

"What? No!"

"It's okay. No one's in trouble. Not even the occasional joint?"

"No," Deenie said, shaking her head.

"Is it possible Lise had been experimenting with someone else?" the woman asked. "Did you have the sense Lise didn't tell you everything?"

"She told me everything," Deenie said coolly. "She tells me everything."

"And that day . . . had you talked on the phone? Exchanged texts?"

"No, but that doesn't mean anything," Deenie replied, which was sort of a weird response and she wasn't even sure what she meant by it.

"I'm sure it doesn't," the woman said. "And how about Lise and boys?"

Deenie felt her body seize slightly, her shoulders clenching hard, a string pulled in the center of her, tight, and her dad's voice seemed to rise up from inside her, though it was really from the hallway, loud and meaningful.

★ ★ ★

"They wouldn't let me go home," Brooke Campos whispered to Eli, across the aisle. "The sub nurse is a class-A bitch."

Eli looked over at her. Beneath the desk, her jeans were unsnapped, her brown pelvis exposed.

"It hurts so bad," she said, rubbing her stomach. "They said it was stress. *Stress* seems to mean 'everything.' "

It might have been the smartest thing Brooke Campos ever said.

"You should go home," Eli said.

She pressed her fingertips on her pelvic

264

bones, jutting from her low-slung jeans.

"It's like something's burning inside me."

"Miss Campos, Mr. Nash," called out Mr. Banasiak from under the blue haze of his PowerPoint presentation.

Looking up, they waited for him to say more, but that seemed to be the sum of it.

The lights dimmed and Eli watched Brooke, shifting in her seat.

"Brooke," he whispered. "Did you ever hear anything about me and Lise?"

"What?" she said, her teeth bright white against her tan skin, teeth sunk into her lips. Like a bronzed beaver, he thought.

"Any stories, about us?"

"No," she said, slowly. Then added, "Well, yeah. I mean, I heard stuff about Lise. But it doesn't have to do with you."

"Who does it have to do with?"

"Some guy from another school. A hockey player."

★　★　★

"Mr. Nash, there's nothing cloak-and-dagger about this," Sue Brennan was calling out, still far behind him. "I've told you where she —"

Later, Tom wouldn't even remember walking, or running, he guessed it was, from the

265

catch in his breath, the wet feeling around his shirt collar, the thump in his chest when he finally arrived in the music room.

His hand rattling loudly on the locked doorknob, he could see Deenie inside, eyes large through the door pane.

Some woman in a dark parka hovering over her like a crow.

"Open this goddamned door," he heard himself say, a voice distinctly his father's rather than his own.

The parka woman turned, a flash of recognition on her face, as if she knew him.

She was saying things, telling him to calm down.

Suddenly, all he could think of was Sheila Daniels's face under the garage-door light, her mouth open, braying.

The door opened, the parka woman saying things to him, and Deenie behind her saying, "It's okay, Dad. I promise."

Before they left school, Principal Crowder caught Tom, made some kind of assurances as they stood at Deenie's locker, Deenie sliding on her jacket.

"You should have been present when they spoke to her, obviously," he said. "Things are just happening very quickly right now."

Tom didn't say anything, grabbing

Deenie's book bag, slamming her locker door.

"And, Tom," Crowder added, "I know I can count on you at the PTA meeting tonight."

"PTA meeting?" he asked, stopping himself from tugging up Deenie's jacket zipper as if she were five.

"Didn't you get the announcements? There's an emergency meeting," Crowder said, eyes darting back and forth between them. "We need you there."

"I'll be there," Tom said. "But why tonight?"

"Didn't you hear?" Crowder looked at Deenie, hesitating. "Can we speak alone for a second?"

Crowder's face, up close, sweat-varnished, as they stood in front of his computer in his office, Deenie waiting outside anxiously.

"It's all over the news," Crowder said. "It's on CNN."

Leaning over, he unpaused the video flickering there.

It was Kim Court again.

"I saw this," Tom said.

"No. This is a new one."

On the screen, Kim looked even more

haggard now, her face lit green, her mouth open.

"Don't believe the lies!" she said in that lisping, tongue-rasping voice. "I won't keep silent anymore. This isn't about some stupid vaccine. Because guess what, everyone? I never had the shot. I'm allergic and I couldn't get the shot.

"So listen! Listen!"

Leaning closer.

"Whatever's happening to us, it's bigger than any shot."

Voice scurrying up her throat, eyes rolling back.

"It's bigger than everything."

Driving home with Deenie, he took the shortcut through the back roads, skipping the lake.

"It wasn't anything, sweetie," he said. "Just another of those videos."

"Okay," Deenie said.

"So tonight, I just want you to stay home and stay off the computer. And the TV," he said. Which was ridiculous, but it must have been a sign of how crazy he was acting that Deenie just nodded. "And no more talking to anybody without me there, okay? Anybody."

Deenie nodded.

He hadn't ever wanted to be one of the hysterical parents, the handwringers, the finger-pointers. But wasn't this different? It felt different in every way.

"And you're sure all they asked you was if you had seen Lise that morning?"

Deenie nodded, eyes turning to the window.

They drove in silence for a moment.

"But Dad," Deenie said, abruptly, "who was that woman, anyway? The one in the big parka?"

"What do you mean?"

"She didn't have the health department thing around her neck. Who was she?"

"She didn't identify herself?" Tom couldn't believe he hadn't asked.

His phone trilled on the gear panel between them. Missed calls: Georgia, Georgia, Georgia.

"I don't remember," Deenie said. "There's so many people at the school now."

"I'm just glad I found you," he said.

She looked at him, and he guessed he wanted a smile or something, but she was staring at his phone, her mother's name flashing.

13

From her bedroom window, Deenie could see her dad standing in the backyard, smoking, which she hadn't seen him do ever, except in the browning snapshots in the photo albums in the hall closet, the ones with the pages tacky to touch, the binding peeled and cracked like everything from the 1980s.

He was leaning against the house, so hidden he was nearly under a corner gutter downspout.

His head turned and she jumped back. She couldn't bear the thought that he'd see her seeing him.

She was afraid to look at her phone. There was something on it. A text Julie Drew had sent, with a new YouTube link.

What if it was Skye? Then she'd be the only one left from the lake.

But she knew it wasn't going to be Skye. Skye would never record a video of herself for the world. Not Skye, who hardly ever let anyone inside her house because her aunt had tinnitus. Not Skye, who told everyone she didn't even have a Social Security number because that was like being in prison, or a concentration camp. *You have to be in charge of your own numbers,* she said. *You can't let them put a number on you.*

But more so this:

Something in her said nothing could ever happen to Skye. She didn't have that thing Lise had, Gabby had, even Kim and Jaymie had. That softness, that tenderness. Easy to bruise.

But then again, Deenie thought, *I guess I don't have it either.*

★ ★ ★

Eli held back Brooke's long hair, twined it in his hand, as she leaned over, bent at the waist.

The noise she made, low and guttural, didn't even sound like a girl's, sounded like the noises players made at the rink, stick in the gut, a wrister off the groin.

"Do you want me to get the nurse?" Eli asked, one hand on her shoulder, twig-brown but cold and goose-bumped in his hand.

271

"I don't think so," she whispered, looking down at her feet. "I thought I was going to throw up. But I didn't."

It was a funny thing to say, as if he hadn't just seen her do it, his hands still in her hair as she righted herself.

She leaned against the wall, her face slick with saliva, her tank top riding up like a crumpled daffodil.

She was staring out the breezeway's glass panels, fogged from the humidity.

Pointing at the tall hedges, her face whitened, her hands covering her mouth.

"That's where. Right there," Brooke said. "Last week. I saw Lise walking out from behind the bushes with some guy. I've seen him before, but I don't know his name. She was sliding her skirt around so it faced front."

Eli couldn't imagine Lise doing what Brooke was suggesting. Anywhere. Much less in the bushes by school. He was sure it couldn't be true.

"I guess I wasn't the only one to see," she said, eyes on the glass as if she were still seeing it.

"Wait," he said. "Why would anyone think it was me?"

"I don't know. He looked like you a little. And he was wearing one of those red interscholastic jackets like you sometimes wear."

Eli didn't say anything, but she shrugged as if he had.

"Lise Daniels," she said, eyes narrowing. "All the sudden she was so goddamned pretty. Some of us have been pretty forever."

It was like she was talking to no one, or to the whole world.

"No one cares if you've always been pretty," she said, palm stretched flat against the glass. "It's the same old news. But if all the sudden you're beautiful, you can do anything. That's what she must've thought, anyway."

Eli looked at her.

When he saw her expression, he thought she was going to get sick again, but then he realized she'd just heard herself. Heard aloud, for the first time, what had been in her head, maybe for a long time.

★   ★   ★

"Listen!" Kim Court shouted on the video. "Whatever's happening to us, it's bigger than any shot. It's bigger than everything."

The clip, which Deenie found on both CNN and Fox News, was only twenty seconds long, edited for the single revelation.

As the headline read, "Afflicted Girl Warns: It's Bigger than Any Vaccine!"

Deenie searched around for Kim's own YouTube channel and found a longer version.

Seven minutes long, with a staggering twenty thousand viewings, including thumbs-up (654) and thumbs-down (245) ratings.

It began with Kim muttering, like the words were sticky in her mouth.

"I told them not to put the glue in my hair," she was saying.

The light was so dim that everything looked brown, murky, and her eyes, amid the haze, looked like black holes.

"Because that's what they did to Gabby and I touched it."

Her fingers were on her throat, and the voice like a gurgle, like she was underwater.

"If I sound weird," Kim said, "it's only because my tongue is so big and my mouth is so small. They're giving me drugs. But if they want to help me, why did they put glue in my hair?"

For a painful moment, Kim seemed to have to gasp for breath. Then she breathed deep, a scraping noise lifting from her.

"I know I was dreaming," she continued. "They said I was. But it was so real. The man with tornado legs. I always dreamed about him, since I was little. And Gabby too! She was pulling seaweed from her throat. The stones that were her eyes. She found Lise down there."

Her eyes suddenly darted to one side, like before, the whites glowing.

Then a light went on somewhere and Kim's hands dropped from her throat, skin bright and raw. Clawed.

She faced the camera again.

"And I heard Deenie Nash is here now too.

"I heard her talking last night. I knew she had to be here."

Kim's eyes burning, the knowing look there as she said:

"Deenie's the one."

Her finger pressing until it turned white, Deenie shut off the phone.

★　★　★

"The parents of Kimberly Court confirmed through their family doctor that, due to an allergy to a component of the vaccine, their daughter never received the HPV shot," the newscaster announced.

Tom had never thought it was the vaccine, never believed it.

But he had the sudden sense, as his phone filled with voice mails from parents, and texts, and e-mails, that everything had become much, much worse.

Now that the definable horror, the specific one, had been eliminated, a pit had opened up beneath them. Beneath all these parents. All parents.

If not that, what?

He picked up his phone.

"Hi, you've reached Diane in Billing. Please leave a message."

Her voice cool, professional, friendly.

He left a message with no confidence she would ever call back.

Then remembering what Deenie had said.

Dad, who was that woman, anyway?

The woman in the parka, who could she have been? CDC? He didn't think so. Sometimes on TV, CDC officials wore uniforms. She didn't even have an ID badge.

And there was something else about her. Her stance. The way one leg was behind her, her hips angled, knees slightly bent.

Like a cop.

Straight-backed, Deenie sat on her bed, thinking about Kim Court, guessing who had watched the video, knowing it was everyone, everyone in the world maybe. All wondering what Kim meant when she said, "Deenie's the one."

And the even crazier part: *Deenie Nash is here now too. I heard her talking last night. I knew she had to be here.*

Like there might be another version of herself out there, in the hospital, with Lise.

Once, Skye told them about a cousin who could astrally project himself. He used to visit her at night and she thought she was dreaming until he asked her once, *When did you get the new pajamas, the blue ones with the rainbows?*

Part of her wished she could do that. She tried to imagine what Lise looked like now, if she looked different, better, something. But then the picture came to her, that mottled buckling in the middle of her forehead.

She turned to face her bedside table. Behind the empty Kleenex box, the gumball desk lamp, there was a picture frame draped in electric-blue Mardi Gras beads. Middle-school graduation, she and Lise, cheek to cheek, cap tassels pressed into open mouths. The old Lise. Lise with a forehead scraped with acne, Lise with a snuggle of flesh around her beaming face.

But it was hard to picture the Lise of now, or of last week at least. The Lise who poked her head around Deenie's locker every morning to say hello, except on the morning it happened, when Deenie never went to her locker. Because of what she'd done with Sean Lurie.

The only Lise she could picture anymore was the one convulsing on the classroom floor. The surprise in her eyes.

It was like the surprise in Sean's eyes. That instant he'd realized the truth about Deenie, knew her secret, or thought he did.

Lise and Sean, their matching stuttered-open expressions.

They weren't the same thing, except maybe they were: *You didn't tell me. You should have told me. You didn't tell me it was going to be like this. You should've told me. Deenie, why didn't you tell me.*

Or maybe it was like the look in her own eyes, Sean pressed hard against her. A look she herself never got to see: *I didn't know it was this. If someone had told me it was this. If.*

She didn't remember turning the phone

back on.

"Mom," she said, the phone shaking in her shaking hand. Had she really pressed her mother's name? "Mom, can you come here?"

★ ★ ★

The phone was ringing.

Not Tom's phone, not anyone's phone. The landline, which almost never rang except right before Election Day, which sat on a table in the hallway like a blistered antique.

"Is this Deenie Nash's dad?"

"Yes," Tom answered.

"Um, can you let Deenie know she doesn't have to come in tomorrow?"

"What?" Tom said, then realized it must be someone at the Pizza House. "Oh, okay. I'll have her call you if she doesn't plan on coming."

There was a brief pause. "No, I mean, Deenie should just take the night off. And Sunday too, okay?"

"What do you mean?"

Another pause.

"We're just being careful, sir."

"So you're closed for business?" Tom said, trying to keep his voice steady. "Who's go-

279

ing to be working?"

"We just don't need Deenie," the man said. "That's all."

"Listen, none of this has anything to do with Deenie," he said. "Though your concern for my daughter's health, since I'm sure that's what this really is, is admirable."

Phones rang in the background, pots clattering, for several seconds before the man spoke again.

"Look, I'm sorry, Mr. Nash, but none of us really know what this has to do with."

"Where did you get this idea? What made you think my daughter —"

"Sir, I don't think anything. I just know I got a call about when she'd last worked a shift. And I hear things. I live here too, you know."

Tom hung up.

Laptop open, he watched the Kim Court video again. The whole video. Filled with gaping eyes and throat clutching and then the worst part. The crazy talk about Deenie being in the hospital too. About Deenie being "the one."

It was the ramblings of a confused, overwrought girl.

The vaccine theory hadn't made sense. Nor had the elaborate theories about bats and toxins. But most of all, the notion that his daughter might be some kind of Typhoid Mary scything her way through Dryden.

He remembered watching a documentary about her on public television.

Her peach ice cream was highly regarded and often requested — that's what they said about Mary, a cook for the wealthy, a carrier who infected dozens of families.

He pictured Deenie at the Pizza House, hands blotted with flour, grinning at him from the back, the steel dough roller rattling before her dainty frame.

The PTA meeting was in a half hour, and he wanted to get there early.

★   ★   ★

"I'm so glad to hear your voice, baby," Deenie's mom kept saying, had said three, four times.

"I didn't feel like talking. A lot's been going on."

"Deenie," she said, "I'm so sorry you're going through all this alone."

"I'm not alone," Deenie said, all the urgency she'd felt when she'd first called draining away and something else, older and warier, taking its place.

"No, I know," her mom said quickly. "I'm

just sorry you're going through it without me."

Deenie grabbed for the Mardi Gras beads, rolling them between her fingers, trying to listen, or not listen.

"I keep hearing all these conflicting things," her mom said, her voice filling the silence. "The vaccine. All those antivaccine people. I remember when you all had your measles shots in fifth grade. Your dad trying to explain to everyone how vaccines work. I bet that's what he's doing now."

Deenie didn't say anything.

"And the congressman keeps talking about the lake."

"What about the lake?" Deenie said, her spine stiffening.

"I always wondered about that lake. That smell."

Deenie felt her hand cover her mouth.

"It used to be so beautiful," her mom was saying, "and then it changed."

"Mom."

"Is it still thick like that, like a bright green carpet on top? Does it still smell like animal fur?"

"Are you coming, Mom?" Deenie blurted, her jaw shaking.

"No" came the reply just as quickly.

The pause that followed felt endless,

Deenie's hand aching from squeezing the phone so hard.

"Come stay here, baby," her mom said, voice speeding up. "I'll get in the car right now. I'll pick you up by midnight. You can stay here until —"

"No, Mom. No!" Her voice rising, that shrill tone only her mom could bring out of her, all those months and months after the separation, slowly understanding what her mother had done.

"Deenie, it's not safe for you there," she said. "They don't know what it is."

"Dad takes care of me."

"I can take care of you. Deenie, I always —"

"You were never good for anything," Deenie said. "Except ruining everything."

★　★　★

Eli's eyes scanned the team showcase.

Glancing at the clock on the wall, he noticed it was almost seven. It had been hours since that smoke with Skye, hours spent on the thawing practice rink that seemed to pass in an instant.

There was a lot of noise echoing from the gym. They were setting up for something. It seemed a bad time to hold a game, a college fair.

He stopped at last year's trophy, a gold-dipped puck presented by the mayor, dusty ribbons, the team photo, sticks slanted in perfect symmetry.

And the big photo from last year's interscholastic banquet.

There were other players from Dryden, and from Brother Rice, Star-of-the-Sea.

He was thinking of what Brooke had said, about the boy with Lise.

In the picture, everyone wore the same dark blue blazers, the same button-down shirts and shiny loafers, the same ironic grins.

They all looked like him.

★ ★ ★

Her head hot and her room smaller than ever, and Deenie couldn't believe she'd called her mom, hated herself for it.

Her phone kept ringing, but she didn't want to turn it off because it might be Gabby.

She was remembering, again, the hundred muffled conversations in her parents' bedroom and doors slamming and her mother crying in the basement, echoing up the laundry chute. She couldn't figure any of it out at first and then finally one night she'd heard it, her dad's voice high and strange through the walls. *Couldn't keep your legs together couldn't stop yourself look what you've done look what happened.*

The next morning, they sat Deenie and Eli down at the dining-room table and she told them she was leaving, a roller bag upright between her knees.

The entire time, Deenie's eyes were trained on her dad sitting there next to her mother, not saying a word, head down, thumbnail gouging a notch in the table.

★   ★   ★

Tom wasn't sure at first where the sound was coming from, or what it was.

But then he moved toward the kitchen and heard the distinctive chugging of the washing machine.

He walked down the rickety steps, thick with layers of old paint.

Deenie didn't seem to hear him at first, the washer grinding to a halt. Quickly, almost furtively, she jerked the lid open, lifting her Pizza House shirt from the depths of the old Maytag.

He watched as she held up the shirt to the lightbulb hanging above.

As she pressed her face against it.

"Deenie," he called out, standing at the foot of the basement stairs.

"Yeah, Dad," her voice came, a hitch in it. She didn't turn around but pulled the shirt from her face, slapped it onto the lid.

It was dark down there, he couldn't quite see, but it felt private. Not illicit, just private.

"You okay?"

"Yeah."

"You said you didn't want to work tomorrow, right?"

"Yeah," she said, still not turning her head. "It just doesn't seem right to go to work. With everything happening."

Her hands were tight on the shirt, red and wet.

14

From the rain-whisked parking lot, Tom could see the gym burning bright as a game night.

Streaking past him, a Channel 7 News van, its antenna corded like a peppermint twist.

In the distance, he could see Dave Hurwich having a heated discussion with a woman in a yellow slicker and matching hat, a container of some kind in her arms.

Walking faster, Tom passed a trench-coated reporter standing at the foot of the building's front steps, a camera light illuminating his face as he spoke:

"Though school officials claim the purpose of this hastily scheduled meeting is to address all parental concerns, it is hard not to see a connection to tonight's revelation."

Another reporter ten feet away, fingers to earpiece:

"If Miss Court never received the much-discussed vaccination, many parents are saying that calls into question the most pervasive theory for the outbreak."

The reporter held the microphone out to a woman in a purple anorak beside him. Tom vaguely recalled her from Parents' Night.

"The vaccine was a red herring," the woman said sternly, leaning over the microphone. "So where does that leave us now? It could be anything. That's just not acceptable!"

Tom kept walking.

A small group was gathered at the school's front door. At the center, a man with headphones and a Channel 4 baseball cap was talking to Assistant Principal Hawk.

"This is a public meeting, isn't it?"

"This isn't a school-board meeting," Hawk said, his face bone-white and wet, his Dryden Stallions baseball cap soaked through. "This meeting was called by the parent-teacher association. We need to respect their privacy."

"But you're a public school, aren't you? What makes you think —"

Tom hurried past, ducking his head, nearly tripping over the long licorice cords snaking from the van.

"Is that the Nash girl's father?" he heard someone say.

He didn't stop. He just kept going.

★ ★ ★

Her mom left two long messages that Deenie let play as the phone rested on the counter and she ate her cereal.

She turned the radio louder so she could hear even less.

It shouldn't have been a surprise that her mom wouldn't come. It wasn't a surprise.

In the past two years, she hadn't spent more than ten minutes in the house, more than an hour in Dryden. When she picked them up, she waited in the car as if there were police tape draped across the entryway.

Sometimes, peeking under the sun visor, her mom would look up at it like it was haunted.

Deenie threw the rest of her cereal into the sink and opened the refrigerator, considered a bottle of beer nestled in the back corner. She had only had maybe ten beers in her life, but it seemed like what you did, what one did in a situation like this. As if there had ever been a situation like this.

The news report came on with that plunky

news music.

. . . called by Sheila Daniels, mother of Lise Daniels, and her attorney, possibly to discuss attempts to move her daughter to the medical center at Mercy-Starr Clark. The press conference will be held on hospital grounds at ten o'clock tonight, after the school's PTA meeting is expected to end. The hospital denies the story, asserting that any such event on their property requires permission to assemble and they have received no such request.

Deenie sat back down, thinking of the hospital, of being in the parking lot the night before, the closest she'd been to the thing that was happening. It was happening there. With Lise.

And then hearing Kim Court's voice, her eyes muddy ringed.

Deenie Nash is here now too . . . I knew she had to be here. Deenie's the one.

She picked up her phone, trying Gabby again.

"Deenie, I don't want to talk." Gabby's voice sounded soft and sludgy, like when she had strep, her tongue furred white.

"But what happened today? Weren't you going to the hospital for more tests?"

290

"Yeah. I'm home now."

"What did they do to you?"

"I don't know, Deenie. More blood, gross stuff. More headshrinking. I don't want to talk about it."

Deenie paused. She pictured Gabby like a ball rolled tight and there was nothing she could do to unpeel her arms from her legs, unfurl her head from her chest.

"Is Skye with you?" Deenie asked, then felt embarrassed.

"What? No."

"Did you see the videos?" Deenie tried again. "Kim Court?"

"No," she said. "No, I'm not watching anything. My mom said I couldn't watch anything. Deenie, I don't want to talk about it. Okay? Please."

But Deenie couldn't stop herself, her voice pushing forward.

"Gabby, we have to do something. What if we went to the hospital? Maybe, with everything going on, we could try to see Lise now —"

"No" came Gabby's voice, loud and urgent. "I'm never, ever going back there. What is wrong with you, Deenie? What do you think is going to happen if you go? That Lise is dying to see you so much she'll come out of the coma?"

Deenie didn't say anything for a second.

"Coma?" she said at last. "What do you mean, 'coma'? I thought she was just unconscious."

There was no sound on the other end.

Then a vague clicking, like a tongue across the roof of the mouth.

"Deenie," Gabby said finally, "people aren't just unconscious for four days."

"But we don't know . . . she may be conscious now. We don't know."

There was a muffled sound, but Deenie couldn't hear what it was, her forehead wet and tingling. She felt so far away from Gabby. Like with everything lately, even before this, all Gabby's adventures with Skye. The only other time she remembered feeling that way was a few years ago. That time Gabby stayed with them for almost two weeks. Every night, Deenie tried to get her to talk and she wouldn't. A few times, though, she heard Eli talking to her downstairs and Gabby laughing, and it had to be Gabby but didn't sound like her laugh, or like Gabby.

Which was funny to think of now, because those weeks Gabby stayed with them seemed to be the thing that had made them best friends. After that, they were closer than ever.

"Deenie." Gabby's voice returned, a whisper. "What is it you're trying to do?"

Click, click, and Deenie felt her own lips, tongue. Was the sound coming from her own mouth?

"Deenie," Gabby said, "we're all sick here."

Ten minutes later, her coat on, she was ready to go.

If I text him, she thought, *he'll say no.*

Tearing a page from her spiral notebook, she wrote a note.

★   ★   ★

The minute Tom walked inside the school, he felt it.

It was loud, louder than any school event he could remember.

The pitchy clamor of nervous parents finding other nervous parents to be even more nervous together.

A flurry of shouts at the door as the sole security guard tried to keep another reporter or producer from entering through the loading dock.

The screeching of gym risers pushed down the hallway, veering hard into the rattling lockers, sending a rolling garbage can careering into the wall.

Two sets of parents shouting at each other, something about a fender bender in the parking lot, and one of the fathers inexplicably crying, humiliating tears of frustration he tried to hide behind his shirtsleeve.

At the gym's double doors, the fleecy-haired student-council president stood as sentry, a name tag slapped across his navy blazer: PATRICK.

"I don't have any information. But don't worry," the boy said, his voice cracking, to the mother speaking fervently to him, her glasses crooked and fogged. "They're gonna explain everything."

He couldn't remember ever seeing the gym so full.

Principal Crowder himself, shirtsleeves rolled up like a junior senator, was directing a letter-jacketed student-council type in how to push open the high windows with the extension pole.

If it hadn't been so hot already, the air outside so preternaturally mild and the school holding all the furnaced breath of months of winter, then maybe the two hundred or more parents packed so tightly would not have radiated so much heat.

The air thick with it, the high windows wisped with condensation, Tom walked through, pushing past the straining masses, the gym starting to feel like some kind of torpid hothouse or sweatshop, the creaking hold of an ancient ship.

And they were all there.

A *This Is Your Life* of parents, current, recent, long past (what was Constance Keith doing there, both her rambunctious, teeth-flashing, hells-yeah daughters and her Adderall-dealing son long gone to state schools, possibly state prison?).

There were the earnest parents, notepads and pens out, clasping copies of news articles printed from the Internet in their shaking hands.

And there were the ones wearing vaguely stunned expressions, the same ones who could never quite believe their children were failing chemistry, had scorched their lab partners' hair while swinging burners like flamethrowers, had referred to other classmates as "pass-around pussies."

And there were the ones, fewer than usual, with their eyes fixed on their phones, just like during Back to School Night, concerts, graduations, their faces veiled now so you couldn't be sure if they were merely biding their time, reviewing the news reports, poised to pounce on the school officials, or if their thoughts were elsewhere (on work, on Scrabble, the Tetris slink).

Standing room only, like a rock concert, and Tom tried to avoid them all, finding a corner by the boys' locker-room doors, against the vaguely damp wall mats smelling strongly of mildew, spit, boys.

Through the aluminum crossbars, fifteen feet away, he could see Lara Bishop in her own hideout, chewing gum with the vigor of a former smoker.

He worked a long time to catch her eye and finally she nodded back, a half smile filled with knowingness. Sometimes she reminded him of one of those world-weary actresses in old movies, the ones who looked knocked around but instead of making them harder, it seemed to make them more generous-spirited.

"You're hiding too," a voice beside him said.

It was the French teacher, Kit, walking toward him, sliding off a tiny leather jacket, tomato red, like her Vespa.

Where did this woman come from? he wondered. And where had she been when he was single? Then he remembered he was single.

A sudden screech from the mike system

made her wince, smiling, her shoulders pushing together in a way that reminded him, unnervingly, of Gabby, Lise, Deenie.

"If I can have your attention . . ."

Principal Crowder began, papers rolled in his hand, pen behind his ear. A cartoonist's drawing of an important person. First, he introduced the murderers' row of officials standing at his side. Deputy Commissioner Sue Brennan, next to the superintendent in his usual taupe suit, then a silver-haired woman introduced as the hospital's "chief information officer," flanked by an unidentified man in a three-piece suit, fingers tight around his cell phone.

And poor Mark Tierney, the PTA chair and a pediatrician, his face crimped and flushed, like a man caught in the middle of a rope pull.

"Thank you for coming tonight," the superintendent began. "Concerned parents are involved parents, and involved parents make our district strong. The safety and well-being of our students is our utmost priority. We are working closely with the affected students, their parents, and health officials to gather all the facts. We ask the community to respect the privacy of the families involved as we progress and that any questions you may have be addressed

297

to Principal Crowder directly."

It was a marvelous string of sentences containing no information at all.

All eyes turned over to Crowder, who momentarily flashed his toothy grin, as if forgetting the occasion.

"Thank you all for coming. While privacy laws prevent us from getting into specifics, we want to be clear that all girls have received or are receiving appropriate medical attention. The headline here is that there's no evidence — and Mrs. Tomlinson from the hospital can back me up here — suggesting we are dealing with a contagious threat of any kind."

The silver-haired hospital woman stiffened visibly, locking eyes with Crowder. It was like watching a couple of battery men at a ball game, still working out their signals. Crowder caught her signal, only a little late.

"But the investigation is ongoing," Crowder said, eyes dropping down to a folded sheet of paper in his hands. "Essentially, what we're trying to do here is walk the cat backward. The district and health officials are working together, trying to determine any commonalities the girls share that might explain their conditions."

"Here's a commonality," someone shouted from the throng. "They all attend *this* school."

There it was. It hadn't taken long, but it almost felt like a relief to get it over with, to have someone start.

Tom could feel the pressure in the gym release momentarily around him and, in seconds, build up again, random parents straining to move forward, others waving for the student with the microphone. The buzz of two dozen or more conversations vibrating louder.

Crowder cleared this throat. "I was getting to that. The department of health is preparing to conduct a full review of the premises, and the deputy commissioner can tell you about that now. I know she's happy to answer any questions."

Sue Brennan stepped forward to the mike stand, teetering ever so slightly on her heels.

Tom focused closely on her, this woman who had spoken so inscrutably, so evasively, it seemed to him now, about his daughter.

"After Ms. Bishop's incident, our staff reached out to officials at the state department of health, including the environmental health and communicable diseases divisions. They're helping us review all available medical tests and sharing epidemiologic, clinical, and environmental data. Several of you have asked about autoimmune conditions, like PANDAS, but none of the girls have recently had strep. We've ruled out many standard infections — *E. coli,* staph. Also neurological infections — encephalitis, meningitis, late-stage syphilis."

You could feel the frenzy in the gym ramp up more and more with each word. Listing all these possibilities, even to dismiss them, seemed like a bad idea. The word *syphilis* felt like a fever in Tom's own brain.

"But it's important to note," she continued, "infections don't discriminate. If this were an infection, we'd see more people affected and not just young girls. But the process is ongoing. The main thing we need is your patience."

"Why would we trust you now?" a voice bellowed from within the body of the twitching crowd. "Any of you? You're the ones who pushed your poison down our girls' throats."

Tom moved forward a few steps, closer to Kit now, and saw it was Dave Hurwich, a tankard of coffee in his hand, a sheaf of curling papers under his arm.

"Lined them up like concentration-camp victims," he added, rising to his feet as the student-council rep with the portable microphone ran toward him.

"Sir," Sue Brennan began, "if you are

referring to the HPV vaccine —"

"Principal Crowder, why did you give it to them?" a woman up front called out, voice shaking. "I'm not against shots, but this isn't like the measles. My daughters can't catch HPV in school. Why did you make it mandatory, given all the risks?"

"Mrs. Dunn," Crowder said, stepping forward quickly, "the vaccine was not mandatory. But HPV *is* a virus. No, you can't catch it from a doorknob, but —"

"Are you going to allow sex in the halls next?" someone shouted. "Because that's the only way they could catch it at school."

Dripping with sweat now, the mounting anxiety in the gym crackling loudly in Tom's ears, Tom shifted a few feet, hoping for more space, more room to breathe.

It was an odd thing, to disagree with everything everyone was saying but at the same time share the dread behind it.

"When are you going to admit we're likely dealing with a hot-lot situation here?" It was Dave Hurwich again, shouting and waving papers in his hand. "You've been playing Russian roulette with our daughters!"

"Sir, if you're referring to rumors that there may have been a bad batch of the HPV vaccine, that's highly unlikely," Sue Brennan replied, her voice just starting to break as she tried to be heard. "Vaccine lots contain thousands of doses. If that were the problem, we'd be facing a citywide or even regional crisis."

Hot lot, bad batches — this was the first Tom had heard about any of it. He felt negligent, wondered if he should at least have been reading up on all this instead of just waiting for someone to tell him what went wrong.

"I wonder what guys like Dave Hurwich did before the Internet," Kit whispered, rubbing the back of her neck, the peacock-feather tattoo flaring. "Don't you sometimes wish you could have a school without parents?"

Tom looked at her and she seemed to catch herself, her eyebrows lifting in mild alarm. "I mean parents like that," she added, nodding toward the rising noise up front.

"Why are we even talking about the vaccine?" a woman shouted. "We know the Court girl didn't get it. That's all been a costly distraction."

There was a low roar of approval from all corners of the gym.

"That's true," Sue Brennan began, her voice nearly drowned out by the noise. "Kimberly Court did not receive the vaccine. Due to a yeast allergy, she —"

"The Court girl's the one speaking the truth here," the same woman interrupted. "Didn't you hear her video?"

"Are you a reporter?" a male voice barked from somewhere. "I've never seen you before!"

The woman stood now, and Tom recognized her: Mary Lu, Bailey's mother. A member of the Dryden Land Trust, of Energy Watch, of Safe Dryden. Tom had signed dozens of her petitions, had once even let her sucker him into a phone bank about pesticide drift.

"My daughter attends this school," Mary Lu was shouting at the man, voice breaking. "And I have as much right as you to —"

Dozens of voices reared up across the gym, shouts and yeas and boos.

"Can we please keep some kind of order here, please?" Crowder was saying, another screech from the sound system as he tried to drag the microphone stand to himself.

A few yards away from Tom, Carl Brophy, the physics teacher, waved his hand vigorously until the student-council kid found him with the microphone.

"Excuse me," he rasped. "What about the obvious explanation? That this isn't something coming from outside but from inside these girls' heads?"

"Hear, hear," an exhausted-looking man in front agreed loudly but somehow wearily from his seat. "As a doctor, I'm pretty skeptical of any epidemiological event that affects only girls —"

A billow of hisses, claps, and shouts swept through the gym.

Tom glanced over Kit's shoulder but could no longer see Lara Bishop.

"It only affects girls because they were the ones shot up with poison," Dave Hurwich said, face surging with blood.

"— and from what I've heard, the affected girls have troubled home lives," the doctor continued. "Girls without fathers in their lives, broken homes. Emotional issues."

A great ribbon of noise seemed to unfurl across the gym, and in the row closest to Tom, a woman leaped to her feet.

"What does that have to do with my Tricia?" she said, nearly bounding forward, looking like she wanted to shake the doctor, any of them, by the lapels. "Until yesterday, she was always a happy, normal girl!"

"Mrs. Lawson —" Principal Crowder tried, stepping toward her.

"Ma'am," the doctor said, "I don't know your daughter, but do *you*?"

More shouts and jeers.

"How does a divorce or whatever explain why her head turned to one side so far I thought it might spin," Mrs. Lawson cried out, her voice splintering. "She said it felt like her skin was burning off. I wanted to call a priest."

She snatched the microphone from the white-faced student-council rep and turned to the audience.

"Tricia hasn't had any trauma," she announced, seemingly to everyone, the microphone piercing with feedback. "She's a varsity athlete. She's a beautiful girl. She never did anything wrong."

"Jaymie was just happy, going along," Dave Hurwich said, rising beside her, voice breaking, touching the woman's shoulder gently. "She was as happy as can be."

At just that moment, there was a loud snap from one of the high windows: its rusty prop rod had slipped loose.

Suddenly, a spray of rainwater shot forth and landed, sizzling, on the audio speakers, which fizzled and crackled.

"Be careful!" Tom called out as several sparks flew, a group of parents jumping back.

The room burst into a new level of noise and confusion, the speakers popping and squealing, a sense of cascading panic.

The superintendent hijacked the portable microphone from the student-council boy himself.

"Everyone stand away from the equipment," he said. "Can we all just try to stay on point here?"

"But you're not listening!" shouted Mary Lu. "This school district spends a king's ransom on refrigerating a goddamn ice rink, but when it comes to protecting our —"

"Mrs. Lu, we've received your e-mails and —"

"You keep talking about what might be *inside* the girls," she said, stepping forward, sneakers squeaking on the wet wood. "What about what's *inside* the school. In the walls. Under the floors."

Tom looked down at his feet, at the splintery shellacked floor. It didn't seem any more likely a cause than the vaccine, or at least not much more, but even he could feel the hysteria. All the things Georgia used to say. About this town, this rotting place.

"The school passed all prior air- and water-quality inspections," Sue Brennan said, her face looking slicker now under the lights.

"Isn't it true that the school is heated by those natural-gas wells just a few hundred feet away?" Mary said, shouting even louder now, voice gaining confidence. "And that those tanks have leaked onto the football field? Some trees died. You walk through it and your ankles are covered with black powder. Wasn't the school told to dig up the affected soil?"

The stir was loud and immediate, the floorboards seeming to thrum, the gathered sense of gathering something.

"That powder is just common grass smut," called out Crowder, but without the microphone he could barely be heard, except for the word *smut*. "We sprayed —"

"It's important to note," Sue Brennan interrupted, talking over him rapidly, "just like infections, environmental causes do not discriminate. If the cause were environmental, we would see a wide range of people affected, not just these few girls."

The cavernous space seemed to explode with diffuse panic: hollers and howls, countless arms raised above heads, fingers pointing like lightning bolts.

Up front, Julie Drew's mother was keeling as if about to swoon from the heat and terror.

"Get her some water!" someone called out, inciting a new spasm of shoving bodies and tumult.

More and more, Tom sensed that if he stayed a moment longer, he would start to feel it too. Feel this sense that nothing could protect his daughter from anything because everything was out to doom her. To annihilate her.

Looking over Kit's shiny head, he searched once more for Lara Bishop. She was definitely gone.

In her place, a pair of oblivious students were making out with long, ravenous stretches of tongue, as if none of these dangers could ever befall them. The cluelessness he wished for all of them, amid this.

Looking past them, through the crossbars of the bleachers, he saw a woman with a long dark braid who looked familiar.

It took a moment, but as she turned to talk to the man next to her, something in the stiffness and purpose of the way her body moved triggered his memory.

The woman in the parka. The one in the classroom questioning Deenie.

She wasn't wearing the parka anymore, just a dark raincoat.

And the man she was talking to was a uniformed cop.

"Isn't it enough that our lake is forever polluted by who knows what sins of the past?" Mary Lu was shouting, her voice strong and searing.

But everything else fell away for Tom. Because it seemed suddenly, palpably clear that his daughter had been talking to the police that afternoon and didn't know it.

The woman and the cop started walking swiftly toward the back exit.

Placing his hand on Kit's shoulder — her body jumping from it — he moved past her and walked quickly toward the pair, disappearing behind the heavy exit doors.

"Hey," Tom called out. "Hey, stop!"

★ ★ ★

There was a thud from the school's east breezeway, something hitting the glass.

A light arced across the floor.

Eli walked slowly toward it, the same spot he and Brooke had stood a few hours ago.

That's where, she'd said, pointing to the bushes. *Right there.*

Outside, there was a blur of movement, the strobing of flashlights.

From the dim corridor, just before the breach into the breezeway, he peered through the glass.

Three figures in dark jackets, caps. Light blue plastic gloves like at the hospital.

309

One of them was lifting something off the ground with a stick. A bit of pink fabric, spattered with mud.

Another was holding a shovel, its tip grass-stained.

A camera flashed and Eli jumped back, as if they were looking for him.

And that made him think of something.

He couldn't be sure if he'd have thought of it sooner if he hadn't smoked with Skye, or if he wouldn't have thought of it at all.

Walking briskly now, he returned to the trophy case. The banquet picture.

The shaggy-haired kid next to him.

"You two are sporting quite the hockey flows," the photographer had said to them both. "You think you're Guy Lafleur or something?"

The forward from Star-of-the-Sea, Sean.

The one who worked with Deenie.

Sean. Sean Lurie.

★ ★ ★

The night air like a wet hand over his mouth, Tom pushed through the doors, caught sight of the woman and the uniformed cop walking purposefully ahead of him, across the parking lot.

Running now, the fierceness in his chest

nearly took his breath away, reminded him of when the kids were little, those moments you'd realize how vulnerable they were. A decade ago, that visit to DC, he'd made Deenie hold his hand everywhere, made her walk on the inside of the sidewalk, her rampart against chaos, against pain.

"Stop!" he called out again, chest clutching.

Both of them swiveled around.

"What were you talking to my daughter about?" He panted, hand to chest.

"Excuse me," the woman said, blinking.

"My daughter, today. You locked her in a room." His voice sounded rough and unfamiliar to him.

She squinted, then appeared to recognize him. "Mr. Nash," she said, "I tried to tell you this afternoon, those were standard questions. The room was not locked."

The officer next to her stepped forward slightly, his hands at his waist.

"You didn't say you were a cop," Tom said. "That's what you are, isn't it?"

"Detective Kurtz," she said. "And I did identify myself. All we were doing was gathering information."

"What do you have to do with any of this?" Tom said. "It doesn't make sense."

"Sir, can you keep your voice down?" she

said, but all he could see was the woman, the flat line of her mouth, and the way everything felt wet and close and she was not giving him anything.

"We're here to help you," she said, "all of you."

"How does interrogating my daughter help anybody?" He couldn't stop his voice from sounding loud, ragged. The way they were looking at him, standing so still it made him feel like he was lurching.

"We were not interrogating your daughter, Mr. Nash," she said. "Do you have a reason to believe we might be?"

"You *know* something," Tom insisted, not answering the question. "Why aren't you telling us what you —"

"Now I remember," the uniformed cop interrupted. "How are you, Mr. Nash?"

Tom pivoted. "What? Do I know you?"

Both of them so infuriatingly calm, their hands at their waists, their feet planted, watching him.

"I was there that time your wife called us," the cop said. "That fistfight between you and that fellow in the district parking lot."

The back doors to the school now rattling open and shut, Tom felt the push of people exiting, gusts of heat and wet insulation and rage, and his chest corded tight.

"Hope things are easier now," the cop added.

Tom stared at him, his glistening rain-cap cover and fogged glasses.

"That was a long time ago," Tom said, breathing carefully, "and that wasn't how it happened."

It wasn't a fistfight, or any kind of fight. There'd been some shoving, like you might see at a ball game, a barbecue, or a bar after one too many beers.

He couldn't believe the officer remembered.

Georgia, he never understood why she'd gotten so upset, that look on her face and crying. They hadn't even put cuffs on him.

And he hadn't known until now that she was the one who'd called the police.

"Mr. Nash," the detective said. "You should go home now, be with your daughter."

Later, he would try to understand what happened next, what tore through him, the words seeming to come from some hidden well inside him, bottomless and newly ruptured.

"Do you have a daughter? Did either of you ever have a daughter?" he said, his voice shredding. "Because if you did, you'd know why I have to ask you these questions, why

I had to chase you out here, why I have to not care what you or anyone thinks. I have to do something, don't I?"

Moving closer and closer to her.

"I have to do it, raise her, protect her. And no one ever tells you what it means. To hurl your kid out into this world. And no one ever warns you about the real dangers. Not dangers like this."

His hand, his pointing finger, a hard jab, perilously close to the woman's chest before he stopped himself, the officer stepping forward fast.

Moving back, hands in the air, and saying, "Did you ever look out in that dark and fucked-up world out there and think, How do I let my daughter out into that? And how do I stop her? And the things you can't stop because you're . . . because —"

"Mr. Nash," the detective started, voice firm, arm out, but Tom could barely hear her, people everywhere now, noise and confusion, and the car lights coming up, "don't make us —"

But both their radios began clicking then and the uniformed cop whispered something in her ear.

From the edge of the parking lot, from the tall hedges that crept along the breezeway, another officer emerged and headed toward them carrying a plastic bag in either gloved hand, his face wet and forearms streaked green.

"Mr. Nash," the detective said, moving to block his view, turning her eyes hard on the officers, "Mr. Nash, you need to leave . . ."

Her eyes suddenly avid, anxious, desperate.

15

Sean Lurie. Sean Lurie.

The sound of Eli's tires thumping the name.

Maybe it was the strange crystal dewiness in the air.

But probably it was because the streets were empty, carless, noiseless.

All the sound sucked out of the world.

He had that feeling he'd get, flying down the wing with the puck, and you know you can't look back, but someone's behind you, someone's catching up. You can tell by the sound of his skates shredding that ice.

And the quick double-tap of a stick, and someone's open and you have to decide: Do I turn my head or do I just send the puck over?

Except, in some way, he was both players. Part of him was charging ahead and the other part saying, *Don't miss it, don't miss it.*

From a half mile away, he could see the

glow from the Pizza House sign.

The hardest-working 510 square feet in Dryden! read the cartoon bubble over the mustachioed man on the storefront sign, his chef's hat tall and tilting.

The whole window seemed to radiate orange.

Skidding to a halt out front, he looked inside.

A gum-chewing boy, face ablaze with acne, stared back at him from the carryout counter.

"Is Sean here?" Eli asked, walking inside, the bell ringing.

★　★　★

Driving home the quick way, skipping the lake, the sky like wine on wood, Tom turned the radio loud, Eli's clamorous hip-hop. Anything to make noise.

Listen, I'm not the bad guy here. That's what the man had said. Georgia's lover.

He'd said it, shoulders hunched into a hapless shrug, to Tom in the parking lot of the Community School District 17 building.

Tom in the car on the way to the hospital, Georgia next to him, her knees tucked against her chest, sobbing. *It couldn't be his, he's nothing at all.* As if that should make him feel better.

This man. The man with whom his wife spent all those hours at Seven Swallows Inn. The man with whom she'd been so careless that maybe she'd even gotten herself pregnant by him, despite her promises at the time (*It's not his. I swear to God*).

Tom couldn't even remember driving to Georgia's building, couldn't remember how long he'd waited before he saw the man.

The man who actually raised his briefcase in the air as if to say, *Who, me?*

In the face of that, who would not have done what Tom did, thrusting his arms out and shoving him, the briefcase falling, spinning like a top on the ice-gruffed concrete.

He could still picture Georgia tapping on the second-floor window, pounding maybe, mouthing, *Stop, stop.*

A shove back, another shove, the man slipping, his elbow cracking. The blood seeping through the arm of his coat, spider-webbing the ice.

Tom could hardly believe it when the police came.

Could hardly believe that the raging man with the scarlet face in the car's side mirror was him.

It wasn't him.

318

The uniformed officer who thought he'd remembered him was wrong.

That wasn't me.

Except it was.

Now, less than seven minutes from home, Tom saw it.

In front of him, the bar's sign winked: TUDGE'S PUB.

He turned the wheel, hard.

The air inside felt cool, artificial, the vague scent of Freon, wood soap, and popcorn. The sulfuric tug from the gold-foil can of Bar Keepers Friend just behind the tap handles.

He couldn't remember the last time he'd been in a bar, a true bar with creaking floors and varnished wood yellow with smoke, with glowing bottles of forgotten liquors (Haig & Haig Five Star, Ronrico rum, green Chartreuse) arrayed pipe-organ style, a long clouded mirror behind them.

Where friends meet, the cursive letters announced, half-mooned over the crested center where the cash register sat. Above it, a pair of hockey sticks crossed.

He'd forgotten all of it. The comforting feel of a nearly empty bar, the bartender's expectant eyes, the red vinyl stools like cherries, the soft black in the middle, where the bar itself met the back tables, the jukebox and its sizzling promise.

That great soft black, like lifting the bedcovers, inviting you in.

"Whiskey, on the rocks," he said, sliding onto a stool, even letting his fingers curl under the wood ridge, shellacked with oil, grime, pleasure.

It seemed only appropriate to order a real drink, even though he could scarcely remember what he liked and hoped it was this.

Why, he asked himself, taking his first biting sip, *did I ever stop going to bars?*

And just when he thought the relief couldn't be greater or more vivid, the jukebox hummed to life. A song he couldn't identify but that had surely been tattooed on his heart, something from twenty years ago, his college dorm room, a car at night with a girl, a sleeping porch.

"Ohh," he said, not realizing until he heard himself that he'd said it out loud.

Swiveling on his bar stool, he turned and saw a woman standing in front of the electric juke. And she was looking straight at him.

"Tom Nash," she said.

"Lara Bishop." He smiled.

All the lights from all the news trucks, it felt to Deenie like a Hollywood premiere.

The hospital's front steps were swarmed over with people, cameramen, women like the TV woman from the night before, panty hose and business-suited, waiting.

Dozens of bright-colored suits, the slick Action News and Eyewitness News seals on the cameras, all under the mounted lights, everything rotating, snapping, and flicking.

From a distance, it looked like one moving thing, like when you peer into a microscope. Like when her dad used to show her gliding bacteria, swaying filaments like ribbons. It made her stomach squirm but it was also oddly beautiful.

Exiting the bus with all the night-shift nurses and orderlies, Deenie had no plan, but something about the way no one spoke, their hands wrapped tightly around their travel mugs, told her no regular rules applied right now.

It gave her a sense she could do anything. No one was looking at her.

The hospital staff, heads down, moved quickly to the back entrance where two security guards stood, hands on belts like soldiers.

It felt as if a presidential helicopter might appear in the sky and land on the front steps.

Nothing had ever happened here, until it did.

"It hasn't started yet."

Deenie didn't see the woman until she was right next to her.

She was wearing a yellow raincoat and matching hat that shone under the parking lot lights. In her arms she held a large Tupperware container.

"Oh," Deenie said. "I'm not here for that."

"Do you know what this is?" the woman said, holding out the container, something orange settled at its bottom.

"No," Deenie said, trying to figure out if she knew the woman, her face dark under the hat brim.

"A fungus," the woman said, lifting it so Deenie could see. "It comes during warm, damp springs after hard winters."

Deenie squinted at it. It looked like the Tang her grandparents used to keep in the kitchen cupboard.

"I think maybe it's just rust," Deenie said.

"All rusts are parasites," the woman said, nodding. "They need a living host."

Deenie tugged at the wool of her jacket

on her neck. "Where did you get it?"

"From the shore of the lake."

There was something scraping up Deenie's throat, a word, a sound.

"The lake water's in everything. So this," the woman said, gazing into the bottom of the container, "could be in all of us."

She looked back at Deenie, one long strand of rain sliding from the brim of her hat.

"But it's definitely in those girls," she said. "The girls at the school."

The woman lifted the container up in the air so the parking lot light hit it, making it glow.

Suspended in the liquid were a few grass blades, hovering. Sticking to them, the smallest of spores, or something.

"It affects the brain," the woman was saying.

It did look, to Deenie, like something.

But who could tell, with the mist-scattered light and the pearly sheen of the Tupperware.

"What does it do?" Deenie said. "If it's in you."

"Spasms, convulsions," she said. "Some people feel like they're burning inside."

The shimmering spores reminded her of the MagiQuarium she'd had as a kid, the

323

dark wonders inside, the hatching and un-hatching. The spinning and seizing of dying things, a briny trail at the bottom of the tank. The sea monkeys that, Eli told her with horror, mate for days at a time. Stuck together, twisting as if trying to strangle each other.

Eyes fixed on them, Deenie felt her mouth go dry. *Inside. Inside a girl.*

"How . . . how does it affect the brain?"

"That's the next stage. Visual disturbances. Hallucinations. Seizures."

"Oh," Deenie said.

The woman turned the bright orb in her hands, catching the light so it looked almost on fire.

Then she said, "It makes you lose your mind."

★　★　★

"Your sister's not working tonight," Sean Lurie said from the back ovens, behind the warming station.

"I know," Eli said. "I'm not here to see her. I'm here for you."

"For me?" He grinned, pushing his hair off his brow. "Well, I'm working now, dude."

"Take a break," Eli said, glancing around at the deserted store, the barren warming shelf under the cone lamps.

Sean looked at him for what seemed like a long time.

It was almost as if he knew why Eli was there.

"Out back," Sean said, very quietly. "Meet me out in the back."

The alley had a dank cat smell, but the parking-lot light gave everything a sparkly look that Eli found hypnotic, like the rink after it'd been sheared to glass.

And the longer he stood there, the more he thought maybe the smell was coming from him, the salty tang of his hockey gear, which seemed to leach into his skin.

He waited three minutes until he realized Sean wasn't coming out.

"Dude," the ruddy kid at the counter said, "he's gone."

Running outside, Eli caught sight of Sean across the street, the blare of his red interscholastic jacket in front of a rusted Firebird.

Spotting Eli, Sean fumbled with his keys, which fell onto the street, then down the storm drain.

"You never were very fast," Eli said, slowing down to a stride. "You just knew how to hook and not get caught."

★　★　★

"I don't see what's funny about it," Lara Bishop said, wiping a slick of cream from the corner of her mouth.

"No, it's not funny," Tom said. "I just haven't seen a grown-up drink a white Russian since 1978. I think that was what my dad used to seduce the neighbor women."

"Well," Lara said, tilting her glass side to side, "I haven't had anything to drink in so long, I figured it'd be best to have something I'd never want two of."

"I know what you mean," Tom said.

"But it turns out," she continued, that whisper of a smile, "I was wrong."

Tom smiled, waving for the bartender. "Two more, please?"

He tried not to let his eyes fix on his phone, silent and gleaming on the bar top.

"Bad taste in drinks, bad taste in men," she said, winking.

"Bottoms up," Tom said, clinking his glass with hers.

They finished just as the second round arrived.

"So," Lara said, "did you stay till the bitter end?"

One of them had to bring it up eventually, though he was sorry for it. And then felt guilty for feeling sorry for it.

"Long past when I should have," he said, flicking his phone on the bar, like the pointer on a board game. Like spin the bottle.

"I figured I'd duck out," she said, looking at her own phone, "before Goody Osbourne took the stand."

Tom smiled, surprised. He wasn't sure what to say.

"And how's Deenie doing?"

"Well," Tom said, then added, "under the circumstances." Eyes back on his phone, he said, "Georgia would kill me if she knew I was here."

"Well," Lara said, tilting her head and leaning back a little. "She's not here, is she?"

"She is definitely not here," Tom admitted.

"Besides, look at me."

Somehow, he found himself taking it literally, his eyes resting on hers, her fingers touching her necklace delicately. In the dim bar light, he couldn't see the scar, but he could feel it. It was an odd sensation he couldn't quite name.

"And, anyway," she said, "it's good they're together."

"Who?"

"The girls. Gabby had me drop her at your place on the way to the meeting. I couldn't leave her at the house alone." She looked at him. "Didn't you know?"

"No," Tom said, a little embarrassed but also relieved for Deenie. "So."

And her smile, under the light of the peeling Tiffany, was so warm, so inviting.

"So," she repeated.

★　★　★

"So, tell me. Are you one of the girls?"

The woman was gaping at Deenie from under her trickling rain hat.

Deenie felt her head jerk. "No. No, I'm not."

"Are you sure?"

"I'm sure," Deenie said, wiping the mist from her eyes.

And it was then that she finally recognized the woman.

She had seen her many times at the public library, sitting in the stacks. Kids used to make fun of her, the way she'd tear off scraps of pink Post-its and mark pages of books no one had looked in for years.

Then one day she saw Jaymie Hurwich talking to the woman and someone told her it was Jaymie's mom, which couldn't be true, because Jaymie's mom lived in Florida, everyone knew. No one had ever seen her.

She was just piecing this all together when it began.

Tire thuds, a swirl of headlights from opposite directions, the long coil of reporters tightening around the neck of the hospital's stone steps.

With alarming swiftness, the woman fled Deenie's side, dashing across the parking lot, the Tupperware cradled in front of her, pressed against her slicker.

But Deenie didn't move.

Moving seemed unsafe, with her head muddled and her throat plugged with humid air and with whatever it was in that container, which felt, suddenly and powerfully, like the thing inside her.

A thing twitching, haired, squirming, fatal.

Before she could let those thoughts take hold, she heard a crackle of static in the distance, saw the pair of security guards bolting toward the front of the hospital, radios to their mouths.

Her eyes returned to the employee entrance. Unmanned.

It felt like it can in a dream sometimes, where you know the door is there just for you. Maybe it wasn't even there until you needed it.

Once inside, the doors shushing behind her, Deenie found herself in some white corner of the hospital she didn't know.

Briskly, she walked through a series of random rooms, one with laundry bins, another with fleets of flower vases on long racks, a tangle of brittle petals in each.

Soon enough she found the Critical Care sign, its long red arrow stretched along the wall.

She walked with purpose, head down, and it was easy because there were jumbles of people everywhere, everything rolling, the clicking casters of IV stands, gurneys, trolleys.

Once, she caught sight of a girl she recognized, a freshman abandoned in a wheelchair, her head dropping to her chest then jerking up again.

The girl's hand was in her mouth, like she was trying to swallow her fist. Lise always could do it, her bones soft like a baby's.

Another corner and everything started to look familiar. The cartoon Band-Aid figure on the bulletin board, the big red lips on the *Shhh . . . Silent Hospitals Help Healing* sign. And posters with dire warnings.

It May Be a Spider Bite.

Would You Put Her at Risk?
You Don't Have to Be Next.

All the posters she must have passed on Tuesday without noticing. Now they felt pointed, urgent, damning.

Turning the last corner, she heard the radio first.

Another security guard, his back to Deenie, stood at the nurses' station talking to a woman with hair hoisted back into a large clip, hand clenched at her side, her face kneaded red.

It was Mrs. Daniels, forty feet away, and no place to hide.

Head turning slightly, her eyes rested directly on Deenie.

For a split second, Deenie thought the guard would turn his head to follow Mrs. Daniels's gaze.

But then Mrs. Daniels's mouth opened, and she was saying something to him.

The guard started nodding.

And Mrs. Daniels kept talking, sliding her phone into the pocket of her coat.

It was like she knew Deenie was there.

Knew and was letting it happen.

"You can't!"

It was Lise's grandmother, standing in front of a room, an empty plastic water bottle clutched to her chest.

The collar of her shirt was gray, her neat white hair now flat like a wet otter's. Deenie wondered if she had even left the hospital since Tuesday. Her eyes, her skin had the look of someone who had not seen the sun in a long time.

"You can't!" she said again.

Deenie didn't say anything, only nodded, walking past her, into the blue swallow of the room.

★　★　★

The swaying way she'd been sitting, the bloom on her face, it had been Tom's idea to make sure Lara got home safely, driving behind her through the black fen of Binnorie Woods.

Walking her to her front door, he'd hit his head on a porch eave, and now he was on her living-room sofa, ice pack to his forehead, water tickling his face.

"But Gabby's dad liked to drink it with peppermint," Lara said, grabbing for a sofa cushion. "Rumple Minze. Which isn't a white Russian anymore. Do you know what it is? A cocaine lady."

"Never a subtle fellow, that ex of yours."

Leaning back, she looked at him, the whisper of a smile amplifying.

"You know, he always liked you."

"Charlie?"

As surprised as he was to find himself sitting, so closely, with Lara Bishop on her sofa in her cozy matchbox of a house, he was even more surprised to watch as, scar blazing up her neck, she began reminiscing about the man who'd put it there.

"Yeah." Then she smiled a little, as if remembering something. Shook her head. "But he always thought you were a secret tomcat."

"What?"

"Well, he said it wouldn't surprise him. He saw you once with somebody. Or something."

"No," Tom said, setting the ice pack down. "He didn't."

She looked at him.

"But that was the thing about him," she said, after a pause. "That was always the thing."

He had no idea what she meant, but he was glad she'd changed the subject.

She tucked her legs under herself, one shoe falling to the floor, her face newly grave.

"You think I'm a terrible mother, right?" she said.

"God, no," he blurted. "What are you talking about?"

"It's not that I'm not terrified," she said. "Just not about those things."

"I know," he said, though again he wasn't sure he did.

"At the hospital, Gabby said they kept asking her about drugs," Lara said, "and she said, 'Mom, like I would ever do *that* stuff.' I was so relieved I almost burst into tears." She paused. "I mean, I *loved* drugs at her age."

She looked at him expectantly, but his thoughts had slingshotted. "Who asked her about drugs? The doctors? Lara, did the police talk to her?"

Lara nodded. "There was someone from the police there. What did they call her? Public health and safety liaison? But the girls just kept coming in. The looks on their faces."

His thoughts blurred back to earlier in the day, to watching the girls in line at the nurse's office. The eerie feeling of something unstoppable, feeding on itself.

"She hated being back in that hospital. All this is making her crazy. I heard her up all night, pacing the house."

"I'm sure it's brought back a lot of bad stuff."

"It's funny," she said, "when you think there's a whole other kid you'd have had if you hadn't done all the things you did to them."

"But you didn't do anything to her," Tom said, leaning forward. "It wasn't you."

She smiled, a smile filled with things he couldn't hold on to.

"You've protected her, you . . ." he started, but the words felt too heavy in his mouth and she didn't seem to be listening exactly, reaching down to the floor to seize the bottle of whatever they were drinking.

He couldn't help but notice the way her shirt pulled, the delicate skin there, a bristle of black lace.

"You know what else is funny?" she said, pouring a little into her glass. "Last week I was worried about what she was up to with boys. Doesn't that seem silly now?"

"No. *That* is something that never feels silly."

She covered her face, embarrassed. "Can I tell you? I found something on her phone."

He felt himself leaning forward.

"I can't believe I'm telling you."

"What?" he said. "Sext — sexts?" The word fumbled from his mouth and she laughed, poking him with her bare foot.

It shouldn't have been funny, but it was because it didn't feel remotely possible. Gabby with her serious face and her cool-girl acumen, her silver-sprayed cello case and her meant-for-college-guys gravitas.

"Sort of," she said, looking at him from behind the hand still covering her blushing face. "A picture. Of her in her underwear."

Tom felt himself go red now. "Well, girls, they . . ."

"I never saw such lingerie. The most alarming purple thong. You couldn't see her face, so I told myself, That's not her. But if it wasn't her, why was it on her phone?"

"I don't know," Tom said, and he couldn't quite separate out all the complicated feelings, the uncomfortable idea of Gabby in a thong, even the word *thong* in the context of a friend of his daughter's.

And then here, Lara Bishop, the top button of her blouse having slid open and the way her body kept squirming girlishly and the way her face and neck bloomed with drunkenness. The way it made that scar look even darker, more striking, a red plume, and he wanted more than anything to touch it.

His head thick and mazy with whiskey and liquors unknown, he couldn't stop himself, reaching toward her. She nearly jumped but didn't stop him, her eyes wide and puzzled and not stopping him.

He put his fingers to it, the scar. Touched the soft fold, which felt warm, like a pulse point, like he was somehow touching her heart, or his.

"I'm sorry," he said, starting to pull his hand back but then feeling her hand grip his wrist, holding it in place.

There was a long, puzzling moment when neither spoke.

"Everyone's sorry," she said, smiling faintly. "The whole world's sorry."

And he could feel the goose bumps on her skin and wondered when was the last time he'd felt that.

Charlie Bishop had been right about something. Tom had had chances, many chances. There were women, other teachers, even a friend of Georgia's who sometimes called after she'd been drinking, told him how lonely she was and that she knew he was too. But he'd never done anything about it.

Hell, he'd had a hundred chances, but he'd never done what Georgia had done. Even though he bet he'd had twice the opportunity.

A few kisses, sure. One with the guidance counselor behind the sugar maple at the faculty picnic, high on foamy keg beer. Five years later, he could still taste the caramel malt on her tongue.

But he'd always stopped himself, and Georgia hadn't. She just did what she wanted and now she treated him, all of them, like they were the blight. That house, its residents, they were the thing. The affliction. The scourge.

"Your eyes," Lara Bishop was saying to him, her skin like a living thing, "are so sad."

★ ★ ★

It was like a doll, a rubber doll, or a vinyl one puffed with air.

Deenie couldn't see most of Lise's face, directed toward the window.

Only the round slope of the cheek.

A bulbous head, the sloping brow of a baby or a cartoon character.

Deep down, she must have thought Lise would look like Lise again, or at least like the girl from the other day everyone said was Lise. The Lise with the dent in the center of her forehead.

But this wasn't either girl, or any girl.

She moved closer, because she could. Because this wasn't Lise. Clearly Lise had been moved to another room, or had left the hospital entirely. And been replaced with this.

Or maybe was in the bathroom, in her monkey pajamas, and would pop out any second and say, *Here I am, Deenie. Here I am.*

Like her outgoing voice-mail message:

"It's Lise! . . . Leave me a message or I'll *die!*"

As it was, without seeing her face, without Lise's strawberry-cream skin and marble-blue eyes and the flash of her teeth laughing — well, it looked less like Lise than anyone, or anything, in the world.

Except.

Except, getting closer, there was the scent of something. Beneath the tubes and wires and the pulp of her ruined face, she caught a scent as distinctive as a thumbprint. A smell of Lise that Deenie couldn't name or define but that was Lise as sure as that butter curl of an ear.

"Lise," Deenie heard herself crying out.

And slowly, slowly, she made her way around the bed.

If I can see her face, she thought, *I will know. I will know something.*

The head so round and enormous, purpled through like the largest birthmark ever, spreading from the center of her face up to her scalp.

The scalp half shorn, tiny baby hairs like soft chick feathers blowing, the gusting air from all the machines.

And, finally, reaching the far side of the bed, too dark to see anything at first, but then something glowing there.

Lise's eyes, open.

Open and wandering, like those plastic wiggly eyes on puppets.

Her mouth a wet rag. A tube snaking in and a violet lattice around it and the puff of her lower cheeks, and it was like something was inside the cavity. Or many things, packed tightly there, like a toy stuffed with sawdust.

It reminded Deenie of the girl Skye had told them about.

The one with the mouth filled with cinders, eggshell pieces, the tiny bones of animals. The things no one would want but that were inside of her.

That girl must have swallowed them, all of them, Deenie realized, her head light with the revelation. She'd swallowed all of them. And now they were hers.

Deenie heard a noise, a loud noise, a loud *oooh,* which had come from her own mouth, from somewhere inside her.

Because there was Lise, one wet eye suddenly on Deenie, its lid pitching higher, as if stuck there.

And Deenie's own mouth opening, as if a cinder would fall from it, moss clumps, leaf smut, grass blades powdered with spores.

"I didn't mean to, Lise," she said. "Don't be angry. I didn't mean it."

★ ★ ★

"And you think it was me?" Sean said, his face grimy from bending over the storm drain, holding up his phone for the light. "With Lise Daniels?"

"I don't know," Eli said, sitting on the curb. "We look a little alike, I guess. And you asked me about her once."

"Why do you care?" Sean said, sitting beside Eli, kicking his car tire ruefully.

"If people think it was me with her . . ." But Eli didn't know how to finish the sentence. The truth was, he wasn't sure why he cared, but the knot in his chest felt tighter and tighter. The sense he was circling something, drilling in.

Sean sighed, leaning back, his elbows on the sidewalk.

"We didn't . . . we were just messing around. We didn't fuck."

Eli nodded. He couldn't say he'd never

341

thought of Lise like that. But he'd always pushed it away. There were other girls. Girls his sister didn't share clothes with, tell secrets to, keep secrets for.

"I'd see her around. I tried asking her out, but her mom's not cool. She wouldn't let her out of her sight. Dropped her off at school, picked her up. So I asked her if I could come before school and we could hang out. She was afraid someone would see us. We found this place behind these big bushes."

"People saw you anyway," Eli said.

"We didn't fuck," Sean said again. "We just messed around. She'd never done anything. She kept laughing and covering her face."

He paused, a far-off look in his eyes.

"It was funny," he said. "She wasn't like I thought. She was so . . . young." He said the last word softly, confusion on his face.

Eli didn't say anything. Picking up a shorn branch end, he poked into the grate beneath him, spotting the glint of Sean's car keys.

"Anyway, it was only a few times. Last week, I guess, and Tuesday. Was that the day she got sick?"

"Yeah."

"She seemed fine," Sean said, shaking his head. "There was nothing wrong with her."

Eli nodded.

"Except," Sean said, scratching the back of his neck. "This weird thing happened."

★ ★ ★

"This way," Lara whispered.

His elbow caught a hard corner as they stumbled to her bedroom.

The crisp smell of night air and pine needles, and the quilt? comforter? on the bed was the softest thing he'd ever felt.

There was the crashing sound, a water pitcher, and a muffled laugh and her hands on his belt buckle.

The sinking sense of future regret hurtled away the instant he saw her tug off her shirt with such vigor a button popped, skittering across the floor.

His hand seemed to hit the warm flesh of her stomach the minute the sound came, the bray of guitar so loud he thought a band had kicked up in the living room.

"My kids," he blurted.

"What?" she whispered, hand on the tongue of his belt.

"My phone," he said. "It's for me."

★ ★ ★

"I didn't mean it," Deenie said, looking

343

down at her hands, not looking at Lise, that open eye. "But you didn't like him, exactly. He wasn't your boyfriend."

She kept starting to say Sean Lurie's name, but it only came out as a lispy hiss.

"And it was after work and we were in his car. I don't know why I did it, Lise. But I just had to."

Which was true. In his car, all the breathing and hands and power of it. Like her body had known something her head never would. Nothing could have stopped her.

Not even knowing Sean was the boy who'd taken off Lise's tights the week before.

And guess who it is, Deenie? That's what Lise had said at the lake, wriggling closer, her fingers over her mouth. *Guess who the guy is. It's Sean. Sean Lurie.*

Waving the milfoil under her chin, throwing her head back, telling her the thing Sean had done to her and how it made her feel.

Hearing it made something inside Deenie twitch, her whole body wanting to squirm. Her face red and hot, like watching a movie with her dad and suddenly there's a scene you don't want to watch with your dad.

That night, though, trying to sleep, all she could think about was how it might feel to have Sean Lurie put his hands there, his mouth.

Watching him at the pizza ovens Monday night, all she could think of was what Lise had told her.

When he offered to drive her home, it felt like it was meant to be.

She never thought of Lise once.

So she didn't meet Lise at her locker the next morning.

In fact, the next time Deenie saw her, Lise was jumping from her desk chair, falling to the floor.

And now here Lise was, or the thing that had been Lise, lying under the cage of wires.

"I'm sorry," Deenie said. "For everything. It's all my fault."

Which couldn't be true, but felt utterly true.

And that's when she saw it. The way Lise's eye gaped, an oily egg rolling.

"Lise?" Deenie said, nearly yelped.

And a sound coming, like a high whistle.

She's saying something, Deenie thought, *inside.*

Like that comic book Eli loved as a kid, *The Count of Monte Cristo,* the corpse with living eyes.

His face is like marble, Eli would read aloud, scaring her, *but from it burned a rage*

345

that could not be contained.

Lithe and cherry-lipped, the real Lise was locked inside this dented and bloated thing, this blow-up toy, but what she was saying inside was *You, you, you.*

And now here she was, her right eye large and gaping and staring at her.

As if she were saying, *Deenie, how could you? He wasn't my boyfriend, but he was mine. I told you and then you had to have him too. And now look what happened. What you've done.*

★   ★   ★

Eli couldn't figure out what it all meant, but he knew it meant something.

"All the sudden she got really nervous," Sean explained. "She said she lost her backpack. No, wait. She said she thought someone took it."

Listening, thinking, Eli felt the branch hit something inside the street grate, heard a jingle.

"She kept saying, *Someone's watching, I know it.* Finally, she just jumped up. She didn't have time to put her tights back on. She jumped up like she saw a ghost."

Eli felt for the key ring, caught it with the branch.

"You . . ." Sean said, watching Eli delicately lift the key ring up through the iron spokes, "you don't think it has anything to do with what . . . happened to her? To all of them?"

"I don't know," Eli said, the keys hanging from the twig. "Did you take them all out by the bushes?"

"No," Sean said, looking suddenly very tired, shaking his head. "I didn't."

With a clean move, like the faintest of wrist shots, Eli flicked the branch back over the grate, Sean's keys falling soundlessly down the bottomless sewer.

Sean started to say something but stopped.

"Sorry," Eli said, then rose to his feet and began walking away.

"Hey," Sean called out. "By the way, how's your sister? She's okay, right?"

"Yeah, she's fine."

"I've been texting her, but she won't text me back."

Eli stopped and looked at him. "Why are you texting my sister?"

Sean stood, shaking his head, not looking at Eli. "I heard she wasn't working this weekend. Just wondering."

Eli looked at him. Slowly nodded.

"You have to leave," Lise's grandmother rasped from the doorway. "They're coming. People are coming."

"I am," Deenie said, walking out. "I'm sorry. But she . . . she was looking at me."

"I know you love our Lise," she said, not even seeming to hear Deenie. "But things have gotten bad today."

"Bad?"

"That other girl upset her!" she whispered, holding Deenie's arm. "I could just tell. A grandmother knows."

"What other girl?"

"The one who came earlier."

"Gabby?" Deenie asked. "She didn't tell me she —"

"No, some girl with hair white as a witch," she said. "She was in there and we didn't even know how she got in."

Deenie felt her flesh tingle.

"And when she came out, she was crying, like an animal. Her whole body. Have you ever seen a snake sidewinding? That's what it looked like."

Deenie didn't say anything, just nodded. She didn't know what it was about, but she knew it was very wrong.

Lise's grandmother leaned closer, so close

Deenie could smell her medicinal moisturizer.

"Who was she?" she asked. "Tell me."

"Her name is Skye," Deenie said. "And you shouldn't let her back in."

*   *   *

No one was home and the house had that spooky feel it always had when the weather changed suddenly. The squeaking and wheezing of floorboards, the walls inhaling and exhaling like a sleeping giant.

Eli read Deenie's note on the kitchen table, the wild lope of her handwriting.

Turning on the TV loud, he collapsed on the sofa.

He was trying to think through everything, but before he knew it, he was asleep.

It couldn't have been more than ten minutes, but everything felt different when he woke up, with a jolt. A noise in the house, in the basement.

It must have been a dream, but it wasn't like any dream he'd had, at least not since he was a kid when he'd run a high fever and go to all kinds of places in his head — the South Pole, Madripoor, Mutant Town, as vivid as comics, as life, but more so — and wake up feeling as though he finally understood everything.

In the dream, whatever it was, he was still on the couch, but Skye Osbourne was with him, her arms hidden in her long sweater, which was like tendrils, and the light came and he could see through it to her breasts, her nipples like gold coins.

One hand, tiny and clawed, suddenly appeared through the bottom of her sleeve and she was holding his phone, as though it had never been lost.

Climbing on top of him, she wrapped her legs tight, waving his phone in front of his face, the picture there. The faceless girl with the purple nails and purple panties.

"You should delete it," she said, craning her neck down, her breasts swinging. He'd never known her breasts were so large. "What if she dies? Then she's on your phone forever."

"Who? Who's the girl? Is it —"

"Maybe it's your fault," she said. "The camera stole her soul."

Her hair falling onto his face as she arched her neck, as she looked at the photo glimmering in her own hand.

"Look," she said. "You can see her heart."

16

"When's the next bus?" Deenie asked a pair of hospital employees smoking out back. "I'm in a hurry."

"Where you going, honey?" one asked, a lady with pouched eyes and a lab coat under her puffer.

"Over by the high school."

"I'm leaving. I'll take you," she said, throwing her cigarette to the ground.

On the way, the woman talked without stopping.

She told Deenie how the pharmacy had never had a day like this, the dispenser beeping ceaselessly, the premixed IVs gone by four o'clock, a tech fainting and splitting her scalp, four girls an hour admitted at first, double that by the time she left.

"I saw you and I thought, *Not another one.* All day, each of you acting crazier than the last."

"I was visiting a friend."

Mind racing, somersaulting, Deenie was trying to piece it all together: Why was Skye visiting Lise? What did it all mean?

The woman glanced over at her in a way that made Deenie's eye twitch.

"A girl came in to visit her sister, and ten minutes later she was spinning around on the floor. We can't get this tiger by the tail. Your eye always do that?"

"I'm okay," Deenie said. "What happened at the press conference?"

The woman kept looking at her, "They canceled it," she said. "Everything's changed."

"What do you mean? What happened?" Deenie felt her eye throbbing, wanted to put her finger to it, make it stop.

"Because of the police investigation."

"What?"

"They found something in the girl's locker. The first girl."

Deenie thought of the people digging through Lise's locker, their gloved hands on Lise's gym uniform, her thermos, her binder.

"What did they find?"

"Look, I can't talk about it," the woman said, eyes returning to the road. "They made us sign all these papers."

The feeling came over Deenie like a rush of water to the mouth, rimy and overflowing.

Please tell me, she tried to say, but her mouth wouldn't do what it was supposed to, and the woman looked at her as if deciding something.

"I don't really know, honey," she said. "But I heard they think someone gave her something that made her sick. Very sick."

Deenie sat for a moment, thinking.

"Like a roofie?" she asked, remembering from health class.

"No. We check for that right away."

"So . . . so that's what happened to everyone? To the other girls too?"

"No. Their tox screens came back negative."

"But that doesn't make any sense," Deenie said, twitching, the vein at her temple like a wriggling worm, her hand jerking up, trying to hide it. "It can't be just Lise."

At that moment, the road rose and the school loomed on the horizon.

"You can stop right here," Deenie said, pointing hurriedly to the nearest corner.

"I can't leave you," the woman said, squinting out the window, the empty parking lot. "It's not safe."

Deenie looked at her. Then it was like

she'd touched a frayed plug. She felt something like sparks, her head jerking against the car window.

She looked at her hands, which tingled.

"Honey, you . . ." the woman started, her eyes leaping to Deenie.

"My dad teaches here. He's inside waiting for me," Deenie said, gritting her teeth to make the shaking stop, which only made it worse. She reached for the door handle. "Stop the car. Let me out now, please."

The woman slowed the car to a stop, looking down the empty street.

"I don't see anyone . . ." she began, but before she could say more, Deenie felt her shoulders vault forward, jaw percussing.

Swinging open the door, she jumped out of the car. And then she ran.

★   ★   ★

It was a little click-click sound and seemed to be coming from below.

Standing at the top of the basement stairs, Eli wondered if it was the dryer, or if it was a raccoon, like once before. For months after, Deenie wouldn't go down there without singing loudly or raking one of Eli's old hockey sticks across the rail.

"Deenie?" Eli called out. "Dad?"

"No," a voice came, throaty, cautious.

Three steps down, he stopped.

She was sitting on the Ping-Pong table, purple rain boots dangling off the edge.

At first he could barely see her face, long hair catching the light and her face tucked behind it.

But then she turned, and he saw her eyes widen, heard the smallest gasp.

"Gabby," he said, walking down the remaining steps.

"I'm sorry for coming in," she said quickly. "Did I scare you?"

"No," he said. "No problem."

"It was raining," she added. Under the lightbulb, her hair glistened from within its deep pockets. All the girls loved Gabby's hair, but Eli always thought it looked so heavy, so complicated, like one of those leathery cocoons you stare into at the science center.

"I had a key from before," she said.

"Good thing," he said. "I was wondering what happened."

"What do you mean?" she said, clasping her phone between her palms.

"To you and Deenie. Where is she?"

Gabby just looked at him.

"Deenie left a note that she was with you,"

Eli said, walking over to the Ping-Pong table.

She said something, but with her voice so soft and the furnace kicking up, he couldn't hear, so he moved closer.

"No. I was just trying to find her," she said, almost leaning back from him, as if he were standing too close. "I came here to find her. I really need to see her."

There was the smell on her of something, something in her hair that reminded him of his dad's classroom.

He must have made some small gesture because she said, "They put glue in, for the EEG."

"No, I —" he began.

"I can't get it out," she said, touching it. "Witch hazel, aspirin crushed in water, nail polish remover. I tried everything. Maybe I'll just cut it all off."

"Don't cut it off," he said, smiling.

She didn't say anything, looking down at her phone. He was a little sick, thinking of Gabby in the house while he was having that dream. Skye and her golden nipples and grinding hips.

"I guess they're all still at the meeting at the school," he said, eager to make conversation, to get the noise out of his head. "Things were crazy over there. I saw them

356

digging around outside."

Her eyes lifted. "Saw who?"

Eli shrugged. "I don't know." He thought about it. The dark coats and the blue plastic gloves. The one with a rain cover stretching over his hat brim. "The cops, I think." And then, fitting pieces together in his head, he added, "By the breezeway. By those big bushes. I guess it had to do with Lise being back there."

"What do you mean?" Her eyes back down on her phone.

He didn't want to tell her, but he was trying to see what the pieces meant.

"Lise," he said, his brain churning, attempting to make sense of it. "She was back there. With a guy. Screwing around, I don't know. What I don't get is why the police . . ."

He stopped.

The look on her face, the way it seemed to collapse upon itself, to wither inside that cocoon of hair. He was the biggest jerk in the world. No one wanted to hear stuff like that about her friend.

"Wait, stop," she said, shaking her head so forcefully it startled him. "I don't understand. Why are you telling me?"

"I'm sorry," he said. What if she was having another seizure, or whatever that thing was? "I shouldn't have said anything. I only found out because there was a mistake. People thought it was me back there with Lise. People were saying it was me."

Her head shot up.

"What?"

"But it wasn't me. I'd never — well, it wasn't me."

"It *was* you," she said, looking at him, eyes black and obscure.

"You heard that too, huh?" He hoped Deenie hadn't. "No way, ever. This guy just looks like me, sort of. This guy, Sean, from the Pizza House."

"It *was* you," she repeated, louder now.

"No," he said, looking at her. "But it doesn't matter. I'm sure it has nothing to do with all this. I'm sure —"

And something seemed to snap hard in her face, like a rubber band stretched too far.

"Oh, Eli, no. Look what happened, and now," she said, her voice going loose, like someone slipping under anesthesia, like when he watched his teammate get his arm rebroken after a game. "Lise. Lise is going to die."

"Hey," he said, gently. "No, she's not."

Her hands gripped the table beneath her.

"She is. She is."

He put his hand on her arm, hot to the touch.

She breathed in fast, shuddering.

"I better go," she said, pressing her body against him for the most fleeting moment, so close he could feel the swell of her breasts, the heat of her breath on his neck.

Before he could say anything, she slid off the table, her jacket dragging behind her as she raced up the stairs.

"Hey," he called out. "How . . ."

But she was gone.

Stuck with the landline, it took him several minutes and a few tries to figure out his dad's cell number.

He could hear Gabby on the front porch, talking into her phone.

After six long rings, his dad answered, "Deenie?" His voice breathless and sharp.

"Dad," Eli said. "Deenie's not here. I don't know where she is."

"She and Gabby must have gone out." It sounded like his dad was even panting a little.

"No, Gabby's here, Dad. She's been waiting for her. She doesn't know where Deenie is either."

There was a pause. Eli thought he heard music in the background.

"Dad," he asked, "where are *you*?"

"Okay, I'm going to find her. I'm going to look for her. I'll call you."

★   ★   ★

Trying to buckle his half-undone belt with one hand, Tom called Deenie. There was no answer.

On the edge of the bed, Lara was talking to Gabby on her own phone. A lock of hair drooping forward, she spoke in low mothering tones.

"I'm not mad at you, Gabby, but . . . okay, it's okay . . ."

Walking into the hallway, he decided to call Eli back.

Just as his call went through, almost in the same instant, he heard the electronic bleat of a ringtone from another room.

Then came the recognition. That ringtone — the shriek of a goal horn. It was Eli's phone. In the Bishop house.

Following the sound, he stopped at the doorway to what had to be Gabby's room.

He could feel Lara behind him now. "What the . . . ?"

"That's Eli's phone. Why would . . ."

Lara's eyes darted around the room. In seconds, she was kneeling over Gabby's laundry hamper, hands rustling through the clothes.

When she rose with Eli's familiar Calgary-red phone in her hand, Tom hung up.

"I don't know," she said, shaking her head.

For several minutes, they stood over the hamper, pushing buttons on the phone, popping the dying battery in and out. It didn't matter. The screen was blank. No call history other than Tom's own call moments before, no contacts, no texts. The phone was immaculate.

★   ★   ★

There wasn't any time to think, just a few minutes, Deenie walking swiftly, a block over to Revello Way.

For a panicked moment, Deenie wasn't sure she'd recognize it. She'd only been to Skye's house a few times, and never inside.

But then she spotted the glint of the gold-rimmed sundial on the front lawn.

It was a ranch house, a rambling one that hooked over a sharp incline on one side. There was the whispery sound of chimes in every window — capiz, bamboo, glinting crystal — and the creaking of its eaves, heavy with old leaves.

It felt too late to knock on the door, but it didn't matter because she saw a light on in the garage.

Making her way up the drive, she caught a flash of white.

T-shirt, bare legs, and the distinct white flare of Skye's hair.

Her back to Deenie, she was completely still, shoulders bent.

Like a picture Deenie once saw of a white cobra, its hood spread.

Girls like Skye, she would never understand. Girls who got away with ditching school and never doing any homework, who could have twenty-six-year-old boyfriends and be able to explain what fisting was and why anyone would enjoy it and had aunts who gave them copies of the *Kama Sutra* and who made everything seem easy and adult and anyone who found it all confusing and maybe scary was just a kid, just a little kid.

Girls who, despite never having been your real friend at all, felt it was okay to visit your oldest friend's bedside and lurk there in that Skye way, like a living ghost, a cobra-hooded witch.

"Skye," Deenie called out softly, wet sneakers grinding up the gravel drive. "Skye."

But Skye didn't move or even flinch, shoulders bony under her thin shirt. Her head down.

Approaching, Deenie finally saw what Skye was standing in front of, a wet-wood hutch on stilts, its front traps open.

"Skye," she hissed, "it's Deenie."

But still her head wouldn't turn, her shoulders hunched, her white figure ghost-like, and a tiny noise of something chewing, gnawing.

"Skye?"

★   ★   ★

Through the window, Eli could see Gabby on the front porch.

At first, he thought she was still on the phone, but then he saw she was writing something in one of her notebooks, writing faster than he'd ever seen anyone write.

He walked through the house, his head starting to feel things again, and badly. Everything seemed to be coming undone, like the ceiling corners, swollen with rain. *The house,* his mom used to say, *is weeping.*

Passing headlights flashed across the front windows and he looked out to the front porch to see Gabby was gone.

The drive back through Binnorie Woods seemed to take forever, twisting down one veiny road after another, while Tom tried to will himself sober. To reckon with the snarl in his head, which included a sneaking sense of relief.

He'd promised to bring Gabby back, had insisted Lara shouldn't drive. And now, the road doing odd, shimmery things, he was pretty sure he shouldn't be driving either.

"I know what it is," Lara had said as he was halfway out the door, still buttoning his shirt with one hand, the other hand crushed over his car keys.

"What?"

"Everything happening," she said, standing in the hard light of the entryway. Saying it quietly, barely a whisper.

He froze, waited.

"It's what we put in the ground," she said. "And in the walls. The lake, the air. And the vaccines we give them. The food, the water, the things we say, the things we do. All of it, straight into their sturdy little bodies. Because even if it isn't any of these things, it *could* be. Because all we do from the minute they're born is put them at risk."

He felt his keys cut into his fingers.

"We put them at risk just by having them," he blurted, not even knowing what he meant. Touched by her words, frightened by them. "And the hazards never stop."

She paused, looking at him. A chill on his neck, he felt as though she could see everything.

"Well," she said softly, her hand in her hair. "We're all at risk."

And she'd slipped back into the house, closing the door.

Now, in his car, he rolled down the windows all the way, tried to breathe. He couldn't really breathe.

He could still smell her on his shirt and hands and mouth, feel her mysterious energy. Warm and unsettling.

In the strangest way, it reminded him of Georgia.

This is why I don't drink, he thought, because a hundred things he'd shut in shoeboxes and hidden in closet tops cast themselves down again.

Like how he'd wanted to grind that guy's face into the icy parking lot.

How he'd called Georgia ugly names, said things in front of Deenie and Eli.

Once he'd even pointed out the guy to Eli at the grocery store. Said, *There he is, that's what your mother did it all for. That loser in the orange tie.*

And that other time. Opening all Georgia's dresser drawers, Deenie in the doorway, balling up his wife's lingerie, her panties, throwing them at Georgia. Wanting to stuff them in her mouth. Stopping himself. He stopped himself.

But that was a short period of time, a long time ago.

How do you get over it? he'd asked Lara Bishop before he left. *Over what happened to you?*

But she just smiled like it was a stupid question, or at least the wrong one.

★　★　★

The streak of her white T-shirt, the hunch of her back, head dipped low, the stillness of her.

"Skye," Deenie said, louder now, the smell of sawdust, ammonia, fur everywhere. "Skye, turn around."

And Skye's head turned slowly, as if she'd barely heard, earbuds dropping to her collarbones.

Her face cool and expressionless and so pale it was near translucent.

"Deenie," she said, her skinny arms inside the open door of the hutch, stroking something. A cherry-eyed rabbit with long ears.

"This is Crow Jane," she said. "Meet Crow Jane."

Deenie stopped short as Skye lifted the animal, its plush fur like the purple foot charm Deenie used to hang on her backpack when she was little.

"His mother tried to eat him," Skye said, fingering a pellet into the rabbit's mouth. "It happens sometimes. When they get scared or confused. Or by accident. Or if they think something's wrong with the baby."

"Why are you out here this late?" Deenie asked, even though she was the one out at midnight, in Skye's backyard.

Skye shrugged.

There was a smell that reminded her of the time the lawn mower sparked and burned up one side of the front lawn.

"What . . ." Deenie began, and it seemed to happen at that same second, the sharp twinge in Deenie's neck, her head bobbing, and Skye saying, "Are you okay, Deenie?"

Something in Skye's calm made her feel crazy, her neck and jaw throbbing.

"Why were you in Lise's hospital room?" Deenie asked, almost a bark. "What would you be doing there?"

Staring at her, Skye lifted the rabbit to her chest, rubbing its body.

"You've been there too, right?" she asked, her fingers nestled in the fur, stroking it with her thin fingers. "I guess the same as you."

"You were never friends with her," Deenie said, voice shaking now. "Not like me."

Something was shifting in Skye's eyes. "No one can be as close to anyone as you, is that it?"

"What does that mean?"

Skye didn't answer, taking Crow Jane by the cowl and setting her, a little roughly, back into the soggy hutch.

A wind gusted up and the smell, sooty and sweet, came strong from beyond the hutch.

"Were you burning something?" Deenie asked, the smell thick in her mouth.

Walking past the hutch, Deenie felt the ground soft with ash.

Skye shrugged. "My aunt does it. We have lots of weeds."

The school's bell tower chimed midnight, an ancient clang, heavy with rust and lime.

Both their heads turned.

That was when Deenie saw.

Through the dark of Skye's zigzagging backyard, the knotted brush, there it was. Its familiar gloomy limestone, veined with soot.

"You can see the school from here," Deenie said.

Something was coming together in her head, sharp fragments, thin as ice, assembling, sliding into place.

"Not really," Skye said. "Until they cut back those trees after the ice storm."

Deenie walked across the yard, straight toward the greening black of trees in the rear.

"Is this the way you get to school? You walk this back way?"

She thought she could hear Skye's breath catch. Heard the hook of the latch on the hutch and then Skye moving behind her, toward her.

"Sometimes."

Deenie walked to the far corner. From there, a few muddy steps and it was a clean path along the long row of hedges that ran up to the breezeway on the east side of the school.

We went behind those tall bushes, she could hear Lise saying now, her legs covered with milfoil. *He took my tights off first.*

"Did you see Lise back there, Skye?"

"Lise?" Skye's eyes narrowed to slits, and Deenie knew she was close to something.

"You saw, didn't you? What Lise did."

Skye looked at Deenie.

"Sure," she said, her voice changed. "I saw. I guess Gabby finally told you. I know Lise wouldn't."

"Gabby?"

"I saw it all," Skye continued. "You should've seen the things your brother was doing to her."

Deenie felt something crack and twist at her temple.

"What? What did you say?"

"Your brother going down on your Lise. Lise's leg twitching like a dog's."

Deenie felt her neck stiffen to wood, her hand leaping to it. She couldn't stop it, or Skye. Why Skye would say —

"She seemed to love it," Skye said, jaw out, her lips white. "She didn't care who saw. Your brother didn't either."

"You shut the fuck up. You don't know what you're talking about. It wasn't my brother," Deenie said. "Stop saying that. It wasn't him."

Skye's hand was at her mouth.

"Skye," Deenie said, voice creaky and high, "did you do something to Lise?"

"She did it to herself."

★   ★   ★

370

For Eli

The note was folded and stuck in the space between the storm door and the wooden one.

It was hard to read, the letters smeared and only the muzzy glare of the porch light. But once he started, he couldn't stop to go inside.

Eli:

The first time I met you, back when Deenie and me were just freshmen, you wore a shirt with a dinosaur on it and you were practicing wrist shots against the garage. You smiled at me and waved and said if I ever had a bad day I should try it, and you showed me the dents your stick made in the door. You put your fingers in them. Deenie kept saying, let's go inside. I couldn't move, I felt it already.

Every time I go by the garage, tonight even, I put my hand over those dents. My fingers fit in all the grooves.

The first time Deenie asked me to sleep over, I ran into you in the hall upstairs. You said you liked my Tupac T-shirt (for the longest time after I wore it every time I might see you). I could smell the beers on you. I couldn't breathe. I stood in the bathroom and held the sink edge. I knew I'd love you forever.

I could tell you a 100 stories like that and you wouldn't remember any of them. If you didn't remember the Ping-Pong, I might die.

That time we went to WaterWonders, I followed you all day. I told Lise and Deenie I got lost. I decided it was going to be the day I told you. But then I saw you talking to that disgusting girl in the white jeans, and I lost my nerve. What if I <u>had</u> done it. What if I had. Wouldn't it be something if you loved me too. If all along you were waiting too.

(Even just now, in the basement, it seemed like you were going to kiss me except my hair smelled so bad. I could feel it. Were you?)

I only went out with Tyler because he was on the team so I could go to the games and watch you. I only ever watched you. I thought I could make him feel like you in my head. I couldn't. And I couldn't make it go away. And sometimes I was sure you felt something. (Did you?) It's what I lived for.

So I have your phone, but I can't tell you how I got it. I had to get rid of the picture I sent you. I was sure you knew it was me, but I guess you didn't. (Except that awful, awful feeling I keep pushing away: you did know it was me and never said anything at all.)

I should have thrown the phone out. I couldn't even turn it off. Having it the past two days, it was like being connected to you. It kept me strong. I even charged it once, held it in my hand like it was part of you. I can't believe I just told you that. I hate myself so much.

I keep thinking about when Deenie finds out. She thinks I need her but she's the one who needs me. I make her feel more interesting. Your sister's a really good person. But she doesn't know me at all. I hide myself from her. I would never want her to know. Now I guess she'll know everything.

I have another friend who gets what I'm really like, and I get her. She scares me. Did you ever see yourself times ten in another person and want to cover your eyes?

I believed her when she said it was you with Lise by the bushes. It was the worst moment in my life, worse even than the other. It wasn't supposed to happen like it did. It was just supposed to embarrass her. I thought it would just. make her look bad, make her head crazy a while. Maybe I wanted her to have to feel crazy for a little while.

Lise is beautiful and there is nothing dark and messy in her. Nothing bad ever happened to her that I ever heard of except her dad dying when she was a baby. She's unmarked. No one asks to be marked up. And nothing was hard for her ever. And then she got to have you too. Or that's what I thought. Now I have to fix things.

I wanted to play Ping-Pong with you forever. Would you have let me.

I'm just so in love with you. I just can't stop being in love with you.

This is the first letter I ever wrote.

xx Gabby

★   ★   ★

"Your daughter couldn't be here, sir," the nurse told him. "Visiting hours ended at nine."

"I know," Tom said, "but I think she might be."

Where else would she be? he thought. Not at home, not at Gabby's — there was no other place.

374

"Sir, we have a lot going on in here right now."

"I know, I do. I promise, I'm not being a jerk. I think she might have gone to see Lise Daniels. Can you at least let me —"

"Sir, have you been drinking?"

"Listen, can you page Sheila Daniels for me? She'll vouch for me," he said, though he had no idea if she would. "I promise."

The nurse looked at him blankly.

Nurses are like cops, he thought. You can't hide anything.

But then he remembered he had nothing, really, to hide.

Together, they sat on pastel chairs in the Critical Care waiting room.

The slump of Sheila's body, so different from the Sheila of the other morning, or most of the times he saw her, always running on nerves and worry. Now there was a zombie sedation about her that made her easier to talk to, but much sadder.

Her hands, chapped, were folded in her lap, the nails lined red.

"Deenie was here," Sheila said, the smell on her like a live presence. "I saw her. I think I did. The pills they gave me . . ."

"When?"

"An hour ago, maybe. I don't know. My

mom saw her too."

"Do you know where she —"

"You know, I've only been home once. For an hour. The coffee table was still tipped over. I keep thinking about that coffee table." She looked at him, eyes yellowed. "That's what did it, in the end."

Something ghastly turned inside him. "In the end? Sheila, is Lise . . ."

But she shook her head, over and over. "Nothing's changed. Except everything. I don't understand. Tom, who would hurt my girl?"

"Sheila, I don't . . . what's happened?"

"I told them Lisey doesn't use drugs," she said. "Is Deenie a drug user now?"

"Deenie? No."

"That's what I told them."

"The police?" he asked, though he knew. "And they were asking about Deenie?"

"All day I've been talking to them," she said.

"Detectives? A woman with a ponytail —"

"They found something in Lise's thermos," she said, taking a crumpled piece of paper from her pocket, reading from it. *"Datura stramonium."*

Tom looked at the paper, a printout from the web. With a picture of a white flower like a pinwheel, smooth with toothed leaves.

D. stramonium — Jimsonweed; thorn apple; Jamestown weed (Family: Nightshade). A foul-smelling herb that forms bushes up to five feet tall. Its stems fork into leafy branches, each leaf with a single, erect flower.

For centuries, *Datura* has been used as an herbal medicine. It is also a potent hallucinogen and deliriant that can generate powerful visions. Legend has it that Cleopatra used the extract as a love potion in her seduction of Caesar.

Low recreational doses are usually absorbed through smoking the plant's leaves. It can, however, prove fatally toxic in only slightly higher amounts, and reckless use can result in hospitalization and even death. Amnesia of the poisoning event is common.

Late signs/fatal reactions: convulsions, cardiovascular weakening, coma.

Tom tried to concentrate on the words, but the noise in his head wouldn't let him.

"Jimsonweed. Someone gave her this?" he said. "Someone gave this to all these girls?"

"They gave it to Lise," Sheila said, swallowing loudly, the paper shaking in her hand. "They couldn't find it in the other girls."

"Do they know why? And what about . . ." There were too many questions and she wasn't listening anyway.

She looked down at the printout, turning it over, showing him the drawing of the plant's chemical composition.

Looking up, she smiled vaguely, her voice rising and pushing the words out: "Blind as a bat, mad as a hatter . . ."

"Red as a beet," continued Tom, an old memory, cramming for a long-ago exam, rising up in him, "hot as a hare, dry as a bone, and the —"

"— heart runs alone," she finished. "The doctor told me that's how they memorize it in med school. The symptoms. Toxic something. I forgot to write that part down."

"Poisoned," he said. "She was poisoned."

The heart runs alone," she repeated, turning from the paper to Tom. "Isn't that horrible?" Then, looking up at him. "Or beautiful?"

★   ★   ★

"Skye," Deenie whispered loudly, moving closer. "What did you *do*?"

"Why would I tell you?" she said, arm lifting to the dark boughs of the tree above her. "What did you ever care about me? The

378

only one who ever cared is Gabby."

"Gabby cares about Lise," Deenie said. *"What did you do, Skye?"*

And that's when Skye's mouth started its clicking sound again.

"I can't believe you never knew," she said. "About Gabby."

"What does Gabby . . ." But already something was happening, a feeling.

"About Gabby," Skye said. "About how fucking much she loves your brother."

"What . . ." Deenie started, but she couldn't make the words come. Because there it was, some private song she knew from far back in a cobwebby corner of her head. A song so faint she'd barely heard it, but now, the sound turned up, she couldn't muffle it anymore.

Gabby, who always walked so fast by his bedroom door. Gabby standing beside her at the washing machine, her hand on Eli's T-shirt. Her fingers. Deenie wanted to look away. A dozen times like that. The way her body battened tight when he came in the room. The way her face . . .

This song, she'd heard it so low and quiet so long, she never really heard it at all.

"She could never tell you," Skye said. "She knew you wouldn't understand, or help her. But she had me."

Deenie felt something drag up her spine. Turning, she said, each word slow and raking up her throat, "Had you for . . . what? *What did you do, Skye?*"

And, stepping farther back under the black canopy of the tree, Skye seemed to draw herself into herself, a small white flower.

There, hidden, her voice low and forceful and insistent, almost a chant, she told Deenie a story, the way only Skye would tell it.

Of how she and Gabby became friends, true friends, because they both knew how to keep secrets. How one night last year, Skye caught her hiding in the tall trees by the school, watching Eli Nash skating by himself on the practice rink. She was so embarrassed, and Skye said she shouldn't be and invited Gabby to her house to do the love tarot.

They sat for hours and Gabby told Skye she'd loved Eli since the day she met him, and he was all she thought about. And that she loved Deenie but that she'd mostly become friends with her because of Eli, whom she loved so much she wanted to die.

It never stopped, the feeling, and watching him with all those girls, once or twice hearing them in Deenie's house, was almost too much for Gabby to bear. Sometimes she even thought that if it weren't for Deenie . . .

But Skye had told her it didn't matter. That was how guys were, trapped for years in the mindless mojo of lust. And together they cast love spells from the Internet, mixing honey, oils, and leaves with things — hair, pens, stick wax, a roll of grip tape — stolen from Eli's backpack, his house.

Once, they used a dove heart Skye's cat carried in from the backyard.

Once, they used menstrual blood.

And then one day it happened, or they thought it did.

I saw him in the hallway, Gabby said, *and you should have seen it, the way he looked at me. I know it worked. I know it.*

To bind it, Skye cautioned, they would have to send him a picture. If it stays on his phone for twelve days, the spell will work. And Gabby said she'd do it. She was not afraid.

But the spell didn't work in time. Or it worked the wrong way. It worked for Lise.

Because one morning, a week ago, Skye was walking to school, late, head full of bad dreams like always, and she saw it all. Saw the secret. Behind the bushes. Lise and Eli Nash.

She told Gabby what she'd seen. And

Gabby could think of nothing else: *I want to die,* she told Skye. *I'm dying now.*

The next day, they'd all gone to the lake.

Gabby was so angry, she couldn't even look at Lise. Lise showing off her body in the water. And that spot on the inside of her thigh, like a moon, a kiss, a witch's mark. The whole time, Gabby kept whispering to Skye, *She stole him from me.*

And so Skye promised to reverse it. And she knew just how.

Sulfur, honey, and dried jimson flowers from the bushes out back, the kind that bloomed at night. They're called love-will. She'd found it in a book. A spell to scare a faithless lover into repentance.

She made the mixture and gave it to Gabby and Gabby put it in Lise's thermos. It was important that Gabby do it herself. It was the only way the spell would work.

And they couldn't be responsible for what happened. In fact, didn't Lise's reaction show that it was Lise who was a faithless lover? Was holding some bad energy inside that needed to be released?

Deenie listened and listened and finally broke in.

"But you gave Lise . . . sulfur?"

"Jimson. It runs wild back here. If you dry the leaves and smoke them, you can have visions," Skye said, stepping back even farther under the heavy branches, only her mouth and chin visible now. "But it only makes visible a darkness that's already there. Maybe eating it like that . . ."

She looked at Deenie, her voice like a pulse in Deenie's brain. "Maybe you bring the darkness inside you. Maybe Lise has it inside her now."

Deenie felt herself sinking, her hand reaching out for the tree beside her, knuckles pressing into its hard bark.

"They'll find it," Deenie said, huskily. "They're finding everything."

"I burned it all," she said, head tilting toward the dredged ashes mixing with the sawdust by the rabbit hutch. That smell Deenie had caught, now nearly gone. "The plants were so beautiful. It's all done."

Pressing her hand to her chest, Deenie tried to get a breath that wouldn't come.

"I'm going to tell," she whispered.

"It doesn't matter to me."

A wind came and Skye's head dipped down from the tree's shadow and Deenie saw her face, hair blown back. Her face bare and clean as she'd never seen it. She looked small and dangerous.

"Skye," she said, softly, "Lise is going to die."

There was a pause. Deenie couldn't look at her, her face so naked, her eyes like hard green marbles.

"I'm not sorry, Deenie," Skye was saying. "And you shouldn't be. We don't owe anybody anything."

Deenie couldn't imagine anything less true. The hardest part was how much we owed everyone.

"You poisoned her," Deenie said, feeling her neck throb from its seizing bursts, her body aching from it. "You poisoned everybody."

"No," Skye said. "She was the only one."

Deenie looked at her, trying to puzzle it all out, including the long, fevered lurches of her own body, heart. How was it possible?

"And it's not poison," Skye said, stepping forward, so close to Deenie she could smell the sawdust, the ashes. "Your brother had some, he smoked some today and he didn't get sick."

Deenie lifted her head, eyes on Skye, the white smear of her face. It seemed to happen instantaneously, her body moving fast across the lawn.

★ ★ ★

384

"Sheila Daniels, please return to ICU."

The crackle from the ancient PA system.

"Maybe she's awake," Tom said, rising, helping Sheila to her feet.

Her body bobbled between his forearms, her hair slipping from its clip, he grabbed for one shoulder to try to keep her upright.

"I'll come with you," he said. "You . . ."

But she had pulled away from him and charged through the double doors with surprising suddenness and strength.

All Sheila Daniels's constant, exhausting vigilance over the years looked different now. It made you wonder if, in some obscure way, she had known what was coming and spent all her days raising the ramparts, doing whatever she could to forestall it, or at least prepare for it.

Except what, or who, had she been protecting Lise from? He couldn't imagine why anyone in the world would want to hurt that sweet girl.

And now he was bounding through the front doors, not stopping to think where he could find Deenie, just knowing he would.

His phone started ringing just as he reached his car.

"Hello?" he answered, not even looking.

"I can't breathe. I can't breathe and I . . ."

And it was Deenie's voice, one he hadn't

heard in a thousand years, and she was saying things, frantically, breathlessly, but with
the sound of everything in the world roar-
ing in his ear, he could only hear "Daddy."

It was five miles or more, even if she found
the right shortcuts, iron spreading through
her chest as she ran.

There was no guessing about it, but a
picture kept coming: Eli's head hitting the
ice, like she'd once seen happen at a
practice, his helmet shorn off, two teeth
knocked out. Deenie had been there, felt
her heart stop.

And her mom running onto the ice, arms
around him in seconds. Scrambling to find
both teeth. Deenie watched as she foisted
them back in Eli's open mouth. And he was
fine. Because Eli was always fine, wasn't he?

Running faster, breathing harder, her face
slicked from the damp, her sneakers nearly
twisting off her feet, she pressed her phone
against her ear.

Her dad was telling her to slow down, to
breathe.

"Where's Eli," she said and it wasn't her
voice now but her voice in an old home
video, long-ago Christmas mornings, a
canoe trip, the time she first rode a bike
and fell elbow first onto the sidewalk.

"Daddy, he's poisoned."

★ ★ ★

A two-liter nestled between his legs, Eli held Gabby's letter in his hand.

He was drinking fast, trying to wake up, to shake off the final dregs of the smoke, to understand what he'd read and what it meant.

There were revelations tumbling through his head — so many moments that looked different now, how he'd read them all wrong — but he pushed them aside for the moment because of the sickly urgency he felt. *Now I have to fix things,* she'd written, a sentence that had a sense of purpose. And finality.

He picked up the kitchen phone again, realized he didn't have her number.

Pulling his laptop out of his bag, he e-mailed Gabby, the first time he ever had.

Gabby, call me. come back.

Then he sat for a second, waiting, hoping. All those times with Gabby, her stern and mysterious face. To matter so much to someone you hardly thought about. To care so much about someone who maybe didn't even wonder about you, or check in much to see if you were okay because that person wasn't thinking about you, not really, and maybe had moved far away, three hours or something, just far enough to be able to put you out of her mind whenever she wanted.

The phone rang.

"Eli, it's Dad."

"Hey," Eli said. "Gabby left. And this thing happened. I don't know —"

"Are you okay, Eli?" his dad said, his voice even more breathless than before. "Are you all right?"

"Yeah, Dad, but Gab—"

"We'll be right there, okay? Don't — just sit still, okay? Just don't do anything."

"What?" Eli said, but all he heard was the smack of tires on a wet road, then a click.

★   ★   ★

She saw the car, the only car in the world, the streets desolate and haunted, like a town during a plague.

"Deenie," her dad was shouting from the rolled-down window.

And the car nearly jumped the curb, spraying her with gathered water.

"You were supposed to go to Eli," she shouted, holding her trapper hat on her head, heavy with rain.

"Deenie," he said, "get in."

She stood for a second, looking at her father, his face red and fevered, hands gripping the wheel.

She felt so sorry for him.

★   ★   ★

Eli kept trying to tell them he was okay, but they wouldn't listen.

Knees up in the backseat, Deenie had her head buried in her arms, and he thought she might be crying.

Dad drove faster than Eli had ever seen anyone drive, faster even than A.J. drag-racing by the old wire factory outside of town.

"Did you drink something?" his dad kept asking. "Did someone give you something? How about in your thermos?"

"What? No. I don't have a thermos," he said. "I'm okay, Dad."

"You're not," Deenie said from the back. "You think you are, but you're not."

The hospital was there, lit so brightly it hurt his eyes, the parking lot like the school's before a big game.

Their headlights skated across a pair of girls, maybe ten or eleven, in flannel pajamas, their mother with an arm around each of them, rushing them inside. They both wore big slippers — lobsters and bunny rabbits — oozing with gray rain, so heavy they could barely lift their feet.

Time shuttered to a stop as Eli watched them, their faces blue in the light, looking at the windshield, at him. He squinted and saw they were older than they'd first looked. The one with the bunny slippers he recognized as the sophomore girl everyone called Shawty, the one who'd snuck into his bedroom months ago, the one who'd cried when it was over, worried she'd done it all wrong. After, she'd stayed in the bathroom a long time. When she came out, her face was bright with pain.

Girls changed after, he thought. Before, she'd been texting him all the time, pulling her shirt up at games, saying all the things she wanted to do to him, flashing that thong at him.

And then after. But it changed for him after too. Growing up felt like a series of bewildering afters.

And now here she was, hair scraped back from her baby face, and she had stopped, and she was looking at him.

Recognizing him, remembering things. A hard wince sweeping across that soft face.

And he wasn't sure what her real name
was.

Then came the girl's mother's burly arm
covering her face, hoisting her along, and
the girl was gone, lost behind the hospital's
sliding doors.

"Deenie," Eli said, turning around to face
his sister, "did Gabby find you? Did you
talk to her?"

And she just shook her head, eyes wide
and startled, mouth fixed.

"Because I have to show you something.
You need to see something."

Reaching into his jeans pocket, he pulled
out the note, damp in his hands.

★ ★ ★

A blurry half hour after he'd left, Tom was
back in the hospital waiting room, this time
with Eli and Deenie.

Eli, glassy-eyed, an arm around his sister,
her face colorless, mouth slightly open.

He hadn't been able to get anything
coherent from Deenie.

Like when she was little and would lose
her breath and all he could do was say it
would be okay, everything would be okay.

I can't breathe. I can't breathe.

Now, his heart still jamming against his

chest, he tried to settle himself. He needed to be ready for anything.

There was something about seeing Eli, his hand on his sister's arm, saying things in her ear, that was beginning to work on him.

To calm him.

To make his breaths come slow, to let him stand back and see them both.

★   ★   ★

When her dad went up to the reception window, Deenie turned to Eli. He had something in his hand and kept trying to show it to her.

It was a piece of paper, like a wet leaf, and she recognized Gabby's tight scrawl.

She read in what felt like slow motion, each word shuddering a moment before locking into focus.

The first time I met you, back when Deenie and me were just freshmen, you wore a shirt with a dinosaur on it.

The things Skye said, they were true.

She thinks I need her but she's the one who needs me. I make her feel more interesting.

She read it and thought of everything that had ever happened with her and Gabby, and all the things she'd held tight to her own chest. About her part of the story, about

Sean Lurie. And how neither Gabby nor Skye would ever find out.

Why should she tell them?

Your sister's a really good person, Gabby had written. *But she doesn't know me at all.*

Maybe we don't really know anybody, Deenie thought. *And maybe nobody knows us.*

★　★　★

The nurse was crazily beautiful, like a nurse in a porno movie, and Eli thought he must still be high, all these hours later.

Her breasts seemed to brush up against him every time she moved, checking his eyes, his pulse. Asking him a series of questions and then asking again.

Fifteen minutes before, he'd peed into a cup, handed it to her.

"Nothing here," she said now, looking at the results. It seemed impossibly fast.

"I haven't done any drugs," he said. "I don't use drugs."

He wondered if his dad, standing just a few feet away, was also noticing how beautiful the nurse was. But his dad didn't seem to notice anything, his eyes set on Eli, his gaze intent.

Another nurse, her scrubs dark with

sweat, rolled a cart past them, the wheels screeching.

"I just don't know how we get out of this," she was saying to the beautiful nurse. "I've never seen anything like this."

There was a frenzy around him, a constant whir that didn't seem to touch him. Or his nurse, her voice tut-tutting, the fine gold cross around her neck, hanging between the tops of her breasts.

And then, as she bent the arm of a light above him, he saw she wasn't really crazily beautiful and was a lot older than he thought, but there was a tenderness and efficiency to her that made him feel like everything would be okay.

"We'll still take some blood but —" Just then a crash came, followed by the yelp of a girl's voice, the skidding of sneakers on the floor.

"Some help here!" a voice rose, deep and urgent.

"I'll be back," the nurse said to Eli's dad, putting her hands on his shoulders to direct him to a narrow waiting area crushed with parents. "Sit tight."

His dad just stood there, watching the unshaven men with pajama tops under their open coats, women wearing slipper boots, one father weeping into his lap.

"Eli," his dad was saying, "I have to make a call, okay?"

No one was looking.

Eli was the only male and that made it easier. No one was looking, so he started walking, exploring.

Hearing a dozen conversations, voices pinched and frightened.

". . . and her throw-up looked like coffee grounds. I heard that means . . ."

". . . explains why she's been this way for so long. All those ADD meds. Maybe this is why . . ."

". . . all these clots when I was doing the laundry. And I asked her and she started crying . . ."

". . . and heavy-metal poisoning, or mold? She kept saying everything smelled like meat. And then she'd throw up again."

". . . like I was floating, and a darkness was closing in on me."

He had been sitting on a small chair, all the exam tables taken, when he spotted, under one of those rolling privacy screens, a pair of soggy bunny slippers.

And then the slippers started to move.

He saw her, the sophomore girl, walking toward the swinging doors.

And he couldn't sit there anymore.

And no one stopped him.

A man in scrubs, his forehead wet, clipboard in hand, called out to him as he passed a nursing station.

"That's my sister," Eli lied, rushing past the man, who started to say something and then stopped.

★　★　★

"I think he's fine. I don't know. They think he's fine."

"Oh, Tom," Georgia said, "what's happened?"

And he didn't know how to begin to answer that question.

He'd planned on telling her everything he knew, but it felt like so many enigmatic scraps, and all of it depended on her being here, on her knowing the teen-girl complexities of Deenie's friendships, of the extraordinary *something* that had overtaken all these girls and everyone in their lives. How did you explain any of that?

He could tell her about finding Eli's phone, and they could try to figure it all out, but he didn't know how to tell her without explaining why he'd been with Lara Bishop at midnight.

"I was always afraid something could happen to Eli on the ice," Georgia said. "That's the thing that kept me up nights."

"Georgia," he said suddenly, "why aren't you here?"

"Because," she said, "I'd only make it worse."

Then she told him she'd tried three times. Gotten in her car, driven nearly all the way to Dryden, three hours, before turning around and driving back. Now she was in the parking lot of a 7-Eleven twelve miles from her apartment.

"Drinking a can of beer," she said. "Genny Cream. Which I haven't done since I was twenty."

And he laughed, and she laughed.

And everything felt mysterious and lonely and half forgotten.

He could hear her laugh in the center of his brain and he thought, *That's not her laugh. I don't recognize that laugh at all.*

★　★　★

Eli lost sight of the sophomore girl quickly.

But down a long hallway in Critical Care, he found what he was looking for.

It was the quietest spot in the entire hospital, a building smaller than their school, which it seemed to be trying to

397

contain right now, its walls swelling and straining.

The doors are always open in hospitals, which seemed funny to him, but he was glad.

Because there she was.

Lise Daniels.

★ ★ ★

It felt like she'd been alone in the waiting room a long time, her thoughts scattering everywhere, jumping to her feet whenever either set of doors opened.

But then Deenie's phone rang, and time seemed to stop entirely.

Gabby, the screen read.

She walked swiftly outside, into the back parking lot to a place hidden by a pair of drooping trees, and answered.

"Hey, girl."

"Hey, girl."

And a pause that felt electric before Gabby spoke again.

"So I'm waiting for my mom. I told them I wanted my mom here before I tell them."

"Where are you?"

"I'm at the police station," she said, voice hoarse and faint. "I walked for an hour and when I got there, I knew I would do it."

"But Gabby, listen to me —"

"Don't hate me, Deenie, okay? Whatever you hear."

"Gabby, I know what happened. I talked to Skye. It was Skye."

"No," Gabby said, with finality. The voice of someone who had decided many things, and now that she'd decided, she was done. *I won't see my dad, I won't talk to him. I'm done with him forever.* "It was me, Deenie. It was me. And I'm not going to tell them about her. You have to promise me you won't either."

"I won't promise! Listen to me, Gabby," she said again, trying to forget the things Skye had said, about Gabby not caring about Deenie, about how Deenie was in the way. "You wouldn't have done it without Skye. It's all her fault."

Then Gabby said the thing Deenie hoped she wouldn't say, never guessed she would.

"When I put the leaves in the thermos, I didn't know what would happen. I didn't care."

And Deenie could hear it, that click-click-click on the other end, Gabby's jaw like one of those old wind-up toys, a spinning monkey slapping cymbals. Deenie could practically see her shaking.

Then, as if Gabby had wedged her hand

under her jaw to hold it in place, the words came fast and Deenie tried to hold on to them.

"Deenie, if Eli didn't love me, why would he have been so nice to me and played Ping-Pong with me and that time he gave me a ride on his handlebars? Why would he have treated me like I was special? Not like those hockey groupies, not like girls like Britt Olsen or those girls from Star-of-the-Sea or that slutty sophomore Michelle. But then I heard about Lise and the bushes by school."

There was a long, raspy gulp, like Gabby couldn't get air in. And when she started again, Deenie could feel everything falling apart for her. Gabby had many things to say, none of which could help her explain any of it.

"And the more Skye kept talking," she said, "the more it seemed right. It was supposed to be *me*, Deenie. He was supposed to love *me*. But we did the love spell wrong. And Skye told me what she saw. It was like a loop in my head. And he was pulling down her tights, that's what Skye said. Thinking of his hands on that . . . that-that-that *skin* of hers when it was supposed to be me."

The way she said it, *that skin of hers*, her voice shaking with anger and disgust, Deenie had the sudden feeling she'd had with Skye. For a fleeting second, she thought it was all a trick, some black art, and it was Skye on the other end of the phone, casting a spell.

"After, Skye said we shouldn't feel bad. She said it's what was supposed to happen. It's how the universe works. Lise's bad energy came back on her. Skye said when she looked at Lise, she saw a black mark, an aura. Just like the mark on Lise's thigh, it was a warning."

Deenie thought of it now, of Lise and the stretch mark on her thigh. And how the fevered mind of her fevered friend might believe anything.

But also, somewhere inside, it felt the smallest bit true. That the stretch mark was a kind of witch's mark, the blot on Lise's body that reminded you of what she had been — a plump, awkward girl — before the lithesome beauty took her place. It was a kind of witchcraft, that transformation.

"But Deenie, I *did* feel bad. It was like it was meant to happen. The bad thing you're waiting for, the thing you might do someday. And then you've done the thing, and there's no going back."

Once, after Deenie said something unbelievably awful to her mom, using a word she'd never even said aloud, shouting it so loud her throat hurt, her mom looked at her and said, *Deenie, someday it's going to happen to you. You're going to do something you never thought you would. And then you'll see, and then you'll know.*

I hope, she'd added, *it's not for a long time.*

"But at the school concert," Deenie said suddenly, remembering Gabby, her cello bow pitching, face scarlet. "Was that all fake?"

"No! I can't make my jaw stop," Gabby said, her voice cracking and a long, low sob. "I can't make my head right. It's like it's everything about me now. It's inside me and everywhere. It was always in me. I couldn't stop myself."

There was a long pause. Then Gabby whispered, "Deenie, I couldn't stop myself. I had to do it. Can you understand?"

Deenie felt her mouth go dry, her head throbbing. "Yes," she said. "Yes."

The clicks started again, and an awful rattle, and Deenie felt the phone hot on her face, beep-beep-beep, her cheek pressed against the keyboard.

Then, suddenly, Gabby's voice came again, low and strange.

"And now he'll never love me," Gabby said. "Now it'll never be me."

Deenie slowly lowered the phone from her ear.

"Deenie, did Eli read my letter? Did he say anything about me?"

★ ★ ★

At first Eli couldn't see her past the wires tentacled over her, the room blue and lonely.

There was just a swoop of a girl's cheek, and a flossy pile of hair, everything blue in the blue light.

And there was something resting in the middle of Lise's head. Something dark. Like in a fairy tale, a black cat perched, a swirl of smoke.

But then he remembered something Deenie had said, about a fall.

She made it sound gruesome, but it wasn't so bad.

Maybe it was because Lise's eyes were so pretty, shining and looking directly at him.

Following him as he walked toward the bed.

Gentle and soft, like Lise. And the light from the open door falling on her, giving her a funny kind of radiance.

Her mouth slightly opening, lips pale but full.

Eyes seeming to smile, at him.

"Do you see?" came the softest of whispers.

And it was Mrs. Daniels behind him, and she was smiling, like watching Lise play "Für Elise" on her flute.

"Do you see?" Mrs. Daniels whispered, her hand gentle on Eli's back. "She came back."

★ ★ ★

Alone in the waiting room, Deenie sat, her phone gripped in her hand.

Everything that day at the lake, just a week ago, started to look different.

The way Gabby looked at Lise, her long legs, like milk glass, thighs so narrow you could see between, like a keyhole.

How Gabby and Skye had stood next to each other, their ankles flecked green from the lake's creamy surface, and Gabby whispered something in Skye's ear, and Deenie had that feeling that she'd had so often in recent months: They are sharing something without me, they are talking about me, Gabby doesn't love me anymore.

And then Gabby wanted to leave, even though Lise was driving.

I can take you, Lise promised, but they were already walking away, their legs greened, never looking back.

And Skye said the lake had bad energy, arms folded, eyes on Lise.

Was that when Skye got the idea? Or had she and Gabby already decided by then?

It felt now like they had. Like it had already been too late.

Deenie wondered how it had felt for Lise, sharing her secret about Sean. Waiting for Skye and Gabby to leave to tell her. Wanting it to be theirs. A thing together. She couldn't know what might happen. How different it might have been had she told all of them.

Deenie thought about what Skye had said, that the whole time, Gabby was so angry she couldn't even look at Lise. Couldn't bear Lise showing off her body in the water. And whispering to Skye, *She stole him from me.*

That day, Lise had been more beautiful than she'd ever been before, her lashes iridescent and her face with an almost unearthly glow. Her body, Deenie guessed, felt her own in a way it only can when you've made it yourself.

Lise did give off a strong energy that day, but not like Skye meant.

And Deenie, she'd said, *Don't tell Gabby.*

Gabby's weird about this stuff.

Deenie, you're my best friend.

Deenie, I didn't do anything wrong, right?

Deenie, am I bad?

Deenie, I hope you get to feel it. I hope it feels like that for you.

It was something powerful, and everyone wanted it.

17

LISE

It felt great, her hands on the wheel.

Lise almost never got to drive, but that day she got lucky and her mom let her drive the Dodge because she was at the ophthalmologist, getting drops in her eyes.

Gabby had been sad all day, like she was a lot. You would only find out later it was because her dad had called or it was the anniversary of something bad with Tyler Nagy.

"She won't even talk," Deenie whispered to her. "Let's try to cheer her up."

So they went for a drive, windows down and Gabby's favorite music and Big Gulps it took two hands to hold. The warmest day in months.

They saw Deenie's brother in the parking lot and Lise beeped her horn at him. Sometimes she wondered if Deenie knew how good-looking Eli was, if sisters could tell. Lise liked to watch him on the practice rink, his hair flying and the faraway look in his eyes. Her mom always said teenage boys only cared about one thing, but watching Eli, you just knew it wasn't true.

On the drive, Gabby and Skye didn't say a word the whole time, but she and Deenie sang loudly to the radio. It was fun.

As they drove past the lake, Skye started telling them this thing that had happened last week. She saw two guys wading in the lake, drinking beers, their car doors open and speakers gushing wild music that made her want to dance.

"They were sexy," Skye said. "One had a tattoo of a gold panther. It went down his whole body, from his neck down below his waist, into his jeans. I wonder where it ended."

Lise could picture the tattoo and the guy. In her head, his shirt was worn denim and he had aviator sunglasses and a wicked smile. And the panther, its gleaming haunches stretched along his torso, the panther's teeth disappearing below his golden hip bone.

"Maybe they're there now," Deenie said, laughing.

And Lise wondered about it, her stomach doing that funny kind of thing, like when Ryan Denning helped her with her fetal-pig dissection, seated on high stools and him reaching for the blunt probe, his hand brushing her lap.

"Let's stop and go in," she suggested, jumping forward in her seat, pressing against the steering wheel. "Let's go now."

So they did, hopping the orange safety fences. The guys with the car and the tattoo weren't there, except it almost felt like they were, the lake glittering with borrowed glamour.

"Maybe they'll show up later," Lise said, running down the bank, nearly sliding on the mud, which spattered up her legs. "Maybe they'll see us from the road."

Gabby and Skye were so quiet. Skye lit a clove cigarette and squinted down at Lise. She was saying something to Gabby, but Lise couldn't hear. They were always whispering to each other.

They were no fun and Lise felt high on all the sugar and soda and was trying to rouse Gabby and she tugged off her tights.

The water looked eerily lovely, like the kind of sparkling lake you'd see in a picture book, unicorns dipping their heads and cloudbursts overhead.

Waving up at the others lined up on the shore, she promised the water felt almost warm and like velvet under your feet and they had to come. It was true. Except it was freezing.

She pulled her skirt higher and spun.

"What's that?" Skye asked, pointing her cigarette at Lise, at her legs.

"Nothing," Lise said, and felt her face go hot.

She knew what Skye meant, the mark on her thigh, a pink crescent. It was from losing all that weight, a tiny stretch mark she put cocoa butter on every night, wishing it away.

"You're just stalling," Deenie shouted at Skye, and Lise smiled. "You're scared."

Deenie hated Skye.

And soon enough Deenie was yanking her jeans up to her knees and wading in too. And Lise was so grateful. Deenie was still hers.

"C'mon, Gabby," Deenie shouted, her jeans already soaked to the thigh. "It only hurts for a second."

And finally Gabby reached down and pulled off her tights, and then of course Skye did too, cigarette somehow still between her fingers, thin as a burnt match.

The water felt soft and globby, like sherbet, but smelled strongly of something Lise had never smelled before.

It was only a minute before Gabby said

410

she was catching hypothermia and the lake was dirty and was making her head hurt. And then Skye said her head hurt too and the lake had a bad aura and you were asking for trouble being in it.

The boy who drowned here, she said, *can't you feel him? He was in the water for days. Do you know what happens? Your body turns to soap.*

And they all looked down in the water as if they would see the boy.

But Deenie said that was kid's stuff, and she scooped up a handful, foam bubbling, and flicked it toward them. That was when Lise knew Deenie was annoyed, or even mad, like she always was when Gabby was being secretive with Skye, which was all the time lately.

It never mattered much to Lise because she'd never felt as close to Gabby as Deenie did. Deenie, who'd never really gotten over the surprise that someone as cool as Gabby Bishop wanted to be her friend. For her part, Lise had realized a long time ago that the way to keep Deenie would be to let her love Gabby just this much.

Skye was the weirdest girl Lise had ever known. Once, a long time ago, in middle school, they'd been to the same sleepaway camp and Skye had the bunk above her.

One night she came down the ladder, her legs snaking around it, and asked Lise if she wanted to see something.

Taking a deep breath, she lifted her nightshirt and showed Lise all these marks, like rosy ridges, on her arms all the way up to her shoulder. She said she'd made them herself, with a Bic lighter, and it had taken a long time. And now they were like the husk, the hard shell. Like finding a beetle or a mollusk shell at the lake, the rattle pods in Binnorie Woods. You shake and it's hollow. The thing inside died. You couldn't do anything to it anymore.

The cabin quiet and dark and Skye breathing hard, her arms outstretched, Lise hadn't known what to say, barely knew this girl. What did you say to something like that? And the next day, Skye wouldn't look at her, and then after that they never talked about it again.

She wondered if Skye remembered it.

"I can't do this," Gabby said suddenly. Her face looked green from the water.

Nodding to Skye, she began walking back to shore, her sweater heavy with water, trailing behind her.

"Come on, Gabby," Deenie said, calling out after her.

Lise bent over and lifted a long stretch of

412

seaweed, draping it around Deenie's neck, like a mermaid's boa.

And Deenie smiled and flicked its edges up and pushed Lise, but when they both turned around again, Gabby and Skye were walking up the bank, their legs stained green.

"Are they going?" Lise asked, looking at Deenie.

Her long sweater sleeves weeping lake water, Skye offered a slow wave.

Gabby didn't even turn around, walking slowly up the slope, the damp edges of her skirt in her hands like petticoats.

"But Lise drove us," Deenie called out.

Except they kept walking, their heavy hair and long-legged elegance, and it was hard not to feel five years old.

So she said, "Swim with me, Deenie," backing up so the frigid water reached the bottom of her pelvis, the green water swimming between her thighs. "Let's do it, huh?"

After a moment, Deenie stopped looking back for Gabby and they stripped off their sweaters and waded in their tank tops and bras, Lise's skirt billowing like a white flower and Deenie's jeans accordioned on the shore.

And then Deenie even put her head under, came up with her hair black and inky.

At first, Lise wouldn't do it. She didn't want to and kept picturing that drowned boy, under the pearling water. *Was he there now? Would he curl his tiny fingers around her toe?*

But then Deenie grabbed her neck from behind and dunked her, and the icy water came so fast she almost couldn't breathe.

Under the surface, her ears hurt so bad she felt like someone had punched an iron rod in them.

But then the pressure broke and it was incredible, her head rushing with the feeling.

And while she was under, she knew it was time to tell Deenie, her best friend.

About the boy, almost as handsome as Eli Nash himself, but without the faraway eyes. The boy who'd looked right at her, rolling her tights down over her legs.

To whisper in Deenie's ear the wonderful thing that was happening and how it felt. She wanted to share it with her.

18

Sitting in his car in the school parking lot, Tom couldn't quite bring himself to go inside.

His gaze fixed on the breezeway beyond. All the hedges had been torn away, shorn stumps remaining, a stray evidence bag, a twirl of police tape. The orange streaks of herbicide dye.

He'd spent the day before driving Deenie the three hours to Merrivale, then turning around and driving home. It was the first time he'd seen Georgia's place, which was cozy and filled with light and fresh air. Deenie insisted on staying only two days, had a history test on Wednesday, had forgotten to bring her books. In fact, maybe she'd stay just overnight.

Eli had come too, had helped with the driving. Deenie kept watching him from the corner of her eye.

At the hospital, they'd tested his blood, even his hair, used enormous machines and tested the electrical activity of his heart. But whatever Eli had smoked with Skye Osbourne, they couldn't find anything dangerous in his body.

"There's nothing inside him," the doctor said. "Whatever it was, it's gone."

Eli told them the smoke had been for something called lucid dreaming.

"Did it work?" Tom asked.

Eli had paused, then said no.

The sharp bark of an engine stirred him to life. Looking out his car window, he saw the French teacher hopping off her Vespa and smiling at him, red-lipped.

"Open that window," she said. "Or invite me in."

He clicked the power locks and watched her glide around the car and climb inside.

Rubbing her hands together, she told him she couldn't take her eyes off the news.

"Gabby Bishop, Jesus," she said. "I never even had her in a class, but I knew about her. The way she'd walk down the hall, girls circling her like little magpies. All that hair and drama."

"Yeah," he said, just to say something.

Her hands dropping to her lap, she sighed. "It's all so freaky. All the other ones who got sick — I sent two to the nurse myself. So they must have gotten some of that jimson stuff, right? They must have smoked it too, like at a party?"

"I don't think so," Tom said. "I don't think they took anything."

She nodded and they sat silently for a moment.

"I remember when I was a sophomore in high school," she said. "There was this girl, the coolest girl in school. Laia Noone. Even her name was cool. She had a tattoo on her stomach: *I've seen love die.* In tenth grade!" She laughed. "All I wanted was to be like her."

"And now you're the coolest girl in school."

"You don't know the half of it," she said. Then she lowered her jacket zipper and, using two fingers, separated the space between a pair of blouse buttons, baring the smallest triangle of flesh. He could see only the middle words — *seen love* — but was sure the rest was there too.

"And so," Tom said, "marked for life."

"That's what high school does."

"And everything else," he said, smiling.

She smiled back, like he knew she would.

"It's funny the things you think of now," she said, yanking the zipper back up. "I

417

remember last year once, Jaymie Hurwich crying in my classroom after school. She said there was something wrong with her mom's brain and it'd started when her mom was sixteen and now *she* was sixteen and what if something happened to her. She said her dad was always looking at her, like he was watching for signs."

Tom was surprised, but then everything surprised him now.

A hundred thoughts started floating in and out of his head, but none cohered.

"It's going to be hard for all of them," she said. "Everyone'll be looking at them. Like they're these damaged girls."

They sat for a minute.

"But not Deenie," she said, smiling. "Thank goodness. No one will be looking at her."

Tom looked at her. Nodded.

19

JUNE

TROUBLING QUESTIONS LINGER AFTER MYSTERY ILLNESS

Six weeks after Dryden High School faced a seeming health crisis among female students following the poisoning of a classmate, local health officials are still struggling to identify the cause.

At least 18 students were treated for symptoms ranging from facial and body tics to hallucinations and even temporary paralysis, but the case began with Lise Daniels, 16, who experienced a seizure following ingestion of dangerous jimsonweed placed in her thermos by a fellow student (see sidebar, "Student Faces Sentence after Plea Deal").

No jimsonweed was detected in any of the other afflicted girls, and health department officials have been unable to find any organic causes for individual cases or any connections among them.

Reports emerged this week that the department is now consulting with experts who specialize in "mass psychogenic illness," a condition in which physical symptoms that are psychological in origin emerge in a group, spreading from one person to the next. "It's not a copycat situation and no one's faking anything," clarified Dr. Robert Murray from the State Psychiatric Institute. "These girls had no control over their symptoms. Which can be terrifying."

Such outbreaks tend to occur within groups experiencing emotional stress and anxiety. "That's likely the scenario here," Dr. Murray said, adding he hadn't interviewed any of the girls so could not speak to their individual circumstances.

At least one parent, David Hurwich, 42, does not accept the diagnosis, and he may not be alone. Last night at a school-board meeting, several parents noted, off the record, that they continue to believe that the real cause is being ignored or covered up, citing ongoing concerns about air and water safety. "Time will tell," said Mr. Hurwich. "But I know my daughter. And that was not her."

Questions also remain for Miss Daniels, who was released from the hospital two weeks ago. Dr. April Fine, chair of psychiatry at Mercy-Starr Clark, warns that what the long-term side effects will be are unclear.

"This girl not only suffered significant physical trauma, she is also the victim of a crime," Dr. Fine said. "The real impact may not be felt for some time, and may emerge when least expected. In some ways, she's a ticking time bomb."

It was one of those painfully lovely late-spring mornings, the kind only Dryden could conjure.

The same obscure meteorology that produced the awesome ferocity of winters kept the lake unusually warm and made for cloudless skies. Only a few popcorn cumuli broke up the brilliant blue that hurt your eyes. It was called the oasis effect.

Waiting for the coffeemaker, or Deenie's sneakers on the stairs, Tom didn't know what to do with himself. He'd stopped reading the newspaper, listening to the news. None of it seemed to explain anything. That morning, though, he hadn't been able to stop himself. *Mass psychogenic illness.* There was a term for it, or so the article claimed.

The main story was about Gabby, who would be sentenced on Friday.

Every day, he thought about calling Lara Bishop, but she hadn't returned his other calls.

That night with her had come to feel like a murky dream, erotic and strange — the enigmatic beauty of it, her scar pulling from her neck, her voice in his ear — and best tucked in a far corner.

It was still hard to imagine. Gabby, the girl he was used to seeing at his kitchen table or nestled on his sofa with Deenie, their hands crackling in potato chip bags. The sushi-pattern pajamas she wore when she slept over. Hair hanging in her face over a morning cereal bowl.

Some days, he felt like she could almost be his own daughter.

Except that wasn't really true. She'd always felt grander, graver. Embossed with the gold stamp of Experience. Something adultlike about her, different. But in the end she was both different and not, burdened by both a girl's crush and a dense gnarl over her heart.

Or maybe he was wrong.

The coffee was ready.

"Deenie," he called out. "Let's go."

The second pot, and stronger. He'd been up awhile, had been lying awake in bed when he heard the click-click of Eli's hockey stick on the kitchen floor as he left the house for practice.

It was strange to think of his son now, after all this. The object of such intense feeling. Lady-killer. Heartbreaker. This was the boy for whom a girl had nearly killed, nearly died. Little Eli, who watched six consecutive hours of ESPN Classic, ate over the kitchen sink, and, despite having had at least one female visitor to his bedroom, never seemed to quite lock eyes with any girl, any woman. Except Deenie, and sometimes Georgia, though Tom hadn't seen them together in so long.

Whenever he looked at Eli now, he tried to find it, as if the answer might lie in some deeper enchantment a father couldn't see.

The skittering on the stairs startled him.

"We'll be late," Deenie said, running in, her hair brushed hard into a tight ponytail. "We better go."

In the car, she was quiet, folding and unfolding a new scarf, pale green like a lily pad. She'd brought it back after visiting Georgia, another visit cut short.

The day she returned, he found her in the basement, holding her pizza shirt up to the light, an errant grease stain still lurking.

"She never had a good reason," she'd said, "for not coming. When everything was happening."

"Deenie, she offered to come and get you. That's the same thing," he said, even though he knew it wasn't, exactly.

Dropping the shirt into the dryer, she looked at him, the longest look he could remember her ever giving.

"You would have come," she said at last.

"Yeah," he said, "but I wouldn't have known what to say. I would have —"

"But you would have come," she repeated.

And it was true, and it was something.

The car rattled as he made the turn onto the lake route, the trees giving way to a swath of cloudless sky.

And then he remembered what today was. Lise Daniels's first day back at school.

"Dad," Deenie said, turning the radio up as she spoke, rising a little in her seat. "The sky hurts my eyes."

★ ★ ★

Lying in bed before dawn, Deenie had heard Eli slip down the hall, the hushed drag of his stick bag against the carpet.

She wondered if Lise was up too. Maybe,

424

over on Easter Way, Lise was nervously combing her hair, covering the violet zag in the center of her forehead, like a lightning bolt.

Or maybe she was doing what Deenie was doing, reading the news article on her phone:

The 16-year-old girl at the center of Dryden's poisoning case faces sentencing today.

They never printed her name, always called her "the girl." It made it seem like it could be anybody, any girl who was sixteen, in their midst.

The article said it would probably be probation, some community service. But it would remain on her record forever, just like they always say about everything you're never supposed to do.

A few weeks ago, Deenie had gotten a long letter from Gabby. It wasn't about Lise or Skye or even Eli. It was about the things she was learning, and how different she felt. She was changing, she said. But she didn't say what the changes were. Only that they were *big* and *important.*

There would always be things she'd never understand about Gabby. And that was the hardest part. That there would be mysteries impenetrable.

Had Gabby herself even known what she

wanted, her fingers tucking Skye's poison
down into the bottom of Lise's thermos,
the same thermos that helped make Lise
sylphlike and beautiful, her body so lovely
and ready for wonder?

And then there was what Deenie herself
had done. With Sean Lurie. And how different it was, and how the same. *I want it too. I
want what she has too. Why can't I get that
too?*

Everyone wanted to be like Gabby. Her
bright tights, the streak in her hair, the big
glasses she wore when she read in class. Kim
Court and Jaymie Hurwich, even Brooke
Campos. Everyone.

Deenie wondered where all that frantic
energy would go now. Did it just disappear,
or did it go someplace else? She wondered
about it for herself.

But Gabby was gone and probably
wouldn't ever be back in their school. Probably she would move away, no matter what
happened.

So where did all of it go, the things she
felt for her?

Because, to her, it was Deenie-Gabby-
Lise, snuggled together in sleeping bags,
behind the bookshelves in the library, on
the soccer field, in the auditorium.

Lise was still there. Today, her first day

back at school.

She'd survived poisoning, which led to a seizure, which led to a cardiac event, which led to a fall, which led to blunt trauma to the head.

Everyone called her the Miracle Girl.

Deenie's dad called her Rasputin.

She said she didn't remember anything about that day, not even the drive to school that morning with her mom. The doctors told her that would happen, and she said she was glad, but it was hard for her to believe about Gabby, and she wasn't sure she ever would.

"What about the hospital?" Deenie asked her later. "Me visiting you?"

"No," Lise said. Deenie pictured herself at the foot of Lise's bed, trying to tell her about Sean Lurie. *And we were in his car. And he . . . or I. Me. It was me.* Lise's gleaming eye. The whistle from her white mouth.

But Lise didn't remember any of that, either. And the first time Deenie visited her at home, she tried again. A twice-told confession.

"No," Lise interrupted, shaking her head, her hair oddly changed, a darker blond and not the same texture where it grew back, the center of her scalp where the dent terminated. "No, no. I don't want to talk

427

about any of it. If I talk about any of it, my mouth fills up."

"Your mouth?"

"My chest, everything. I don't know, Deenie," she said, breathless. "Just stop."

And Deenie's dad told her that there could be emotional stuff for a long time, that it was a kind of trauma, and that Deenie shouldn't take it personally.

The word *trauma* seemed to cover a lot, a whole world of things, and it was the word they'd always used for Gabby, before what happened to Lise. To Gabby and Lise.

But it wasn't only Lise's hair — nothing was the same. Even her walk, the jut of her hip, the weight of her feet on her bedroom rug.

And most of all, it was something in her eyes, like when Lise first collapsed to the classroom floor that day, like something black, like a bat flapping.

★　★　★

Every morning, Eli woke from the same dream. Of riding in the passenger seat of a car and feeling something catch around his ankle, soft, light as air. Reaching down, he never found it.

Sometimes, he felt it when he was awake,

in class, or even during a game, sweeping down the rink and feeling, even through his thick hockey socks, the boot of the skate, something both delicate and tight there on his ankle, grappling for him.

He tried not to think much about Gabby.

In a funny way, he was angry, and he didn't like the feeling. He'd always tried, very hard, not to feel mad at anybody, ever.

But there was someone he thought about more than Gabby, every time he walked by the double doors leading to the loading dock. Other times.

The night after Lise woke up, he and Deenie had stayed up late, sneaking beers from the fridge and talking. She told him about Skye, about everything. Or at least everything enough.

He could tell Deenie thought Skye was a monster.

But Gabby won't tell on her. It's all Skye's fault but Gabby won't tell. So now I can't.

He didn't point out that she didn't have to do what Gabby said. She could do whatever she wanted.

Instead, he just nodded, and nodded, and teased her about slurring her *s*'s.

And then she said, *I think Skye told me she gave you the jimson to get rid of me. And then she could run away. She knew I would have to find you.*

And he thought that part was probably true.

Then they watched *Meatballs* on cable, which their dad always loved, and Deenie fell asleep and snored just a little.

It was the best night ever.

And they hadn't talked about any of it since.

Stepping out onto the practice rink, he looked off into the backfield, the ground shorn of all its foliage, and the smell of ashes always now.

His skates hitting the ice, just starting to soften, he thought of Skye out there somewhere.

He'd heard her uncle had contacted the police, saying Skye had called him, collect, but he was already on probation and couldn't risk any trouble with the law. And besides, he was worried about her out there. She was just a kid.

Sometimes Eli thought he spotted her, a white flash in the corner of his eye.

No one had seen her since Deenie left her in her backyard the night Gabby confessed. The police were looking for her as part of the presentencing, were unsure of her role, if any, in what Gabby had done. They were following rumors, mostly.

Skye was a rumor now, a whiff of smoke drifting.

Now he thought he kind of understood what she meant about energies, the way they can be passed to you, can live in you even when you don't know it, until it's revealed to you. She was wrong about Lise. She didn't have any dark energy, or any powerful energy. Everyone else did, but not Lise.

When he got his phone back, he thought of Skye taking it, slipping it from his backpack as they sat on the loading dock. He wondered how long she'd had it before she gave it to Gabby.

Did she look at it, did she somehow see into him?

It was like his dream, Skye's thighs locked tight around him as he lay still. And her mouth opened and he could see inside, and . . .

There was a witchiness to her that was terrifying. And there was something else. Part of him wished he had put his hand on her back that day, on that twisted spine of hers, which she'd offered to him, asked of him.

But those were early-morning, predawn thoughts, out on the ice, dreaming.

431

The early spring had meant everything arrived early: the school grounds bursting with red shoots, the lawns thick with creeping phlox, other things he couldn't name.

Tom held the school door open for Deenie, her arms heavy with that monstrous book bag of hers.

The building smelled so different now. They had gone through the entire facility, the dropped ceilings in the basement, every stretch of the HVAC system. Scooped out every hidden cavity, scraped matter from each crease and furrow.

And they found many things.

Deep in the upper and lower corners of the old school they found pipes, fans, dampers, ducts coated with prehistoric sediments, gypsum board and ceiling tiles furred with mold, lead paint over older lead paint. PCBs in the caulk, the fluorescent lighting ballasts, the transformers that powered the school. Radon, mercury, arsenic in the water pipes, on the wood of the track hurdles, in the modular chairs, tables. The only thing they didn't find, other than, maybe, uranium, was asbestos. Everyone got rid of that a decade ago.

Trace amounts of a dozen or more things,

most of which they'd removed over Easter break. The rest to be removed over the summer.

None of it, officials pointed out, had anything to do with what happened.

Because even if it isn't any of these things, it could *be,* Lara Bishop had said.

We put them at risk just by having them. And the hazards never stop.

But now, everything just smelled like nothing.

You wouldn't have thought nothing would have a smell.

"It's time, Dad," Deenie said, pointing to the old mounted clock, its brass casings stripped of green and newly shining.

"Right," he said, reaching down to hand her the new scarf, which had drifted to the floor. "Have a good day, D."

"Okay," she said, smiling a little, a half smile that was new to him. Wise and wary and not a girl's smile at all.

And he watched her walk all the way down the corridor, head lowered, hoodie half up her neck.

Each time her sneaker took a swivel on the bright polished floor, he felt his heart lurch.

There were only sixty seconds before the second bell, but everything seemed to slow down.

Shutting her locker, she put her hand on Lise's door, wondered where she was.

Walking through the halls, she saw all the girls with legs bare now, even though it was still too cold. A few of the boys were even wearing shorts.

She'd worked only one shift with Sean Lurie since everything happened.

He hadn't looked at her once, just took the order tickets, his nails greased. He was even wearing his cap, first time ever, so she couldn't see his eyes.

She didn't want to look at him anyway.

That night, a text came, the same unknown number as before. But this time, he said who he was:

Hey, u, Sean here. Sorry, k? we cool?

We cool, she'd typed back.

Then, somehow, they were never on the schedule again at the same time.

But he didn't go to Dryden High, so it was like it never even happened. She'd never told anyone other than Lise, and Lise didn't remember, so maybe it hadn't happened.

Except she could still feel all of it, but that

was okay.

Turning the corner into the east wing, the breezeway unusually warm, the sun pounding on the glass, she saw Brooke Campos, laughing loudly at something a boy had said, her mouth like a shark's.

All those girls, she wondered what they felt now. No one said anything, really. No one talked about the girls who'd been so sick.

Except for one of them, Kim Court, who'd transferred to Star-of-the-Sea after staying a long, long time in the hospital. Her videos were the only ones still online, and once in a while, the address still stored in her browser, Deenie would start typing and the video would come up, and there was Kim, talking about the man with tornado legs, about Gabby pulling seaweed from her throat, about Deenie being in the hospital, about Deenie being the one.

"Are you ready, Deenie?" It was Jaymie Hurwich, books clasped to her chest. "It's time."

And Deenie nodded.

The classroom door was open, and there was Lise, seated at her desk. The same spot she'd been in nearly seven weeks before, her legs tangled beneath her. Her chin tilted, looking out the window.

It was Lise, but it wasn't.

And Lise smiled at her, sort of. And Deenie sat down, and the bell rang, and everything shuttled back into place.

She'd never thought it would, that the fever would break. But the Lise who returned didn't seem like the same Lise. There were all these different Lises and none of them was Deenie's.

Looking out the window too, following Lise's gaze, Deenie saw the hedges, shorn to the ground.

And she could see through to the other wing, and there was Dad, charcoal sweater and handsome, talking to the French teacher again, showing her something on his phone. Giving her the smallest of smiles, the one her mom used to call the Croc.

All the trees and foliage had been torn away during the investigation, the remediation. Bushes razed, the earth seemingly shaken to its core. You could see everything now, if you wanted.

And though homeroom had begun, Eli was out there, outside, jacket off, on the practice rink, skating.

It was almost like fall, branches strewn across the thawing ice. Prickly globes split, seeds spilling, white petals pulped, spores that split red onto ice.

Each turn, graceful and lithe and hypnotic, she watched as his blades ran over every one.

ACKNOWLEDGMENTS

There are not thanks enough to offer the incredible Reagan Arthur, nor Michael Pietsch and the magnificent, creative, and generous-spirited Little, Brown team, especially Theresa Giacopasi, Miriam Parker, Sarah J. Murphy, and Peggy Freudenthal. I'm honored to work among them all.

Immense gratitude is also owed to Paul Baggeley, Kate Harvey, Sophie and Emma Bravo at Picador UK, and to Angharad Kowal, Maja Nikolic, and Bakara Wintner at Writers House and Sylvie Rabineau and Jill Gillett at RWSG. Thanks also to James Lavish and Vicki Pettersson, for an invaluable assist.

And foremost to Dan Conaway, without whom, in all ways.

My debt to the following just grows and grows: Phil & Patti Abbott; Josh, Julie & Kevin Abbott; Jeff, Ruth & Steve Nase; and the one and only Alison Quinn. And, as ever, thanks to Darcy Lockman, Kiki Wilkinson, and, of course, to the FLs. This year, I'm particularly grateful to the good folks of Oxford, Mississippi, including Jack Pendarvis, Theresa Starkey, and Ace Atkins.

And, as writer and reader both, I'm certain the greatest debt is owed to booksellers everywhere.

ABOUT THE AUTHOR

Megan Abbott is the Edgar Award–winning author of six previous novels. She received her PhD in literature from New York University. She lives in New York and currently serves as the John Grisham Writer-in-Residence at the University of Mississippi.

The employees of Thorndike Press hope you have enjoyed this Large Print book. All our Thorndike, Wheeler, and Kennebec Large Print titles are designed for easy reading, and all our books are made to last. Other Thorndike Press Large Print books are available at your library, through selected bookstores, or directly from us.

For information about titles, please call:
    (800) 223-1244

or visit our Web site at:
    http://gale.cengage.com/thorndike

To share your comments, please write:
    Publisher
    Thorndike Press
    10 Water St., Suite 310
    Waterville, ME 04901